# The Silver Llama

L. H. May

authorHOUSE®

*AuthorHouse™*
*1663 Liberty Drive*
*Bloomington, IN 47403*
*www.authorhouse.com*
*Phone: 1 (800) 839-8640*

*This is a work of fiction. All of the characters, names, incidents, organizations, and dialogue in this novel are either the products of the author's imagination or are used fictitiously.*

*Published by AuthorHouse    01/14/2016*

*ISBN: 978-1-5049-5818-9 (sc)*
*ISBN: 978-1-5049-5817-2 (e)*

*Print information available on the last page.*

*This book is printed on acid-free paper.*

# Author's Preface & Disclaimer

This novel, <u>The Silver Llama</u>, is the fourth and last of "The Tihuantinsuyo Quartet", the first being <u>Riders On The Niño Storms</u>, EBook ISBN9781456764968, AuthorHouse, 2011, $5.99, the second <u>The Gate Of Two Snakes</u> by L.H. May, EBook ISBN9781491823392, AuthorHouse 2013, $3.99, the third novel is <u>The Coca Bums</u>, ISBN97815049118181, paperback, AuthorHouse 2015, to order call 1-888-280-7715 or 1-888-728-8467. Portions of <u>The Silver Llama</u> were originally published in <u>Return To The Corner Of The Dead</u>, since withdrawn, out of print and chopped for the present production. "Corner of the Dead" is the translation of the Quechua 'Ayacucho', the Peruvian province where the bloody Maoist Sendero rebellion arose in the Seventies and Eighties. The title was changed because people confused the book with The Walking Dead and zombie fiction. The only problem with 'Llama' in a title is that most Americans pronounce it 'lama', but trust me, the correct pronunciation is 'yama'. None of the persons or events depicted in this or any of the previous novels of The Quartet are real.

"The heart has its own reasons." Pascal, <u>Pensées</u>

# Line 71 In The Wasteland

"That corpse you planted last year in your garden, Has it begun to sprout?" Eliot, <u>The Wasteland</u>

Lima, Peru
December 15, 1996

It was a nice day to be digging in his garden until Jim's three-prong fork hit a root of the fig tree that had invaded his compost heap, or at least he thought that was the snag until he saw the shoe. The dead man was dressed in a brown gabardine suit and a card in his wallet said that he was Nestor Aurelio Lenguado. Jim contacted Police Captain Leoncio Fregosco, whom he'd known for over ten years and who reported after a week of investigation that the man was a minor civil servant whose wife was involved with a politician. He said the murder was undoubtedly a crime of passion and had nothing to do with Jim, whose house on a cul de sac happened to be convenient to the main drag of Avenida Arequipa, with many trees around and his garden wall easy to scale with the planting wells on the outside, so a perfect dumping ground.

"How did they get the body in?" Jim said. "That guy was pretty hefty."

"Jumped the wall and sprung the gate—have you been away lately? Do you have a security system?" Fregosco asked.

"Yeh, Senora Sanchez up the street," Jim said. "I asked her to watch the place when I went to Philadelphia. She's got an eagle eye and she didn't see anything."

"A lot of walls in these old places have broken glass on top set in cement," Fregosco noted, looking at the substantial garden wall and the limestone flags at the base. "Nobody made any threats to you lately? No irate investors?"

"I don't have any irate investors," Jim said. "And there are only the general threats that Sendero would have for a Wall Street lackey."

"Nah, the senderistas are on their heels," Fregosco said.

Jim did believe the captain on that point. Ever since Abimael Guzman, the charismatic leader of the Maoist Sendero Luminoso rebels, had been caught in 1992, the movement had been dramatically weakened. President Fujimori's popularity inversely rose spectacularly, even after he suspended Congress and gave free rein to the military to mop up the rebels. Now the tourists were back flocking to Machu Picchu, bringing the foreign exchange so vital to the Peruvian economy, as the rebels had known when they were crippling the country with terror added to the everyday misery and poverty there, conscripting children to kill as soldiers or be sacrificed as suicide bombers to pay what they called 'the quota of blood', the price of revolution. It was no longer like the days when Sendero controlled half the country; they were now down to maybe seven hundred armed rebels, making money doing protection for the campesinos in the Upper Hualaga valley, a rich coca growing region. Peru had finally discovered a commodity more dear than the gold, silver, guano, fishmeal or Amazonian rubber of previous booms, namely the coca leaf from which was derived cocaine, so successfully employed by Sigmund Freud, Kentucky horse breeders and big deal American salesmen. Zounds, Cambridge archaeologists had even found Peruvian coca residue in pipes recently excavated in Shakespeare's garden, (along with Danish hemp), raising the spectre that the Bard was coke high when he cooked up MacBeth.

The DEA was pouring chemicals on the coca bushes, it just reminded him of Agent Orange, and it wasn't going to stop it, just acted as a price support. And now they wanted Jim to check up on his clients. What the hell? He should add a question to his intake form: 'Where'd you get your money? Was it dirty drug dollars? Or did it go back to a royal grant from the time of The Conquest?' They want me to get them to fill out a form, but nobody at the ticket gate at Disney Land asks you where you got your shekels.

"Like a beer and a sandwich? I've got pastrami and provolone, some good French bread from Panificadores?" Jim said. "Hot mustard and pepperoncini. I also have some eggnog with bourbon for Christmas cheer."

The portly Fregosco enjoyed the pleasures of the board, answered 'all of the above' and reassured Jim this was a random incident probably due to his absence in the U.S., and wanted him to know it had nothing to do with him personally or his being an American citizen. Though Jim expressed no doubt about the captain's judgment, some questions lingered in his mind—just because Sendero wasn't targeting him, it didn't mean somebody else wasn't. After he got the mollifying police report, which found no matches for the drips of blood at the base of the wall, nor the fingerprints on his umbrella stand and basement door, Jim decided to put in a call to his old friend, Harry Stein, a retired foreign correspondent who knew Peru and kept his ear so close to the ground that grass grew in it, and asked him to check up on this Nestor Lenguado who'd ended up in his garden.

—m—

They arranged for Jim to come over to Harry's place the next Thursday for holiday lunch.

"How has the old reprobate been?" Jim asked Rosa, his housekeeper, who greeted him at the door.

"Intolerable, though he's been drinking much less," Rosa said. "Sometimes I wish he'd drink more if it made him less sour."

"I'll take that as an order," Harry said, shuffling out to greet him. "Jim and I will tipple and discuss hard tacks."

Rosa brought them a chilled quart of Cerveza Cristal and two plates of her exquisite picante de camarones, and they went out and sat on the patio. It was evidently true that Sr. Lenguado, a mid-level official in the Fisheries Ministry, had a wife who'd been involved romantically with a naval liaison officer to that ministry. This confirmed most of Fregosco's story, though he'd said the paramour was a politician. Harry pointed out that Fisheries had been nationalized under the leftist Velasco military government, before being privatized again, and said the officer was doing lobbying on the side and possibly eyeing a political career. Many theories were suggested besides a crime of passion, including an effort to smear the reputation of a promising candidate, and then the deceased Lenguado had evidently been taking bribes to gain favors and perhaps these hadn't been forthcoming as expected. Fujimori needed men and the officer had been on the ship that blasted open the walls of the island prison that Sendero prisoners took over in '86, so marine commandos could storm in, freeing all the hostages except one who was killed. Harry had gotten the sense from Fregosco that the officer was well connected, the navy was traditionally the most conservative of the services, and there were really not many answers to be had in the case. Oh, one other thing, after the operation to quell the prison riot in '86, this naval officer had served in Ayacucho Department in the sierra, where there was no ocean, but there was a detention camp where suspected Sendero rebels or their sympathizers were interrogated.

"You haven't been up to Ayacucho recently, have you?" Harry said.

"Not since '69," Jim said. "I did meet several communists at the time, but like ninety per cent of the faculty at the University of Huamanga was leftist."

"But no recent contact?" Harry said.

"I do go down to the soup kitchen in the ayacuchano barrio here, but all those people are loyal, hell, they got displaced to Lima by Sendero," Jim said.

"Or by the government, depending on how you look at it," Harry said. "Did you know the name, Ayacucho, means 'corner of the dead' in Quechua? I don't know if that comes from the Incas' bloody defeat of the Chancas there in the 15th century. Or maybe it's because of the starvations when the rains don't come to the sierra. It's been a hard land from time immemorial, and a fertile ground for rebels."

"When I talk to Sra. Paucharimac, I always ask about the latest news from home and some of it ain't so good," Jim said. "Not from the barrio neither if the army comes kicking down doors. I can find out if somebody's been around asking about this gringo, Jim Hiram."

"I don't think you need to be afraid, but I did get the sense from Captain Fregosco that there weren't many answers down this road," Harry said.

"Um, say, doesn't lenguado mean 'sole' in Spanish, as in 'filet of sole'?" Jim said.

"So a good name for a fishery official, right?" Harry said. "You shouldn't worry. Fregosco likes you. He said you've done all right for his pension account."

"I'd have done even better if Garcia hadn't screwed things up with the IMF in '86," Jim said. "Now Fuji's the man of the day. Didn't he win over sixty per cent of the vote?"

"Things can change quickly," Harry said. "You've heard his new nickname, Chinochet?"

Chinochet was a combination of 'chino', Peruvian slang for anyone of Oriental descent, and of General Pinochet, the rightwing Chilean dictator who'd deposed Allende. As far as 'chino', Fujimori was Japanese-Peruvian, so like Jim's buddy Milt Takita said, it showed even with stereotypes, Peru couldn't get it frigging right. As far as the fascism, Fuji had dissolved Congress in '92, and though the Clinton administration's threatened sanctions had made him hold elections in '95, which he won big anyway, now there were questions about how he did it. His chief of the secret police, the SIN, the National Intelligence Service, Vladimiro Montesinos, had been accused of wire-tapping his congressional opponents with the aim of recording them taking bribes to assure their cooperation and silence.

The third member of their triumvirate was the Chief of Staff, General Hermosa, who'd allegedly tried to put together a coup when he invited all the other generals to his birthday party in Lima, but Fuji got wind of it and sent all the generals back to their posts. No happy birthday, no ice cream, no cake, maybe the triumvirate was more like a 2.5-umvirate, but now the focus was on the dirty tricks of Montesinos.

"Is the triumvirate a Latin thing?" Jim said. "It didn't work out so great for Mark Anthony."

"If things don't work out with one of your allies, you've always got another to turn to," Harry said. "Unless, of course, you're odd man out."

"My dead guy in the garden didn't even make the papers," Jim said. "I'm not complaining, since that couldn't be good for business. I'm guessing the grieving widow's been quiet too, considering her position in this."

That evening Jim was having a nitecap and thinking about Montesinos and the SIN, their national intelligence service, humming 'who put the SIN in MonteSINos' to the tune of who put the ram in the rama-lama-ding-dong. It wasn't real funny because he knew some of its connection to a death squad the Colina Group, but then kittens pounced, pawed, clawed and bit as they played in preparation for the time when they would grow up and hunt. The feline was a feature of mythic fear in Andean iconography, they still had masques with jaguar dances in Ayacucho in the sierra where some of the worst massacres had occurred during the recent civil war. Jim snoozed off recalling high school American History and the description of the Alphabet Agencies of FDR along with his packing the Supreme Court, an insult to American constitutional institutions, rank treason and apostasy, and his dream involved The Master of Acronyms in a game where you could be out if you missed just one question. This interlocutor looked sort of like The Penguin in Batman, in his tails and spats and grinning with his cigarette holder in his teeth. Question: 'And now for our next question, Jim, who is buried in your garden? Is it Chester or is it Nestor? Nestor is of course: (a) the sage Greek counselor who advised against hooking up with Hester; or (b) a venerable and wise old man. Jim's Answer: Both of the above. Ah, a wise guy, Master Pengy said, with that game show host grin. 'Fool, think you're so smart, who built the step pyramid of Zoser, who did William tell, who's buried in Grant's tomb, and who came not to praise Caesar? Get all those right and move on to the next level, Sonny Boy Jim. How about Acronyms for a category, the ABC

countries and you are presently in P. On our radar. Bewilderment—
Jim: 'Wait, what was the question again?' Master Pengy: 'Sorry, kid,
if you don't know the question, you can't get the answer, can you?'
'Oh give him a clue, Pengy,' Miss Dolores in her satin bustier pleaded
for him. 'Keep this under your hat,' Master Pengey said. 'Try looking
up TS, old man.'

"TS," Jim said, waking up and jotting down the details in his
dreambook, the notepad he kept on his bed table for that purpose, all
the while thinking 'what is this TS, the standard US FBI acronym
for Technical Surveillance?', which he'd learned back in his antiwar
days when Jedgar was listening to him tinkle. Not that he thought the
IRS or the DEA would be lobbing bodies over his wall, but if they'd
been bugging him to access client information, that was a horse of
a different color, they might have an informal sharing agreement or
an agent making money on the side. What an irony: he'd filed all
his 1040s for years, didn't keep two sets of books, wasn't protesting
Vietnam, was feeling good about a centrist Democrat in the White
House.

TS, the IRS, it didn't make any sense, he was off on a false trail.
Now, exactly what was it Emcee Pengy said in the dream, 'Try
looking up TS, old man.'

'Old man', is that from Gatsby, or English usage like 'old chap'?

Nestor is the wise old man, and also the name of the very old
man in his garden, as in one cannot get any older than when one is
in Eternity, then he remembered the place in "The Wasteland" where
the poet recalls Stetson being at Mylae, a battle in the Punic Wars,
'a war of commerce', and asks whether the body in his garden has
sprouted yet. The reference was to Romans and the community of
the faithful.

"Oh, God, the TS is for T.S. Eliot," Jim exclaimed, getting up
out of bed and finding a modern poetry classics anthology with

"The Wasteland" and quickly locating the line about the body in the garden. It was in Line 71.

Soon after, with his mind on acronyms, Jim remembered NAL were not only the initials of Nestor Aurelio Lenguado, deceased recently in his garden, but also of Norman A. Larsen, chief counsel for Seymour Industries, also deceased in Jim's garden 1986, Lima, Peru, but fortunately not buried there. NIMBY (not in my back yard) was a good rule when disposing of bodies, not dead by his agency but at a time it would have been terrible for the Seymours, especially Helen's mother, who'd gone off her rocker right after her husband died up in the sierra. Well, after managing to kill Harry Seymour in the sierra, Larsen had arranged for his body to be lost at sea, not to make it home to Philadelphia and possibly prompt an inquest that could void a multi-million dollar insurance policy on the CEO. And Larsen hadn't readied a coffin for Harry alone. He'd also made provisions for Jim and Pedro, a med student who'd done toxicology tests on Harry to confirm Jim's suspicions of foul play. It wasn't Jim who'd shot Larsen in his garden; it was either Jim's brother-in-law to be, Peter Seymour, or Pete's lover and future wife, Holly Abbott, Jim hadn't seen which. The S.O.B. was blackmailing Holly, threatening to tell all about her old days in the life, and ruin her marriage plans with Pete.

That episode with Larsen had been ten years ago, and virtually nobody knew about it back then, well, at least nobody who'd want to talk about it. Norm Larsen had been muscling Jim when Holly Abbott showed up and Norm shot at her first before getting shot. She and Pete didn't even know Larsen was already dead when they left his place, because Jim told them he was going back inside to call an ambulance. But Norm was already gone when Jim got to him, lying down in the cellar stairwell. After he'd horsed Larsen's body into the SUV and the coffin, which he locked and drove to the docks of Callao, Jim saw the coffin loaded on the boat that later sank offshore. The old InterCon hulk called the General Ochoa had exited Callao harbor pumping bilge and exuding a heavy oil smoke, needed an engine overhaul bad, went down in about 10,000 feet in the Humboldt Current, so even with a Jacques Cousteau in a diving bell, it'd be long odds ever finding that wreck.

Jim had thought at the time there might be some back-flack from the case, but there was nothing substantial. Two insurance agents did come to Lima about Harry, the first guy Hansen arriving the Monday after the Sunday Jim had shipped Harry Seymour's body home on a private flight. That Monday Jim was in Valparaiso pretending to be Larsen absconding, and when he got back to his office Tuesday, Hansen was waiting. He'd heard this bogus press release Norm had prearranged, that Harry's body had been lost at sea in an explosion, was unaware that Harry was already interred back in Haverford Mills. Hansen was pretty hot and thought Jim had snookered him, so they sent another guy to follow up, Pirasini, a young Italian-American attorney who recalled a big city, clean-up prosecutor. After inquiring about Larsen, he'd noticed the recent excavations in the garden, and Jim had made some crack about the backhoe and the massive root ball of the fig. Oh God, did the insurance Johnny think Jim was just in his face, like 'yeh, Norm's takin' the long nap in my garden, whatchu gonna do about it?' Ach, that was crazy too: insurance men didn't throw bodies into the gardens of those suspected of insurance fraud. They might know T.S. Eliot, but they didn't as a rule lob bodies over your garden wall. It had to be somebody else besides Pirasini, or Piranesi or Pirandello as he and Helen occasionally referred to him when talking about the case and the days after Daddy died, as those days receded in the taillights of time. It wouldn't likely be Pete or Holly bringing up the subject of old Norm now, because there was no statute of limitations on murder, in the U.S. or in Peru.

It was like when he'd lost his keys or cell phone or wallet, before he called to cancel all his credit cards, he felt he had to go back and trace things and haply for him, the muse of memory was like a forgiving mother, and let him recall every detail.

Oh, there was that Juan Stelzer. That was the name on the accounts in Lima and Valparaiso, Chile as a co-signer with Larsen. Jim had always assumed that Stelzer was his straw man, if he were a real person at all. The Chilean police had identified Stelzer as a suspect in Larsen's disappearance, in part due to Jim's work in extending Norm's life by the miracle of impersonation. Maybe Stelzer was not an alias, was Norm's partner and a friend, we all need friends, even the bad boys. Maybe the cops gave Stelzer trouble after Larsen's disappearance, and now he was coming after Jim on the tenth anniversary of Norm's being gone. Still, most con men don't know a lot of T.S. Eliot. So many maybes, and a frustrating lot of theories.

When at a total loss for a reasonable explanation, go back to the last thread of it, or talk to somebody smart with a detached view, so he called his old friend, Frank Mathiessen, in La Paz. After they had discussed empty nest, which Frank and Luz were suffering with their two eldest off to college in the States, he got down to business.

"Hey, Frank, you remember back about ten years ago you put me in touch with a man named Benavides to act as an agent on the docks at Callao?" Jim said.

"Benavides was a top notch guy," Frank said. "Didn't he act as a go-between for you and some shipper? That was after Helen's dad kicked in the sierra."

"Yeh, an outfit called InterCon, the boss there was named Ugarte," Jim said, explaining that Norman A. Larsen had disappeared about that time, and now Nestor A. Lenguado had appeared dead in his garden, and his fear was that somebody was playing some morbid name game with acronyms, maybe an old associate with an eye on blackmail. "Could you maybe check up on this?"

"Probably just a coincidence, man, life's full of them, but sure, if it'll make you happy, I'll check up," Frank said. "This T.S. Eliot idea, that's kind of wild though. So now you're back to batching it alone? How's that going for you?"

"Not so great," Jim said. "I don't do well without a woman. I need one to keep me steady, or like they say on the talk shows, to complete me."

"Or to complete sentences for me because she knows what I'm thinking before I say it, that's what Lucita would say," Frank said. "So Helen's staying in Philly a while longer? She's already been there a while, right?"

"Her mother's not good, it's Alzheimer's," Jim said, realizing it was the same thing he said the last time they talked, and Helen had been back home almost two years. "Her mom just didn't adjust to the nursing home, was continually trying to leave, saying she wanted to go home now. Can't really blame her much with compulsory crafts class, who needs clay slip mess, just reminds you Mother Earth's waiting, and the big Wurlitzer booming out 'Alley Cat' to keep the somnolent awake. Helen thinks I could get a lot of investment clients there, but I don't want to start all over now. It's not easy to be without a woman. There are putas to help me make paja, but really I need a woman, and Helen's not coming back. Plus, the air fares, I can't afford to commute one month out of four. Especially if I'm getting bodies dumped in my garden when I'm away."

"You need to get away to La Paz for a visit," Frank said. "Lucita's been in an empty nest depression now with Elena gone this Fall. Her brilliant little girl has gone off to Stanford just like her big brother before her. Frankie loves California and only calls every couple of weeks. He says, Papa, you mean you voluntarily left California to go to Bolivia? I tell him it was so I could meet your mother and procreate you, kiddo. Come up, Jimmy, and we'll go out and get blotto. She has a niece aged thirty-five and just divorced. Still young stuff."

It felt good to say it out loud to Frank that he knew Helen was never coming back to Peru. He thought she'd go home years ago, the day when the Tupac Amaru Castroist rebels set off a big bomb that left a crater a city block wide, destroying a statue of JFK and leaving forty dead, Helen as usual was a night owl and it woke her, and she thought it was an earthquake. Miraflores was a quiet, affluent south-side Lima suburb, and Helen had been a gracious host there whether his clients had come from the upper echelons or from the ayacuchano barrio where he'd helped with a micro-investment cooperative. He'd fallen in love with the 'Cuch' scenery that summer of '69 when Frank and he fished the streams and lakes of the province, with the rugged beauty of the Andes, a hard land and the men and women made strong by it. And then, next in their trail of tears, came the Manchay Tiempo, the Time of Fear that Sendero created, the Vietnam of the Andes it was called.

No, it wasn't fear of Sendero or TupacAmaru rebels that had sent Helen home to Philly. It was her mother's advancing Alzheimer's, and the decision to put her in a nursing home. It didn't work out well, when her mother kept saying she just wanted to go home, and Helen couldn't bear hearing her mother needed to be restrained from leaving the nursing home. Her brother, Pete, was not going to be the one to help. She was the only one. She moved back into the family mansion in Haverford Mills, with those porches that seemed to go on forever curving around the house like you'd reach the Poconos if you kept going, the place so large that most of it was closed off and her mother and the practical nurse and Helen lived in six or seven rooms. The place was immense beyond that, with a carriage house, summer cottage, cabana, pergola, fake Greek temple, and had gingerbread carpentry that needed high maintenance, not to mention that Joan Seymour didn't want any bushes or trees cut or pruned, so these immense overgrown woody mock orange with invading grape vines from the arbor reached the porch gutters and clogged the downspouts with roots, blocking the light so that it recalled the House of Usher, depressingly gloomy to him in a way she couldn't comprehend, telling him they could live there and he could remodel her dad's den in the carriage house for his office. He'd gone up there and found squirrels had gotten in and taken up residence, making nests with old press clippings, a notice for all German military to report to Allied authorities, his war medals and French francs and German marks. Jim evicted the critters, repaired the holes in the eaves, cleaned it up and made it a nice storage space for his own old files. He'd done enough rehab on his house in Lima, he liked things the way they were there and didn't need to take on any new projects.

Helen's question to him was why he didn't just roll up his business in Lima, and come back to be with her. She thought they had enough money, but her perspective was of one who'd always been rich. He wasn't so sure about her money, so he wanted to keep his business going. His buddy at Seymour Industries, Vince Scarlatti, told him of problems there where family ownership had now dipped below forty per cent with the outside creditors working behind the scenes to acquire controlling interest. They'd been contacting shareholders, and complicating the situation was the substantial block of shares which Peter Seymour had, because he had been a spendthrift and cocaine addict for a long time, and it wasn't clear how many of his shares he may have pledged in the past. In addition to her own stock, Helen possessed a general power of attorney for her mother, so she controlled the largest single block of shares, but there had also been moves by the board of directors to increase the number of shares issued, which could dilute the pool of existing shares. There'd also been a proposal to reduce the dividend on preferred stock, which was income Helen took from her trust to support her lifestyle, which was not frugal. She'd never been on a budget, and liked Gucci shoes and looked good in them. Shoes were wearable Art, Art was sacred, ergo Money was no object there.

His first financial advice to Helen had been to diversify her I.R.A. out of Seymour stock, which she was loaded up on, and he'd been able to make her money in the Clinton bull market on the money she pulled out of the company. She still controlled the biggest block of family stock, which had survived the Chapter Eleven reorganization and creditors' composition, though her family lawyer, Dev Smith, agreed with Jim that the 'Chicago creditors' were happy now because the company was making money, maybe because Norm Larsen wasn't skimming profits now. But how long would that last?

Dev told him after Norm's disappearance that he'd pegged Larsen as a crook from when he was first brought in by the Chicago creditors as counsel to the board of directors, and wasn't at all surprised that he'd absconded with three million, and faked his own death in Chile.

"He's sipping a marguerita on some tropic beach, I have no doubt," Dev said.

"He was a sly one," Jim said, thinking 'no, Dev, Norm is in Davey Jones' Locker in very deep water off Peru, while his victim and your mentor, Harry Seymour, is at rest in a classy Pennsylvania cemetery. It had a nice symmetry, Harry put away in East coast North America, or Norm in West coast South America, like a global yin yang, like a classic myth instead of a pair of unsolved homicides. And it had a moral symmetry: Harry's company was safe from takeover for the time being, and his killer, Norm Larsen, got his shortly after his victim passed.

Dev was a great lawyer and had been an immense help in expediting Harry's funeral and interment, and in quashing an insurance company motion for disinterment. He gave straight advice and agreed with Jim it would not be an easy road for him to repatriate and get clients there, the Seymour's crowd was old rich Republicans mainly. They already had trusted financial advisors, so Helen was being unduly optimistic about his prospects, love but verify.

Helen did know some big contributors to the arts through her museum work, but that didn't necessarily translate into clients for him and he'd never had much success with the old boy networks, though that was a big sales feature for the Ivy League. It reminded him of his sophomore year at Yale right after he learned of his dad's big stroke, when he it was his last year there with the situation at home, and vowed to take advantage the great lectures there, settled on an Egyptology talk and stumbled into this room with antique desks and tweedy, WASP rich, and thought, well this is certainly a world I never could have imagined without seeing it, Egyptology must be the hobby horse of preference for the East Coast idle rich. Yeh, he tried to improve himself there, saw classics at the Yale Film Society for a buck a show, the same as three packs of Winstons, it was so sad when they showed <u>Citizen Kane</u>, and all the preppies got teary when it got to Rosebud, since so many had been sent from home at a tender age.

Jim could have made more of an effort to socialize when he visited back in Philly, but he only wanted to be with Helen when he was there. She'd missed him and was very responsive. He was like a camel drinking at an oasis. There was one oracle of Apollo in a Libyan oasis, crazy huh, it was like he was on it there, though he tried to keep it in.

Back in Philly for a Thanksgiving visit, the Mummers were tuning up, it was a nice turkey day and he got a chance to play tennis with Vince Scarlatti, the old family friend and protégé of Harry Seymour with whom he shared the Seymour Industries scuttlebutt after a couple of sets. Vince was around fifty and in good shape, had been a linebacker prospect at Penn State, could make the quick lateral and forward-backward moves of tennis. Since he was eyeing early retirement from the company, he kept up with things. It seemed that Pete Seymour's shares were the object of the most recent push by the 'new Chicago creditors', as Vince called them, though they'd been in Seymour now for over a decade. He used to say about them, it's like we don't have enough wise guys in Philly, they got to bring them in from ChiTown. The shipping business was legit and making money, despite some rake-offs by young Turks like Larsen and their kids or nephews, and the old guys were getting a good return on investment, but they still wanted a controlling interest. Jim had thought that Pete in his Baudelairean course of self-destruction to spur creation, had probably pledged all his shares, but no, his father had the trust written so Pete received distributions in five year steps all the way to forty-five before he inherited fully. So Pete, who was still composing now more into New Age with a jazz influence and Tibetan prayer bells, quenas and whale songs, still had many shares coming to him and that was of interest to the Chicago boys. And they weren't the only ones. Holly, who'd always taken care of business while Pete was in a creative trance, was now asserting claims to the dividend income.

"They had some kind of blow-up recently," Vince said. "Either he was messing around with someone, or she was, or they both were. They had to call the cops to a motel in New Jersey where he was just trashing the room, threatening to tell everything, and she said 'no problem, I'll kill you if you don't stop talking crazy, nobody's after you'. But actually I think the creditors were after him. He has elephantine appetites and no concept of finances."

"So has she filed?" Jim said.

"My understanding is she left and filed in Wisconsin, then withdrew it, or put it on hold," Vince said.

"Wisconsin?" Jim said. "What's that about? She was in a foster home there when she was younger. Wait, it's a community property state. Maybe she's trying to get to the income from this next bunch of shares coming to him before the Chicago boys put their mitts on it."

"Helen probably knows more about this than me," Vince said.

"He doesn't tell her everything," Jim said. "She's saved his bacon so many times she prefers to live in blissful ignorance. And she tells me, oh, just retire and we can live here, after the board's share dilutions and cutting preferred dividends. Six per cent is still fat, but who knows what tomorrow brings. I just hope you get out of it clean."

"They're trying to cut the pensions too," Vince said. "It's like they're rewriting my future. If I'd been siphoning off money, I could understand them saying you been taking from us, we take back from you, but hell, I'm here every day making things work. It's their kids, they've gotten jobs for them, now they're skimming like Larsen."

"Larsen was their man, even though he was skimming from the start," Jim said. "I met him once in Lima. A real schmuck. Didn't they trace him down to Chile?"

"One story is he was murdered in a deal that went sour there, and his body sent out to sea," Vince said.

"Yeh, Dev Smith thinks he staged the whole thing, is alive and sipping a cool drink in a hammock while a winsome native girl fans his brow," Jim said. "How about you?"

"I wouldn't be one bit surprised," Vince said.

'Swell,' Jim thought, 'if that remains the official story, and as for the unofficial one, close enough, maybe a few miles north, rest in peace, Norman, in the Peru-Chile Trench, the deepest water in the Pacific this side of the Marianas Trench.

"Say, he didn't have any close friends that you know of?" Jim said.

"No, he was a loner," Vince said. "Nobody knew he was taking off with the dough. The big boys did a thorough internal investigation."

Still, there was the 'press release from the dead'. Somebody had to send that to the papers because Norm was planning to fly to Santiago the night of the anticipated loss of Harry's coffin at sea. There had also been prior financial transactions in Lima to arrange that burial at sea, including at least one joint account with his straw man or alias, Stelzer. Most of his pass-through accounts for a rainy day getaway had been in Santiago and Valparaiso, which coincidentally made the trail Jim laid down in Chile and the scenario of absconding more credible. InterCon, S.A., had been the shipper of the funerary freighter, had been a Seymour lessee, subsidiary or agent before, but Jim thought poking around there might stir up more trouble than it was worth. Frank's friend, Benavides, could find things out more discreetly. As far as Chile, where Norm had taken advantage of the secrecy of Pinochet's regime to channel money to a hoard in the Grand Caymans, Turks and Caicos, Austrian and Swiss banks, and in preparing the path of his own departure, had laid the foundation for Jim's obfuscation, Jim had no reason to revisit that scene.

Regarding the press release, he could call his journalist friend, Tommy Davila, whom he'd recruited to guide him to find Pete in Tingo Maria, and who helped him drive Harry's body back to Lima after he had the big one at a sierra resort. All the tour books advised taking two or three days to adjust to the altitude, but Harry was impatient to a New York minute. They iced Harry down in the back seat of Jim's Satellite, got him to Lima and Tommy took him on down the coast to Chincha Alta for a private flight back to the States, a practical expedient since Joan Seymour was already mentally unstable, and could not have stood up having her spouse's corpse poked and prodded by insurance investigators, or made the subject of a criminal investigation.

—◊—

Tommy knew all about Harry's case, but fortunately little about Larsen's, and nothing on the subject of whether he was dead or not. That fated Sunday evening Tommy had arrived at Jim's to pick up Harry's body, unaware that Larsen was already in the coffin in the big black SUV, waiting for Jim to run it down to the Callao docks. The place felt like a damn mortuary for a while. Tommy could maybe track down that press release, it would be somewhere in the morgue of some Lima paper. They kept good records, maybe a mixed inheritance from colonial days when everything official in South America had to go through Lima. When Jim had been researching an article on the Two Hundred Mile Limit in a ministry archive, he'd found a copy of the letter from FDR's State Department thanking Peru for adopting this expansion of territorial waters, aimed at keeping Nazi ships from refueling and resupplying in South America. Now the war was over and done, the U.S. tuna fleet wanted back the old twelve mile limit to access the rich waters off Peru, which wanted it for itself, to control its own resources, not a hard call for Jim, didn't indicate he approved all expropriations, just he knew the history and had seen hunger and malnutrition there. He liked international law and it did come in handy in the investment business, where there'd been better money for him.

"Hola, Tommy, how have you been?" Jim said. "Want to get together for a drink this evening? You remember that Harry Seymour case? I kept telling you to be careful about it. These people are rich. They bump into things because they're big and don't even realize it."

"Sure, we drove Harry's body down to your place from the sierra, then next day I took him south to that airstrip at Chincha Alta," Tommy said. "They put Harry right on the plane for home and I saw it take off. It got there, didn't it?"

"It did, but the strangest thing now, that case may have come up again after all these years, and I wonder if you could check out a story that may have appeared in Lima papers the next morning," Jim said, refreshing his memory describing what would likely have been a short piece reporting the loss at sea of the body of American business magnate, Harry Seymour, after his decease in Oxapampa. Tommy knew the story from Oxapampa down to Lima, where they stashed and iced the body in Jim's wine cellar, while Jim conferred with Helen about arrangements. With her okay, Tommy then took Harry's body south to Chincha Alta for the flight home that Sunday night, saw him put on a small jet to the U.S., and didn't even know

Larsen had been at his place that afternoon, much less about the shooting or his final oceanic resting place. Tommy did remember that Hansen, the first insurance agent who interviewed him, mentioned he had learned of a report that Harry's body had been lost at sea, but Tommy told him he knew nothing about that report. He knew Jimmy suspected Larsen of Harry's murder, though he didn't share that with Hansen, and to him also it seemed highly likely that Norm was now sipping a piña colada on a white sand beach behind shades with a chica linda applying sunscreen.

"You think Larsen may be back on the tenth anniversary to settle old scores?" Tommy said.

"Him or a buddy of his, I have no idea, man," Jim said, thinking 'you'd appreciate the irony if I could tell you, because Norm and I wanted basically the same thing, for Harry not to be tested, but then Norm also didn't want me or Pedro around with any evidence of foul play, and the final irony was him unwittingly prearranging his own burial at sea. "I'm totally in the dark. I thought maybe your intern could check on that press release."

"No problem," Tommy said. "The trip was crazy from the start. First finding prodigal son, Pete, in that bar in Tingo, then Harry on ice in the back seat of your car. It reminded me of Juana La Insana hauling King Philip's body around in her carriage. She couldn't bear to part with him."

"Was that Philip the Fourth, or Philip the Fair?" Jim said.

"By the end of Spanish summer, it must have been Philip the Foul, waiting for it to blow over, and why have not ten years time done that for Harry Seymour?" Tommy said. "Is this some kind of weird anniversary thing?"

"Oh, it gets weirder, but I don't want to bore you with arcane details," Jim said.

"No, by all means bore me," Tommy said, but then when Jim explained the same acronyms in the Larsen and Lenguado cases and the link to T.S. Eliot, he shook his head. "Jimmy, you should have been a literature professor."

"Yeh, but no," Jim said. "How great is a profession that took seventy-five years to see Moby Dick was a classic?"

"Only problem with your theory, how many mugs know T.S. Eliot?" Tommy said. "I have a couple sources in Fisheries and on the docks. How much of a rush are you in? Are you about to go back to the U.S. for Christmas?"

"No, I was just there," Jim said. "It was depressing as hell. It's like the House of Seven Gables. Helen's the main caregiver for her mother, who has Alzheimer's. I don't know if she'll ever come back here."

"And when I saw you last, I thought you were starting a family," Tommy said.

"We were, but she lost the child, and it affected her," Jim said. "She went into a depression."

"I'm sorry, I didn't know," Tommy said.

"We'll have to get together, I've just trimmed my evergreens for Christmas wreaths and the place smells like a bottle of Pinesol," Jim said. "Call and come by for a drink. Wassail and all that."

"Wassail and salud pues," Tommy said. "I'll see what I can dig up for you."

Three days later Tommy called him back and they met at a bar-restaurant with umbrella tables that flapped in the wind rising over the Miraflores cliffs, so with the street noise of late rush hour, even with a shotgun mic it would have been hard to hear them. Journalism wasn't always the easiest profession to follow in Peru—back to the days of Velasco's press restraints from the Left and now Fuji on the Right had taken over a leading TV station, Channel 2, and was suppressing criticism of the regime. Tommy used to describe himself as an armchair anarchist, probably closest in outlook to APRA on the left, though their first elected president, Alan Garcia, had disillusioned him after initially inspiring hope in 1985.

It was windy as they walked out the promenade and heat lightning played in the sky over the ocean.

"My intern found that story you asked about," Tommy said. "It was sent in to the Correo night desk and got picked up by wire services. Eminent U.S. businessman dead in Peru, his body lost at sea. The editor remembered it because they printed a retraction. And he said the man who sent it in was a Sr. Ugarte."

"At InterCon Shipping, right?" Jim said.

"Yes, InterContinental, SA, has received some fat government contracts and has connections in the U.S.," Tommy said. "Bribery and corruption mixed with amigismo have been around here since Creation, so it's old news to say something's rotten in the state of Peru. But the present exceeds the lowest lows of the past. The government buys friends and kills critics. These are people who wouldn't talk to me if they knew I were a journalist."

"You went down to the docks on this?" Jim said.

"Not me personally, I have people I know," Tommy said. "You want me to keep on digging?"

"You've done great, but maybe let things settle a while, if it is Larsen come back to haunt me," Jim said, or possibly Tommy could figure out what Jim had done that Sunday night, since musical bodies seemed to be the jeu du jour.

"I'm working on a big story now, but I'll let you know if anything new comes in on the feelers I already put out," Tommy said. "It interests me Jimmy, because I have a nose for a story. A fictional death at sea, what was that line from the Wasteland?"

"Oh, that T.S. Eliot thing was nuts, man, I was going around in circles, grasping at straws," Jim said. "That was wild-ass idea. Once I said in a paper on a Dryden funeral ode there was a play on the word 'mold'. The prof said 'absurd', and I said, yeh man, that's what I was going for."

"There does seem to be this maritime theme though," Tommy said, smiling as he dropped the subject or rather transitioned it to general terms of how old cases sometimes reopened, mentioned the rumor mill at Fisheries was buzzing about the Banchero case and possible links to Klaus Barbie's discovery in Lima by a German immigrant employee who'd seen in a German paper a time-enhanced photo of 'gorilla ears', as Resistance prisoners called him, recognized him, and reported it to Banchero, a shipping and fishing magnate, who in turn vouched for his veracity in a letter.

"Wasn't that back in like '71, has that come up again?" Jim said, well aware of the original investigation because Lima police searched the mansion of another ex-Nazi officer, a currency dealer and money man, where Barbie had been recognized at a social function, and found a concealed safe-room in the cellar. Capt. Fregosco had alerted Harry Stein and Jim, who were researching Haberman, that his name appeared in a second set of books found there, along with that of Alois Meidel, who had also sold looted art in South America. That had helped Jim track Haberman down in La Paz, but nothing indicated a link with Barbie, and his friend, Frank Mathiessen, told him that Haberman had closed his bank accounts and warehouse there.

"The cops said it was a crime of passion by the gardener, but a lot of people questioned that," Tommy said. "You knew the CIA was running Barbie in counterinsurgency."

"Yeh, he claimed credit for hunting down Che Guevara," Jim said. "I always wondered if the company brought him to Peru for the same job. It would have been embarrassing for them, the Butcher of Lyon on U.S. payroll."

"They disclaimed all knowledge, but a ministry official in La Paz says otherwise," Tommy said. "Peru sure dumped him back on Bolivia quick. An army colonel ran him up to Desaguadero in January in a VW. Talk about brand loyalty."

"He's dead for his murders now," Jim said.

"Yeh, the Banchero case was twenty-five years ago," Tommy said. "It is interesting how things crop up again. This Larsen is only gone ten years. Maybe he thinks it's safe to surface."

"I don't know," Jim said, thinking 'not likely to surface from the depths with that amount of mahogany and the lead liner in the coffin, Norm picked it out himself for Harry at the Paz Eternal funeral home, never dreaming it would be for himself, which was why it always pays to get top of the line.'

Everything was still a bunch of theories, making Jim glad he'd saved the CYA evidence on Larsen, from the tape that included his confession to Harry Seymour's murder, to his gun he'd been firing at Pete and Holly, a slug from it dug out his trellis that showed he'd been firing, his bloody tie that Jim had used to try to stop the bleeding, but you can't tourniquet a shot to the heart, all this in zip-lock plastic bags, along with little notebooks that chronicled his thefts from Seymour Inc. and books for Santiago banks and some passwords for Turks and Caicos and Swiss accounts.

"I'll get back to your case, but I've got a big story now," Tommy said. "You know if Montesinos goes down, we can get Chinochet out."

As he drove home, Jim kept hearing echoes of the conversation with Tommy, like 'police called it a crime of passion,' 'they say the gardener did it, but some doubts remain', and 'there seems to be a maritime theme here'. He went to his basement to get a bottle of wine when he got home, inspecting the masonry work he'd done there ten years before to create a receptacle for the Larsen files, with eight by sixteen cement blocks with an inch thick parging and bright white stucco finish to create what looked like an unbroken wall from colonial or pre-Columbian days. His thick oak basement door with a dead-bolt and double locks seemed not to have been breached during the recent Lenguado incursion, but he needed to get his wire man back in there to sweep for bugs and these new transistor cameras. He picked up a bottle of Ocucaje merlot, grapes did great there just like in Napa, and he didn't look around much except to see it all looked smooth and no dust on the table or chairs down there. Call the wire man, put that on your list, just something else to survive on your own, not much help from Uncle Sam on this one, might even be Sam pushing on me, the gov types down here tended to be rightwingers, it was a U.S. major who set Barbie up in Bolivia, so no surprise if they shared files on former protesters, they still blamed them for losing the war, heh, after defeating Tojo and the blonde beasts, the Red Threat was numero uno and Barbie was on our side in the holy war. LBJ had his library back in Texas, probably no push-button recordings of his speech 'we will not ask American boys to do the job that Southeast Asian boys should do' and after he won a landslide, he turned right around and did just that, thought he had a mandate in Nam. Not so, but it's hard to tell the Emperor he has no clothes, that the horse led to water is not drinking and the river is burning, and the children are crying at Kent State.

His basement wall had not even a hairline crack in it, neither invasive jackhammers, nor temblors of Lima had cracked it, he thought of it like a sealed tomb of a high official in the time of the Pharaohs' Dynasties. Strange that today that a president had more power than Ramses the Great or Caesar Augustus.

His wall looked like a solid if you didn't know what was there behind it.

—m—

Tommy had said he'd get back to Jim on the Larsen case soon, but another big story intervened when the MRTA, the Castroist Tupac Amaru rebels, took over the Japanese Embassy at a holiday reception and took more than 90 people hostage. It was a slap in the face of Fujimori, after he'd captured the Sendero chief Guzman and effectively defeated the Maoist rebels, a significantly greater threat than MRTA, which never numbered more than a hundred or so fighters.

Jim had been sitting on his couch watching a TV documentary on global warming with these immense glacier cliffs crashing down into the sea, and thinking 'this is just like my love life, first it heats up and then it falls apart'. Then the news came on about MRTA taking over the Japanese embassy during a reception.

The hostage situation dragged on drearily through Christmas and into the New Year. Tommy complained in February that the hostage story was driving everything else onto the back pages, while he was getting more reports on the bugging of Congressmen taking bribes from Montesinos. Monty was videotaping them taking his bribes to ensure their support for Fujimori, so an arm-twist secured with tape. Who knows how they might have voted without the mordida, the bite, the slang for bribe, but they didn't get elected to national office for their wives to go around in old shoes. Chinochet had shut down Channel Two for criticism of his corruption, but it was one thing to call foul and another to have proof. Now for Fuji to get punked by the Tupac Amarus after bringing down Sendero, it was like getting treed by a hound after killing a bear. But he was busy at work, though the Tupac captors kept releasing hostages to show their good faith, and had settled into a routine where they were playing their daily intramural soccer for recreation when the marines poured out of their tunnels dug quietly over weeks by expert miners under the embassy walls, and took over the compound in April with only one hostage casualty.

All of the Tupac captors died in the raid, many allegedly in execution style after they had surrendered. There was no great sympathy for the rebels. Peru had been beleaguered by terrorism for over a decade, and MRTA maybe had a message in taking the Japanese Embassy with an undercurrent also against a perceived new colonialism. From an indigenista perspective, Peru had been ruled by foreigners since Pizarro, so now with a Nisei on top, it was like Fuji was putting the country on sale, like selling your sister to Ming the Merciless.

"It began before Christmas and ended with Easter, like a passion play," Tommy said, who was naturally suspicious, even speculating the hostage crisis might have been a ploy set up by Fujimori to divert attention from his autocratic excesses, but Jim told him he was being paranoid, everybody knew MRTA was Castroist, so it might as likely have been Fidel pulling it, though of course the rebels weren't talking because they were all dead.

They'd gone out to a café at the shore in Miraflores, because Tommy thought he was under surveillance, got drunk and it was a windy summer day. He loved to hear Jim tell about his childhood in Ohio and vice versa as he did of Tommy's in Lima, not Lima, Ohio, which was named in gratitude for Peru sending quinine to relieve a yellow fever epidemic in NW OH Maumee region, mosquito-ridden swamp before they drained it, good muck soil, onions and sugar beets and nitrogen fertilizer run-off that was creating massive Lake Erie algae blooms feeding the invasive zebra mussels that clogged the water intake grates, all that after the Cuyahoga River caught fire, like bad news from home apocalyptic Rust Belt images, before the Rock n' Roll Hall Of Fame came to Cleveland, bringing bright modernity to this dirty old part of the city, maybe in tribute to Alan Freed, the DJ who coined the term and got persecuted for playing that sexy, subversive music. Downstate Chiquita Brands had its headquarters in Cincinnati, and due to its advertising every American knew that you should never, never refrigerate bananas. Then one night Pocha told him to get the bananas out of the refrigerator for fruit salad and he thought 'what?'—and they did have brown skins and like a week old from the market, but inside were firm and snowy, not inedible or even gastronomically compromised. So Chiquita Banana had lied to him, a corporate mendacity, it was like Johnny Lennon had it right when he sang, Can you believe the lies they told us, how they controlled us? Chiquita might have heard the Peruvian jungle had some dark predatory history in the rubber barons of the Putumayo whose murderous rule of terror Sir Roger Casement described as the Amazonian Congo, comparable to the colonial terror the Belgian police imposed on the Congolese peoples. But it was still like 'what you don't know, can't hurt you'.

"It's like Big Brother watching," Tommy said, hinting by nodding his head back to an apparent tourist with a camera at an umbrella table beside the parapet wall at the edge of the cliffs down to the Pacific. "Big story, I've been working on. If it's right, it could cook Montesinos' goose, even get to Chinochet."

"Oh boy, I came to you about this Lenguado case thinking you might do some discreet investigation, and maybe I just muddied the waters," Jim said.

"Not actually," Tommy said. "I did go down to the Callao docks before this big story broke. It's lucky you warned me again about that Seymour case. I went disguised as a chef from the Hotel Crillon."

His intern had done research on InterCon, and found on their list of goods shipped was produce and seafood. Tommy said he saw no evidence of either on the docks that morning, while a secretary went to find her boss, who was around. When Ugarte came in, he said there was no seafood today, was an old businessman who didn't see much business in Tommy, who persisted if there were fresh asparagus or other produce available, he'd been a buyer when Seymour Lines had an operation there.

With that mention, Ugarte looked him over, and said 'perhaps you need to speak with their agent, I will call him', whereupon he went to the window and called down to a man on the docks, 'Pedro', a tall gringo in his late thirties wearing anodized shades and a light cotton suit like Dan Duryea used to wear in Singapore intrigue movies, a dude with long blond hair and when he turned to answer the call, Tommy said he saw it was Peter Seymour, he was sure though it had been ten years since he'd seen the prodigal, and he took off before Pete came upstairs to the Intercon office.

Ten years back Larsen had claimed that Pete was his man in Tingo Maria, checking to make sure cocaine bricks went out on flights while he fed his own coke habit at discount rates, this because his old man cut him off financially and was suing to have him declared incompetent. Pete had inherited a large sum when his father passed, but his dynasty trust still had stepped age limits of five years up to 45 for full disposition, and he was an addict and a spendthrift. Jim had calculated back then, if he had a $90,000.00 a year habit, especially with steep interest if he had to borrow when he was squeezed, he could well have spent everything, including pledging future interests, again at a steep loan rate. They didn't talk at all about money when they last got together in Haverford Mills a couple years ago, didn't even ask Jim any legal questions, as if Holly were just eternally grateful for what Jim did with regard to Larsen, and she seemed to have a thing for Jim, which made him somewhat uneasy, given what he knew about her.

So Pete Seymour was back in Lima, evidently back to working for those Chicago creditors who had been moving in on Seymour Industries for a decade, 'the new creditors' Vince Scarlatti still called them, and suspected there wasn't just jumbo shrimp from the Humboldt Current in those refrigerated holds, a nice operation, scampi for restaurants, and white powder for lines on mirrors for secret fun in the New Prohibition. Ah, the Puritan spirit of America, if it's fun, it's likely bad, and for some like Pete, it was bad, he couldn't restrain himself, justified it as necessary to create his music, but then he might have been an alcoholic like his late father, if it hadn't been cocaine.

"Hmm, the prodigal returns," Jim said. "Helen didn't know where he was when I was back in November. I wonder what exactly Pete is doing here and how long he's been around?"

"I can't say," Tommy said. "You said to hang back. I didn't know if Pete would recognize me after ten years, even with a beard and a chef's jacket, and playing the maricon. Did I do right?"

"Perfect, man," Jim said.

Jim briefly considered disguising himself to check up whether this was Pete, quickly decided it would be easier to call Helen and have a long chat. They did talk every few days, with international rates just coming down after the Supreme Court broke up AT&T. Sometimes he'd call and get the answering machine, and then she'd call back that night or the next day.

Tommy was right about the surveillance. Someone did tail Jim home that evening, but after he put in a call to Captain Fregosco, the tail disappeared. It was Tommy who was the focus, because he was working on the story that eventuated in covering the intrigue that led to a terrible political murder. He had seen a lot of darkness in the politics of Fujimori, who had suspended Congress in '92 and might not have held elections in '95 if not for threatened U.S. sanctions. Congress was back in session now, and though the nation would be eternally grateful to El Presidente for ridding it of Sendero, many felt it was time for a change, and the functioning of political parties such as APRA was building resistance to the administration.

Anyway, Clinton did something for Peru by supporting civilian government and elections that kept congress in session there, and a U.S. President hadn't done much for the country probably since JFK and the Alliance For Progress. LBJ had in effect hastened the fall of Belaunde over the IPC oil controversy, by invoking the Hickenlooper Amendment (cut-off of foreign aid if you expropriate US co. property, irregardless of the corrupt and fraudulent nature of their contract). And funds for the OAS and Alliance For Progress dried up as Vietnam occupied more of the budget. Nixon didn't have a warm place in his heart for where his motorcade got stoned by leftist students from Universidad de San Marcos when he was Ike's veep back in the Fifties. Yeh, neither Lyndon nor he had much use for Latin leftists. After LBJ sent the 84th Airbourne and 22,000 combat troops into the Dominican Republic to prevent a Castro-type government (Juan Bosch was no Fidel), and it was suggested the OAS might take over security, LBJ commented 'these people couldn't pour piss from a boot if the instructions were written on the heel'—folksy, and the takeaway, the OAS was not going to be as important in inter-American relations as the big stick. And Reagan had the Iran-Contra scandal, so yeh, now it was good to feel better about U.S. foreign policy. As far as Nancy and the Just Say No anti-drug campaign, it was admirable but he didn't see much change in the amount of coca leaf produced—they'd wipe out eight thousand acres and forty thousand new would be planted, the growers just moved to another part of the jungle mountain slopes if they had a

DEA-sponsored eradication program at one site, like crop-dusters spraying the same formula as Round-Up and the farmers and their children were getting skin irritation and breathing problems, and damned if the whole thing didn't remind him of Agent Orange in Vietnam, which caused such long-term injury to the Vietnamese and also to American servicemen who were in the area, but you could see why the gringos weren't always so popular in Peru. The War On Drugs really wasn't being won, and the greatest hypocrisy was on the part of the U.S., which was the prime consumer of all that stuff. America sucked it in through all these barriers meant to discourage it, prohibition providing price support, and it enriched criminal syndicates like it had during the Prohibition against alcohol, and created more crime to fund the users' illegal habit. Tommy and he agreed, it was hypocrisy that put the legs on a story—if you were a thug and thief, nobody expected much good from you, but if you were a senator or a priest, you were assumed to live by a higher standard.

Another thing Tommy said was that on his hurried exit from the Muelle d'InterCon, he noticed a man in a nice SUV with two bodyguards go in and shake hands with Pedro Seymour. Maybe now they were routing some of the coke through Lima, rather than flying it out of Tingo and having to pay $15,000 per flight.

"I wonder if Pete was in town when Sr. Lenguado showed up in my garden," Jim said.

"I know how you love your garden," Tommy said. "You do all the work yourself, you don't have a pongo. It's like corruption seems to taint anything of beauty here."

"Chirk up," Jim said. "Look through the clouds, Sendero's gone, Fujimori's on the defensive. People say Velasco's reforms are gone, but a lot survived. Getting rid of the literacy requirement meant new voters and with a $33 fine for not voting, you get better voter turn-out than the U.S."

"It's always fun to talk, Jimmy, it's like going to a Chamber of Commerce booster rally," Tommy said. "Even as I walk in the valley of the shadow of Mt. Fuji, and it can be quite cold on the backside."

"Arriba Peru," Jim said, making the ascending circular sign which was one of the creative logos selling progress during the Velasco years.

As Jim drove home imagining Tommy in the role of a gay chef from the Hotel Crillon, he remembered he needed to inform his amanuensis, L.H. May, to change the name of the Hotel Bolivar back to the Crillon for the shooting scene in "The Gate Of Two Snakes", the second novel in the <u>Tihuantinsuyo Quartet</u>. The Bolivar is a real four-star hotel in downtown Lima with excellent accommodations, service and security and an impressive lobby with crystal chandeliers and polished brass, and might not appreciate being cast as the scene of criminal activity. The Crillon was also a top-flight downtown hotel, in fact John Wayne had stayed there when he was filming in Peru, and that's where the actual shooting of Doc Penny and Haberman's driver had occurred. He'd however visualized the scene in the Bolivar, which has a classic marble staircase, and which the wounded Haberman falls down, evoking the scream from one of the English wives drinking gin and playing bridge in the lobby, someone like Maggie Smith, old enough to remember sirens and scurrying to shelters with bloody Germans up above. It would be great if his agent could sell the film rights and shoot in the Bolivar and they could name it the Hotel Sucre instead, or they might have something grand in India if he had to go through Bollywood. Certainly Luc-Goddard wouldn't be interested after his criticism of the Maoist Sendero atrocities, foggy London Town could simulate Lima, but y'know Politics and the English, big fogs and lapdogs. The Bolivar would be perfect and he could go there and watch shooting on location and eat watercress sandwiches in the lobby like the British did, kept them from getting scurvy, and revise the novel's proof to rename it the Crillon for the film version. That was where that action happened anyway, and the old Crillon was being torn down, so they wouldn't sue for defaming their establishment, and if there were a new Crillon, Jim could say he was writing about the Old Crillon and not the new.

—⟋ℳ⟍—

It was after supper the next day Jim got around to calling Helen. She wasn't in and he left a message that it wasn't urgent, he just wanted to talk. While he was making long distance calls, he decided to get in touch with his favorite Windy City gumshoe, Rad Ratkowski, to ask him about the recent incident of Pete and Holly at the New Jersey motel, the state of their marriage and Pete's recent travel itinerary. He got his answering service, and Rad called back on his own nickel because he had ABD in philosophy, which was Jim's minor in college, and liked to talk.

"Hey St. James, what's shakin' in the Ring of Fire?" Rad said.

"I have just this one question, Professor, if this is the best of all possible worlds, why aren't I happier?" Jim said.

"Either you're not drinking enough, or your woman left you and you're drinking too much," Rad said.

"Bingo, you're right on the money and that's better than Leibnitz did for me," Jim said. "I didn't know monads from gonads. It makes me wonder whether he cribbed calculus from Newton."

"It was simultaneous invention," Rad said. "Reminds me of this joke about Mutual Climax Insurance. This divorce lawyer has the wife in deposition asking about insurance, then moves on to the subject of sex. He asks 'And do you have mutual climax?' and she's distracted and answers, 'No, I think we have Prudential.'"

"That's a scream, Rad," Jim said. "And insurance is not irrelevant to cases at hand, since you remember about ten years ago, you helped me on that Harry Seymour case, and there was a multi-million dollar insurance policy on him, was there another big one on the chief counsel, Norm Larsen?"

"I think there was also like a thirty-five million policy on Larsen," Rad said. "The beneficiary was his last foster home mother in Skokie or Milwaukee. As I recall, they never found a body."

"Yeh, well, see if there's been any action, and also check up on an incident at a New Jersey motel last Fall, maybe October, involving Peter Seymour and Holly Abbott," Jim said. "And check his recent travel. Also a financial snapshot on the insurance company, large cap, small cap, cash reserves, new investors, pending investigations, you know the drill."

"Sure, and Holly Abbott, where do I know that name from, oh yeh, aka Holly Beitel, she was in that same foster home in Skokie as Larsen, then they got sent to a Gertrude Pinaro in Milwaukee," Rad said.

"They had kind of a twisted history," Jim said.

Rad had the old file from ten years back when Harry Seymour had died in the sierra looking for his wayward son, Pete; also deceasing shortly thereafter was Norm Larsen, possibly as a result of blackmailing Holly about her past. With all the names and numbers, it wouldn't take Rad long to bring him up to speed on what was going on back home.

Helen called back after he'd gotten in bed and was reading Proust, who always gave him perspective on matters of the heart. It had been a rough day with Mom, who in addition to the Alzheimer's was suffering from diabetes, so she'd been put in the position of denying food to her mother, who then threw a tantrum, so unlike the Joan Seymour of ten years ago, so refined, so gracious then. Joan would listen to Jim, and if she wanted another opera cream, he would pretend it was the last one and he'd had his eyes on it, and she'd say go ahead and take it. Helen cried over it, just another chocolate but it would send her blood sugar through the roof, and then she cried again that he wasn't there to wipe away her tears and give her warm comfort.

"I wish you were here," Helen said.

"I wish I were there too, darling," Jim said. "Need to keep the business going though. Did you get to the Christmas concert?"

"We were ready to walk out the door and she said, 'I don't want to go there, what ever made you think I did', and I said, because you've always loved The Messiah, and she said, I have not," Helen said. "When you're here, it's more rational because there's somebody else who knows I'm the sane one, at least relatively speaking."

"I had a drink with Tommy Davila today," Jim said. "His eldest son is in law school now. It seems like yesterday he was just a kid on a bike. Tommy knocks lawyers but I think he's glad the boy didn't go into journalism like him. I fortunately got him to put some money from your Dad's case into Microsoft, so in a way we helped the kid get through law school."

"I always liked Tommy, back from when he helped you find Pete in Tingo," Helen said.

"He was asking me about you and Pete, and I said you were fine, but I hadn't seen Pete in a couple of years, when was it?—back when we had Joan's ninetieth," Jim said.

"I saw him in October, though I wish I hadn't," Helen said. "I didn't tell you about it because it was just depressing. He and Holly got into a screaming match in a motel in Ft. Lee. It was the night after he had the premier of his Jazz Concerto #137 in a Village club. The few reviews were harsh, like the whale song bits were faddish cant, intellectual bedwetting, et cetera, and he got high and started ranting against the critics, I'll kill the ignorant bastards, then sequential rants against bourgeois society, against the Establishment, and the last rant against her and her female culpability. Holly said she'd taken enough crap in the relationship, though she loved Pete, he was out of control, busting up things and telling her she could go to Hell. She called the police, and they took him in. I had to drive there with his bail money, because he'd spent everything on the club, the musicians, the gala reception, open bar, champagne, shrimp cocktails, hors d'oeuvres, the works. I don't know where he went when he got out, but he didn't leave with Holly, and she was threatening to call a divorce lawyer."

"You didn't get in touch with him after that?" Jim said.

"You know what I go through on a daily basis with mother," Helen said. "Honestly, no news is good news when it comes to Pete. He did say something when he got out, it's going to be all different now."

"Did that mean he was going on the wagon?" Jim said.

"Even if that's what he meant, it doesn't mean that's what he'd do, you know people just say things sometimes," Helen said. "Dev Smith called and said he'd published a notice in a legal newspaper that neither the trust nor I would be responsible for Peter's debt. Oh, and he also told me the board has no grounds to cut our preferred dividends."

He'd talked with Dev too, who was a good lawyer and said it could take a while to challenge the board's decision, and he was also very circumspect in talking about Peter, who was of course affected by this action. Jim cried a couple tears after he got off the phone, had a couple heartaches over being apart, but he'd seen bankruptcies of grand old firms fallen on hard times, and it could look like the skeleton of a Leviathan stripped by sharks. Helen still thought of herself as rich, but he'd been over the books with Vince Scarlatti, and thought there were a lot of bumps in the road ahead and he was doing her a favor to worry about the money.

"Good night darling, I'll fall asleep wishing you were in bed next to me," Helen said.

She wanted him to come back for Valentine's Day, but the international air fares were high and he wanted to get the facts in this Lenguado case sorted out first.

—ᴍ—

Frankie called him about three nights after that. He'd gotten in touch with Benavides, who told him it was odd since his was the second call he'd gotten in the last couple months about Larsen, and about Jim Hiram too, from someone who said he was an old friend of Jim's trying to track him down. Benavides had been retired for four years, but knew about the Lenguado death because he was in the same dockside Tontine as the deceased—for non-lawyers, a Tontine Trust gives all to the last to die, or last two or few depending on its terms, like life insurance with a gamble—and of course he thought it odd to get two calls about the same ten-year old affair that close together. He didn't recognize Larsen's name, but he did Jim's, though didn't acknowledge that to the caller, since he was already suspicious. When the caller became persistent, he said Ugarte of InterCon might know more about it. The caller said 'that's who sent me to you', and Benavides said that was all he knew about it. It gave the retiree Benavides a chance to renew some old friendships on the docks, and shinnying the other way up the tree, he also confirmed that InterCon was a subsidiary of Seymour Industries, and further that they were now quite friendly with the Fujimori government. He also saw the man who called him on the phone, or more exactly heard the voice he recognized as that man, glanced around a steel mooring pylon and saw a 'gringo grande'. Trying to connect up dots and thinking of Pete, Jim asked whether he might have meant a tall gringo, but Frank said that was all he knew and he had more interesting news. It seemed he'd called a friend at the Lima Chamber of Commerce to track down Benavides, which friend remembering Frank was an avid collector of Andean artifacts, had sent him a slick catalogue from a new upscale auction house in Lima, which catalogue Frank was perusing while having morning coffee and he nearly spilled sugar on the counter.

"It was the Silver Llama," Frank said. "The same one we found back in Ocros in '69."

"Are you sure?" Jim said. "You know that's a standard Inca form. Didn't you buy another one just like it yourself?"

"But the Ocros one had those markings on it, you remember, you sketched it when we were recovering in that old hacienda," Frank said.

"And that was the last time we saw it," Jim said.

They'd both been in and out of consciousness recovering from hypothermia, soroche, extreme exhaustion and mortal fear as the Andes began to shake and a driving freezing rain had begun to fall, sending a mudslide down that caved out the ground where they'd found the Silver Llama and the ichu grass, signs of a capa cocha burial—capa cocha was an Inca child sacrifice to appease the god of the mountain. The Spanish priests destroyed these as they did other mummies and huacos, since these were worshipped as idols by the Indians, but they didn't find all these sites because the Andes had many peaks that the priests didn't hike out to. Peru was about 98 % Catholic and about 60% Indian, who had retained traditional beliefs also, so an American mining company comes in and then discovers that the gold in them thar hills is in a sacred range of the local Quecha campesinos, then culture-clash, demonstrators with placards saying don't tear our mountain down, boards of directors of mining companies wondering how serious native sentiment is and what obstacle it presents to the extraction of proven deposits of gold. The American mining companies should have hired some out-of-work anthropologists during the Tenure Crunch, who could have told them, no, they're serious, the mountain is sacred to them, they're like natural environmentalists, they don't need any politicizing. It was just hemispheric cultural disjunction, which the company might jump by paying bribes to take the gold out—and when it tore the place up and the solvents they used got into the water, no clean-up funds. Jimmy had always pushed for foreign investment in Peru, and said they ought not be hostage to the spectre of IPC, which was a classic J.D. Rockefeller Standard Oil rip-off in a distant land with enough deposits at La Brea that they were the main source of revenue for Peru for decades. A crucial page eleven of the IPC contract had turned up missing and one wondered if old J.D., though he was a good northern Baptist who didn't smoke or drink, and went to church on Sundays, might have been up to some of the old tricks he used to ruin competitors back in the U.S., since business was business and church was church. Ah, but all that great art at the Cleveland Museum of Art, a statue so lifelike you'd say 'it moves, it lives'.

His other senior law essay besides the one on IPC had been on the Two Hundred Mile Limit in international law. The California tuna fishery industry and the Japanese trawlers liked to take rich catches from the Humboldt Current, and wanted the limit set back to twelve miles. The Velasco government was trying to keep them out, had confiscated vessels in a Third World defiance of international norms, but then overfished it themselves and the catch had declined catastrophically. This lead to another stress on national finances, after incurring big debts for arms purchases from the Soviet Union, another straw on the camel's back that lead to the Tacnazo coup twenty years back by the military against their own generalissimo, Velasco, the old warrior wobbly with health issues affecting his judgment. Gone, but not without effect, with a law abolishing the literacy test for voter eligibility, enfranchising millions of Indian campesinos, who were of course illiterate because of the malfeasance of blanco governments in Lima. It seemed like a long time ago with the shift to Fujimori—Velasco came in in '68, was out in '74 and

Father Time was pushing on toward a new century now, so it didn't just seem like a new time, it was a new time, though time was like an animal with natural camouflage that could hide most of a day. His friend, Frank, had married a lovely Pazena in the early Seventies, a conjunction happy and prolific though they were now experiencing empty nest syndrome for their second child, Elena, who had also gone off to Stanford, like her brother, Frank, Junior, before her, and she loved it there, it was so free. Carlos, their youngest, was still in prep school, like his big brother a good tennis player, a smart kid but not much of a scholar, so Jim thought they were babying their baby, of course, and the kid liked the fact that Jim sympathized with his rebellion. Oh yes, there are small personal rebellions that may affect our destinies as much as grand revolutions. It was strange to have some years of life behind him and see how things had worked out, like hiking up to a panoramic view, broader than when you were in your Twenties.

"You think you might go to an auction for me next month to check up on this?" Frank said. "You know it actually did change my life. I could have gotten tenure if I'd brought back that piece."

Sure, Jim had regretted losing that Silver Llama, he'd hoped they were going to be in National Geographic, but it wasn't going to affect his legal career one way or another. They'd both slept all the way back to Ayacucho, and assumed it got swiped from their packs during the trip. He was mainly glad to wake up in the hospital, suffering only from hyper-exhaustion and dehydration, and glad to be alive.

"You know where that sketch of the Llama is now?" Frank said.

"It's buried in a box of books in my cellar, totally inaccessible at the back of the storeroom, I'd need a forklift to get to it, but I'd be glad to go to an auction for you," Jim said. "Oh wait, that notebook may well be back in Philly stored in the carriage house. You know the Seymour mansion had a carriage house. When they built it, they still weren't sure automobiles would work. Basically I don't know where it is. I did save it, so when they research me for posterity, they'll know it. But where it is now, I'm clueless."

"Anyway, find out who the seller is beforehand if you can," Frank said.

It was around ten fifteen at night when the front bell rang, clanging because his doorbell had shorted out probably from water in the conduit when he soaked his garden. It was a brass ship's bell so Jim ran down to keep from disturbing the neighbors further, and when he opened the front gate, there was Liz Teris standing before him, camera case on her shoulder, carry-on bag on the pavement next to the idling cab.

"Hi, Jimmy, I wanted to see you but didn't know if you were in," Liz said. "Or whether you'd even want to see me again, if you forgave me."

"Of course I'm delighted to see you," Jim said. "Come on in, and you know I forgave you before you left. It was a crazy time."

"I need to talk to you in private," Liz said. "Is Helen in?"

When Jim explained that Helen had not been 'in' for a couple of years, Liz sent the cab away and they went inside to talk. She had been back in Peru for extended periods during the last five years, explaining she was reluctant to contact them because her old friend, Helen, knew of their romantic past, and she didn't want to rock that domestic boat. She'd been back in Ayacucho recently, the impoverished sierra province where they met and fell in love almost thirty years before. This was one of several visits she made in the Nineties, many of which included photographic and tape recorded documentation of human rights abuses, many by the military, many by Sendero. In her recent travels back to Mother Peru, she'd met many academics for whom she'd done photo work over the years, who with the onset of peace had returned to do research in the area, including Irv Cohen, an anthropologist they knew from the old days, who filled her in on some former acquaintances. It seemed someone had filed a complaint with the American Anthropological Association against Rob Emerson, another of the old gang, now a respected authority in pre-Columbian archaeology, alleging unethical behavior.

The word was that Rob suspected it was Frank Mathiessen, Jim's friend and now successful La Paz businessman, because Frank had been denied tenure at California and had engaged in trickery against Rob in Cordoba, upon which Rob didn't elaborate much to Irv because it involved Rob trying to sell a gold Chimu set of armor on the black market, in which deal he got snookered himself. But Frank was outré and Rob was top notch, so who was Irv to believe, yet Irv, who didn't drink much himself, was around a bar in Trujillo when Rob said he was going to get back at that sonofabitch Mathiessen and his lapdog money launderer Hiram. Irv always liked Jim, who liked his Catskill poniard humor, and he knew Liz was at a dig about twenty miles outside Cuzco up the Urubamba in the Sacred Valley of the Incas, so he made a special trip up to tell her about this. Although she'd avoided a visit so as not to rock any boats romantically or domestically, she knew she needed to tell Jimmy about this because of Rob's past history with him, which was not good, involving Rob's knife attack on him in a Cuzco café and then Jim's logistical assistance to Frank in screwing Rob on the Chimu piece in Cordoba.

"Thanks for giving me the warning," Jim said. "Don't you think Rob may have just been blowing off steam? I haven't reported any black market activities to the Anthro Assoc, and I doubt Frank has, since that's where he buys the most of the stuff he gets. You know he's got me going to an auction next month here. It's one of those silver llama statuettes they put in with the capa cocha burials. He thinks it's the same one we found at Ocros in 69."

"What makes him think that?" Liz said. "I mean they're not real common, but they're not all that rare."

"Some markings on it," Jim said. "It's odd though about it coming up now, given this other stuff with Rob and ethics and the black market. He was doing that before, but I'd have thought he'd have gotten out of it when he rose to international stature. You know he's a big cheese now."

"Sure I know, which was why I wanted to tell you about this," Liz said. "He has, like they say, connections here. He may have just been blowing off steam. On the other hand, why take a chance if he's really off his nut. He was before."

"I appreciate your coming to tell me about this," Jim said, letting her in on some of the strange happenings with him recently, including the body of Nestor Lenguado in his garden.

"You don't see any relation of this to Rob Emerson, do you?" Liz said.

"I don't see any relation of this to anything yet, just a web of shadows," Jim said. "Even if he's on the war path, why come after me? I helped him get the seventy-five thousand from Frank."

"And then you gave him another thirty thousand to bail him out with the Colombian dealers," Liz said.

"Twenty-five thousand, though with five per cent interest over twenty years, it could be a hundred thou now, yeh, I have the note I had him sign that night at Pension Inglesa before we took the cab to the airport," Jim said. "It was like I won't darken your door-step, do likewise with me and no action will be taken on the note. Never had any trouble with him after that. I saw his articles after the Prince of Sipan was discovered. I wasn't even jealous, even after he recaptured Marilyn."

"You were involved with her then?" Liz said.

"Yeh, after he stabbed me and ran off with you, she came around to see about me," Jim said. "Like an angel of mercy with chicken soup and comfort. We went to tango classes for joint therapy for cuckolds. In fact it was her dad who got me into stocks. But ultimately, she did go back to Rob. You recall Milt's wry wit. He said they'd won the Bay Area Open Marriage Couple of The Year award several years in a row, so I guess I got snookered like the rest, but she was primo just like you, sweetheart, and I never regretted much. I won't lie—it was a pain in the butt hunting you down in Juliaca."

"Those were crazy times, I'm sorry I put you out," Liz said. "And I'm grateful you saved me. You know I could have died in Puno after he abandoned me. I had to hock all my camera equipment. But why go there? I rarely even drink now, and I avoid all drugs."

Wondering whether that included the anti-psychotic ones that Frank said had been prescribed as far back as when they were living together in Berkeley in the Sixties, well, why question the good intentions of an old female friend who was also quite hot for a forty-nine year older and was sitting right there in his study drinking his quality Tradicion pisco brandy.

"I avoid drugs too, except Aleve for tennis," Jim said, telling her about having tennis elbow, which spread to tennis neck, which next caused tennis back, so now he had tennis body, and creaked all over, in so many places it was symphonic. "I jogged three miles before breakfast, and I feel weak, but that may be happening because I'm looking into your eyes."

"I have to ask you about Helen," Liz said.

"Helen's gone home, and I'm still here," Jim said. "It's like Lima's my home now. I guess I like things creole. Does it seem like

Evangeline and we were separated by events beyond our control, and we're reunited now."

That seemed a plausible narrative and after a couple more Madeiras, my dear-ah, Liz and he were reunited. It felt like total release and resurrection to him and she fell asleep in his arms and he thought 'I'm back in business now after all this loneliness'. As for the other hassles, they paled in comparison to having new love. And not just a new unproven love, someone he had been in love with and who understood him maybe as well as Helen did, even though she'd been out of his life for twenty years now.

New love, crazy at fifty, right? But if you thought you had it put away and taken care of at twenty-five, love was a river that could run its own course, in or out of its banks and maybe not the same as you imagined. Oh, good-o, Liz still enjoyed being on top and riding and he could have ridden a cock horse to Banbury Cross and beyond to Channel Two, she was probably banned on those fronts, he knew her and was able to make it just fine though she was on the left side.

—◊—

'What a lovely day', Jim was thinking as he went out his front gate to get the morning paper, waving to the milkman and to Sra. Sanchez and sharing with her his praise of the weather. She always asked about Helen, whom he explained was confronting the challenges of Alzheimer's with her mother, but of course the senora had eyes.

Liz was sleeping in, so he read stock quotations from The Journal in his home office until ten o'clock, when he heard her down in the kitchen.

"Morning, darling," he said, embracing and kissing her on the scruff of the neck like she liked as she sat at the island drinking her coffee, then kissing her on the mouth when she turned around.

"Um," she said when they broke. "Pardon the coffee breath."

"To me it's sweet as rosewater," Jim said. "Like a croissant, some sausage or bacon, I'm not half bad as a short order cook now. I can do your eggs right, sunny side up or over easy, scrambled, however you like."

"Thanks no," she said. "When you fell asleep last night, I got up and raided your refrigerator. I was just famished. Hope you don't mind."

"Not at all, a quarter for a beer gets you lunch at the bar, no charge extry," Jim said, swinging around beside her onto a stool at the island. "What is it you have there?"

"It's a group photo from Vinchos '69," Liz said, sliding it over to him. "I took it myself with your old Zeiss Ikon with the delay that let you run around and get in the picture."

"I have a copy of this somewhere myself, though I haven't looked at it in years," Jim said.

"Me neither, until the police in Trujillo asked me about it," Liz said. "You remember Val Davis? He worked with Stephenson and Emerson. He was an expert on projectile points."

"Oh yeh, Val, nice guy, very retiring, scholarly, he told me about paleo points ad infinitum once, convinced me anthro grad school would be even more boring than finishing law," Jim said. "Hey, that's him circled in the top row."

"When the police showed up at my door, and I thought, oh shitski, they're here about the photos I just took up in Ayacucho, but no, it was about Val," Liz said. "They found him in his hotel room, dead from blunt force trauma to the head. He had this photo on him, like placed on his chest. Rob Emerson came down from Chan Chan to i.d. him. This was after Irv told me he was upset about that ethics inquiry, and raging about Frank and you."

"Oh great, now with Val dead, Rob's even more likely to be paranoid about us," Jim said, thinking not a moment later 'now there's a person who'd know T.S. Eliot and who hates me, and that $25K note he signed back then wouldn't discourage him now if he's a world authority pulling down big bucks as a big gun in the Ivies and he'd have had to have friends here in high places to keep working through the Terror, connected here, connected there, make the conegtions, man, oh so maybe now Old Rob the Emir is the snake in my American Eden which makes me an American Adam, innocent or maybe just ignorant, and one thing made clear in Eden was the Devil was clever, well degreed and skilled in the arts of deception. Peruvians understood and sometimes cultivated maya, and it could be a task to find if Rob were behind it, but Jim was not without his own weapons, since he kept elaborate notes on Rob's black market deal to sell the Chimu Armor in Corboda to Haberman, the ex-SS officer to whom he'd been fencing for some time. That CYA file, including the photos he got of the old fox in San Pedro, and inventories of looted art from pre-Columbian to French Impressionist that he fenced, that file was in his home office safe. "How could Rob think I give a rat's ass about his ethics inquiry?"

"Don't ask me," Liz said. "I was just happy the cop wasn't there about Ayacucho. I shot a series of a memorial procession of the survivors of a village where half the people were killed in the war. It was quite moving. And I talked to people. The war's supposedly over, but the government still likes to keep a lid on coverage."

"There's an undercurrent against that now," Jim said. "It's like Fujimori was the strong medicine needed to defeat Sendero, but now the medicine is sickening the patient. A journalist friend of mine said there's talk of a National Reconciliation Commission like the one in South Africa after the end of apartheid."

"What, so they can pardon the death squads?" Liz said.

"I don't know what they'd do about the Colina Group," Jim said. "They were involved in that Bar-B-Q Massacre back in 91, another in 92, and who knows what since. I get the sense the nation is weary of violence, and of Fujimori. APRA is the only surviving political party. Garcia, their last man in, back in '85 messed up the economy big time when he challenged the IMF. Now the economy's back, and Fuji's still here. The void will be filled though. You know politics in Peru is never dull."

"Fujimori and SIN are still in charge," Liz said. "I'm not sure Val's murder isn't related to me. I mean, this old group photo from Ayacucho, I'm photographer of that and more recent bad pictures. I'm just back to working in Peru, and maybe it's a warning not to rock the boat."

"Wouldn't you look in Rob's direction first?" Jim said. "The guy had a temper, especially when he was high on coke, he was dealing through his grad students, discreetly importing, was in the huaco black market too. Maybe Val got called as a witness on the ethics matter, and Rob didn't want that to happen."

"If he wanted to lean on me, he could have just mentioned the two dead at the Bolivar that night," Liz said.

"Rob didn't know bullshit about that shooting, he was hiding around the corner in a closet, it could have been Penny who shot Haberman's driver," Jim said. "That was a terrible night. I hate to think its shadows are casting our way."

He told her more about the late Sr. Lenguado turning up fallecido in his garden, about T.S. Eliot and acronyms and his various theories or flights of paranoid suspicion masking as theories, not mentioning about Pete Seymour being back in Lima, because he didn't want to remind her or himself of his relationship with Helen.

"The one good thing, even with this new mess, is that we're together again," Jim said. "I don't worry about it. My main worry now is that you'll fly away right after arriving, mi picaflor, because I remember you always had itchy feet."

"I've settled down, really I have," Liz said. "After Dieter left me for his twenty-five year old mistress, I felt very old. Like a wadded-up washrag souring in a corner of the tub. I tried meditation, but I'm not very good at it. Then he convinced me to go to an analyst when I was clinically depressed. She really did help me sort things out. Cost a bundle, but it was worth it for a me that works. Who knows, if I'd gone to that analyst in La Paz you wanted me to see, we might have stayed together. At the time it was like I was defending my sanity in resisting. One thing about knowing yourself, I did find it's easier if you have some outside help. Also back then I didn't like the idea of my mind being dissected."

"So you've settled down, my little runaway," Jim said. "I always remember you telling about jogging all the way home from Senior Skip Day beer bash to evade the Iowa State Patrol because you were afraid you'd lose you scholarship to California."

"Or get locked away by my father," Liz said.

"How is the old autocrat?" Jim said.

"He died five years ago," Liz said.

"I'm sorry, I didn't know," Jim said. "Please excuse me."

"No apologies needed," Liz said. "Frankly I felt free afterwards. Whenever his ghost comes around, I say, No, father, this is 1997, it's a different time, go back to your time. Also this is a very different place from Iowa or Hungary. That works well because he was always so distant when he was alive."

"I recall things hadn't always been smooth with Dad," Jim said. "Did the analyst help you with that? And did you tell him about me?"

"Her, and yes to both questions," Liz said. "Because father was intellectual, abstract, didn't like emotion, and you were different. I worried about commitment. And I ran. But I've slowed down."

She'd gone to a top-flight psychiatrist who'd studied under Luce Irigaray, a disciple of Lacan and a noted feminist analyst, to sort out the detritus of paternalism, and came to the conclusion she had fled from love with Jim because she was afraid of getting close, Herr Professor had always had this enclosed Plexiglas lectern from which he issued his dictates. So she ran around, physically, going off on road trips at the drop of a hat, and romantically, like with that young Adonis with the guitar and tie-dyed T who crashed with them in their Cuzco place and his Daphne who was seducing Jim in tandem, or more seriously with Rob Emerson, a high and mighty prof like her dear old dad. Maybe it was true that Time healed all wounds: at least that one he didn't obsess over now like he had at the time, jealous and distraught at the thought of them making love. You may fire when ready Grimsby, oh I faint at the prospect. He just thought of it, we really were a crazy lot.

"This photo takes me back to another time," Jim said. "Remember Mac, there's Friedrich, and Irv, there's Emerson, Stephenson, Val, who is that on the end?"

"That's Penny," Liz said.

"No need to warn him, poor guy, gone on," Jim said. "We ought to contact Mac and keep in touch with Irv about this. Who else? Frank told me Stephenson is back in the Ivy League and doesn't do fieldwork here anymore. Hell, why risk getting held hostage by Sendero when you've got it made in the shade with lemonade? If Miller isn't in academia anymore, if he's in business in Sinaloa, why would he come here, when he's already at the end of the supply chain for the big mark-up before the stuff hits the streets in major cities across the U.S.of A.?"

"I talked to Frank right before I came here," Liz said. "I told him about Val and the photo. Incidentally and in the way of confession, I did ask him about you and Helen. He said she'd abandoned you for two years."

"Frank never warmed to her," Jim said. "So you came here with an already formed intent to seduce me?"

"Yes, I did," Liz said, going back to the photo and perusing it, perusing in Peru. "Is that a crime? You're a lawyer. Take me in. Report me to the authorities. I have adult sexual desire, acted upon, is it a crime, a faux pas, what would you call it?"

"A crime, crazy in this world that love should be a crime, more like a good job, a damn fine job of seduction, I bow to your mystic sexual prowess," Jim said. "You know though, you could have told me. I wouldn't have been so prissy."

"What, and spoil the surprise?" Liz said, going back to looking at the 68 Vinchos photo.

"Okay, there's Friedrich—he's in Paraguay now, doing Guarani-Spanish bilingual research," Jim said. "There you are, and me, and Frankie, there's that boor, Miller. Are you sure he's in Mexico now? Irv said he left the Ph.D. program. Talk about somebody not warming to me. That was even after I saved him when he was hammered and about to get gored by a bull at the campesino corrida. It was like, oh, maybe you're okay."

"That was because Miller suspected you of being a narc since you were in law school in Ohio," Liz said. "You knew he was supplying the entire anthro staff that summer? Last I heard of him he'd relocated to Mexico, and that was like ten years ago."

"He was a big bruiser, Frank's six foot three, and Miller was taller by an inch or two, and just big," Jim said. "He tried to beat on me one night at the Colmena. I don't know how much time I have to look for that lard-ass now. I've got a lot on my plate. Why would he be here anyway? I'm behind on my quarterly stock newsletter. And here I've got Liz a la mode."

"Please, please," she said, squirming away as he kissed the nape of her neck, blew on her ear lobe and leaned against her. "Hasn't time at all banked the fires of desire?"

"I'm lookin' at the big five-o and after a half century on this insane granite planet, I'm still not satisfied with my life," Jim said.

"Me neither, I get up running each morning and it's like I've gotten one-thousandth of the way to where I want to be, " Liz said. "You just need to keep running, got to keep moving in the right direction."

"Right, but one other thing emerges as clear to me from this new mess," Jim said. "We need to stay close for protection."

"Yes, I was thinking that myself," Liz said. "In case an SIN squad shows up and wants to confiscate all my films."

"We won't go to the door," Jim said, caressing her again. "We'll say we're watchin' a DVD. Something good. Bedtime For Bonzo or Clockwork Orange or All Must Die."

"Which reminds me, I've got to go to my photo lab downtown and pick up several rolls of film there, so please no more hanky panky now, Mister Jaimito," Liz said. "Can I offer you a nooner? That is, assuming I get done on time?"

'Oh my God, what will I do til noon,' Jim thought, '?putter in my garden, better avoid heavy lifting, want to be in top-notch shape as far as energy level, though not Viagra, Cialis or Levitra had been necessary to get it up last night, pure Liz and the sweet spot. Instead of plotting his own insane lust he fell asleep reading Proust and his passages on Albertine, his libertine runaway, recounting his classic love obsession buying ridiculously expensive gowns for her to dress her like a doll, reminded Jim of chasing his own runaway, Liz, all over the altiplano and finding her sick in Juliaca in a hospital gown. He had a dream where she was an angel without wings, a luminous female form, seemingly nude though diffuse in outline and detail, there in the center panel of a triptych in his bedroom, sat down there and was like a vital restorative or even an apparent secular salvation by passion. Love could work for you like that, just call this 800 number for your own personal reading.

He was chilling while swinging in the garden hammock listening to the drip fountain, like a cocoon about to open into a luna moth fluttering toward the pheromone of the female of the species, when he thought he heard her come in. But why she'd gone up to his study he didn't know and when he called out to her, it was like he was still in the dream, also somewhat bombed. Then it was silent for some moments before he saw a man come bounding down the stairs, saw him in the garden and going for the front gate, but the bolt was sticking now since Jim hadn't fixed it after the Lenguado case, so the man came running into the garden. Jim thought he was coming at him and dodged and grabbed the ditching spade he'd set there to put in zinnias for Liz who loved them from her days on the American prairie, but the intruder went right by him, climbed the big fig tree like a Chinese acrobat and went over the wall.

This incursion was disconcerting enough, since his Emerson file was in his office safe and his suspicions had been turned in that direction. Maybe the misinformed scholarly bunghole was firing another volley across his bow, but Jim originally wasn't going to tell Liz about it and ruin their scheduled romance, a nooner where the bedroom venetian blinds opened to admit the barest bars of a cloudy sun would create a grid on her rising like Venus in the surf above him.

So much for dreams. When Liz got back three hours later, it was obvious she was in no mood for the sex he had so anticipated.

"Sonofabitch, the bastards confiscated all my film," Liz said. "This lab went out of the way to help me back in '68 and '76 when I had photos of massacres. They must have really twisted some arms this time."

"They'll do that," Jim said, recalling for her that Fabian Salazar, a columnist for the La Republica, was watching leaked videotapes of Montesinos telling the head of the electoral commission how to rig the next congressional elections, when SIN agents broke in, confiscated the tapes and sawed his arm to the bone. "Fortunately, the guy who broke in here didn't have a saw."

"Oh Jimmy, did he get my carry bag with the duplicate negatives," Liz said. "Oh please God, let him not to have gotten that. It was that dark blue triangular bag with the zip up and a lock at the end."

"I don't think so," Jim said. "It's in the wine cellar. He'd need a chain saw to get through that oak door."

"You always had good sense, I don't think I appreciated it back then," Liz said. "But could we just go down there and make sure?"

They descended the stair to the sotano and the heavy oak plank door was inviolate and her camera bag was inside, not far from where he and Tommy had put the body of Harry Seymour twenty years ago when also Norm Larsen was trying to take it, got himself shot and killed that night on those very stairs, two bodies to go then, and also not far from where Jim had encased the CYA (cover your ass) evidence of those crimes. Liz didn't need to know anything more about the Larsen episode now; she'd only been in on it in Act One,

Scene One, when she introduced Jim to Helen, a friend of hers who worked in a Paris gallery, trying to find her wayward brother in Tingo Maria. His notes of that episode had already been fictionalized in The Coca Bums ($3.99 see p. 41, to order) by his amanuensis, L.H. May in New Mexico. Ah, Colon, ah patron, ah Columbus, N.M., ah Pancho Villa, ah Cisco nada, ah me, the Gringo Grande and Uncle Sam will drive the rebels from our land. After Cuban crises and Mexican standoffs, Jim was just happy to be making money in Peru. When he found her camera bag, she calmed down, and they went ahead with their afternoon date, though occasionally through the act she would exclaim 'm.f.' or 'the bastards', but why let them take anything more from you?

After sex, she talked about going into analysis, Dieter was ten years younger than her, had been doing the Broadway Boogie Woogie for three years on the side with an artiste half their age. Liz was deep into her forties and had a panic attack. She said she felt like an old dishrag, and she resolved to change her life. The root of her incredibly good physical conditioning became clearer as she described throwing out all the liquor bottles, running in her first marathon, and mentioned she hiked in the sierra now and could run Diet's little bit of fluff into the ground. Her father had been very distant, a professor and she was always drawn to smart guys. Jimmy was different in that he was smart, but he also had a heart, though she reacted by fleeing when his impulse to closing and commitment was growing.

"So your Paris analyst is a Freudian and a feminist," Jim said, as they lay in bed afterwards. "I was just reading a feminist critique of D.H. Lawrence's male fascist streak, blood in the loins, male dominance, but it's good to recall the priggish, hypocritical side of Victorian society he was rebelling against. It was like nobody wanna have fun, and that's pure justice."

She'd always liked his bedtime stories, and if she thought her parents' marriage had been bad, he told her about DH's parents, his father a coalminer who came in soiled from work, and his mother a schoolteacher, who taught him so well he went away to the great university in England, and became a great writer, believed in blood in the loins and sexual energy, but also thought the man should hold the woman back from climax, which was maybe a step up from Freud, who didn't even believe in the existence of female orgasm. Why deny it and why prevent it, was Puritanism so pervasive it infiltrated even the minds of the liberators? It's like one third of U.S. women have never had it. So why is there no campaign for female orgasm? It's the bread and butter of divorce lawyers and after them, bordello owners. Mister Jim say bring on the love challenge we' go over Niagara together, no barrel needed. Why harsh on DH for being behind the times when the times were behind him, in fact Jim wrote a story where Lawrence is out on a picnic with Mabel Dodge, and the climax of the story is when they experience climax together, simultaneous, it freaks DH out so bad, he sees a rattler go into a hole under a saguaro cactus eating baby chicks until the crow gives him a mud chick and the snack strangles the snake, isn't that just proof the female orgasm campaign has legs, what do you think, does it have potential, get it published in <u>Ladies Home Journal</u> and send copies of the article along with the Kinsey Report to all the members of the Supreme Court and Congress, so they can see what a sticky situation it is. What do you think? Silence from Lizzie, and success in some form. He'd been able to put her to sleep again with his crazy stories.

Then he woke her up inadvertently when he went to the bathroom. She got cozy with him again and the joyous friction began to bridge the gap of the primal opposition of the sexes. He must have been having a good dream because it was up for her and on and quickly off. Snatches of the tune, <u>When Sunny Gets Blue</u>, played in his head as his eyelids flooded deep blue and green Technicolor visions in the aftermath of orgasmic synchronicity. As she showered, he tried to remember the Dante sonnet that begins dui donna, what was it Boccaccio said about the Poet, that Dante was troubled by the sin of lust even into old age. Such trouble we all should have, Jim thought, since it was a trice till the final dinner, a mere millisecond in the grand scale of time, nano saith the worm.

As he lay waiting for her to finish showering, he remembered their trip to the Peruvian Amazon and the big house a French ethnobotanist maintained outside Iquitos, which catered to tourists, who sat in a circle and were given atahuasca to drink. Jim didn't have any desire to lose consciousness in Amazonia and didn't drink, though he held the bowl to his lips. If Clinton didn't inhale, he sure as hell didn't ingest jungle LSD. Liz told him afterwards the effect was of intense tropic colors and a sense of traveling through the jungle, running and seeing a jaguar and at times being that jaguar. The idea was that they were supposed to see their spirit animal in the trance. She had been given the name of jaguar and he had been given dragonfly. To him it was like the Transcendental Meditation craze where each sycophant was given his or her special mantra. Then later you discovered others had the same special word so it wasn't secret. He was glad he hadn't lost consciousness in the jungle. He'd already seen clients in nursing homes who didn't have a grasp on reality, he knew what a delicate thing consciousness was and how incredible it was that any of us perceived the world with any success of correlation to its underlying reality. In the jungle it was wise to sleep on beds raised off the floor, so the snake wouldn't come in and take you off the floor. Back then it was Liz's wild side that drew him to her, something that would make his life exciting, keep the square block of his life interesting to live in.

—⟨⟨⟨—

As it turned out, the security agents and SIN had other, bigger things to worry about than Liz and her Ayacucho photos. Montesinos, the security chief, had instituted a Plan Operativo "Tigre 96" to control press leaks by military personnel, since he'd been secretly bribing congressmen to fix the last election for Fujimori and wanted to keep on doing so. Goons like the Colina Group had been around since before Fuji came in. In the late Sixties Liz and he had seen leftist organizers for an agricultores'cooperative laid out on a hacienda porch in Ayacucho, and she had shots from the Mancay Tiempo, the Time of Fear, and the massacres of the Sendero guerilla war of the Eighties and early Nineties until Fuji cut off the head of the serpent with the capture in 1992 of El Presidente Gonzalo, as Guzman called himself. He was well hidden in Lima where the rebels brought the war after their arms source through FARC rebels in Colombia had been interrupted; interestingly, Fujimori was sentenced in absentia in '06 to having sold 20,000 assault weapons to FARC, fascinating to explore the Machiavellian dimensions of how that deal arose from he who defeated terrorism in Peru, but was maybe not so passionately against it in his neighbor, Colombia. Since Fuji was also implicated in money laundering and drug trafficking, which FARC was involved in also, it might have been not germane that their founding ideology was leftist, now making cash through kidnappings and supplying cocaine and arms to Europe including through the I.R.A. Incidentally, the capture of Guzman of Sendero in a posh Lima apartment was brought to the screen by John Malkovich in "The Dancer Upstairs", starring Javier Bardem, a cubano actor in the lead role of the cholo detective, based on the novel by Nick Shakespeare, a credit to his tocayo and ancestor, the Bard of Avon, ding dong, Avon calling.

The nation was shocked in '97 with the murder of Mariela Barreto, a sergeant and victim of Montesinos' Tigre 96 plan, after she leaked videotapes of her boss bribing congressmen to fall in line for his boss, Fujimori, who of course denied complicity. Her military associate had also been tortured, though not killed like Mariela who had leaked those incriminating tapes to the news media. The brutality of her murder, abducted by police agents on her way to a hospital for a pre-natal check-up, tortured and quartered with surgical instruments, shocked the nation of Peru. This was on top of the revelation by one of the hostages of the Tupac siege at the Japanese ambassador's residence, a top government official who resigned in protest, saying he'd seen alive two female Tupac Amaru rebels who'd surrendered right after the Marines had secured the compound, and were later found shot execution style. Similar allegations were later made by a Japanese hostage. Since Fuji had published his own account of the resolution of the hostage situation, extolling his micro-management of the crisis and downplaying the role of Hermoza and the military, the charges of murder clearly went back up the chain of command. Having taken credit for everything, he had implicated himself in responsibility for everything. It seemed like a turning point for the nation in that, though the people were grateful to Fuji for having defeated Sendero, it was like 'what have you done for us lately?' and how grateful must a grateful nation be, now that it's you who's ripping us off. Since now their bloody civil war was over, the question remained of how much was owed for prior services. Montesinos had reportedly ransacked the treasury for as much as $264 million, and Fuji had perhaps as much or more socked away in Swiss accounts and Singapore. The third of the triumvirate, Gen. Hermoza, was the weakest thief, able to amass a personal fortune of a mere $22 million.

Perhaps the chaotic history of Peru accounts for its people's suspicion that all politicians are thieves in some degree, and of course all foreigners might be CIA agents or pirates, like Sir Francis Drake and his American successors who acted from greed and rapine under the guise of protectors per the Monroe Doctrine. Tommy even suggested once when they were well loaded and discussing the Japanese Embassy hostage crisis, that this all went back to the China Opening, when as a bone to Japan for this tsunami-like change in international relations without prior notice, to compensate for this shock, Peru had secretly been given to Tokyo, just like in 19th Century Europe they'd hold a Congress of Vienna or a Treaty of Paris and give this territory or that to this big power or that. Of course Tommy was talking yang here, Fuji was as Peruvian as chifas, but Jim did recall his jest later when Tokyo denied repeated requests from Lima for their ex-presidente's extradition to stand trial in Lima on corruption, theft in office and human rights charges, well, maybe blood is thicker, the old law.

It was not too long afterwards that Montesinos went into hiding—the joke went around that maybe he was hiding out with Saddam—because his opponents were continually locating new funds he'd appropriated, and more instances of corruption. The noble warriors against Sendero were being daily reduced in stature by new charges by the press hounds like Tommy, because they were willing to dig up the truth, even when whatever powers wanted whatever crap covered up. Fuji vowed he'd track Montesinos down, something few Peruvians believed, and things looked different for the prez with his strong arm man gone. He'd been their local J. Edgar Hoover or Luria, the job description involved sticking it to traitors, a category Jim had fit in back during Vietnam, so he was not without some experience in the matter of government control of the press. It was like Tommy said, I write for the souls of the wronged dead and of the living who want a better life. He and Tommy got together for a light lunch and a few beers at a windy costal bar Cinzano table with the umbrella flapping in the breeze. Jimmy always liked to criticize his own first, like the proverb of 'keep your own house clean, before you talk about your neighbor's dirt', tho they'd never erect a big brass statue of Montesinos like they did of Jedgar in front of the FBI HQs, the question remaining if he had surveillance of Rev. King, why could he not also have had protection. And then what he did to the anti-war protestors, DC conveniently forgets Martin was against Vietnam, even in honoring him as an African-American hero along with General Clayton Powell. Anyway, no statues of Jerry Rubin and it would be years of planning to get a forklift to relocate Jedgar just like they moved Pizarro from the National Cathedral after the Sendero bombing there. Tommy said nothing matched fresh hypocrisy for news value. The new scandal can be made old by the denial of unconfirmed reports. Then also old crimes long covered-up can be made new when they see the light of day.

Fujimori had responded to the new allegations by placing the blame squarely on the shoulders of absent Montesinos and was planning to run again in 2000 for a third term. Only two terms were permitted by the constitution, but he claimed this would be only his second term under the new constitution, which he'd gotten passed. In this house of lies, the dismembered body of Barreto had been found at four points around Lima, like an echo of the execution of Tupac Amaru II two centuries before, his body having been drawn and quartered. It was horrible brutality and it seemed like the country was going back in time, receding into barbarity. Not that the Spanish were alone in such cruel execution, an aging Good Queen Bess had Southey drawn and quartered for inciting rebellion, had his remains sent to four parts of Britain—it was a political act, it was a warning. Tommy was not using scribblers' hyperbole when he said something's rotten in the Republic of Peru.

"Most people think Fuji is hiding Montesinos," Tommy said. "Maybe he's forgotten where he hid him, like an old Easter egg."

"I read Vargas Llosa the other day saying Fujimori was the worst of Peru's many terrible dictators," Jim said. "I wonder what it would have been like if he'd been elected President."

"If philosophers were kings, the world would be perfect, isn't that Plato?" Tommy said.

"Vargas Llosa's a novelist, not a philosopher," Jim said. "Anyway, didn't the powers that be in Syracuse send Plato packing back to Athens?"

"Do you really think a novelist could run a country, even one as screwed-up and hungry for any sane, non-piratical leadership as Peru is?" Tommy said.

"Well, both novelists and politicians are always plotting, putting out their narrative, so maybe it's a transferable skill," Jim said. "As for me, an economist would be my first choice. What Peru needs most is prosperity, and not just for the top dogs. Poverty is the enemy. Without the abject poverty of the sierra, do you think Sendero could have taken root? Don't deny it, Fuji won the war against Sendero, and that's why he has so many apologists. It's like Coriolanus, except he can go to Tokyo. The tourists are back with dollars. The mining companies are investing big time. China's building and needs copper. Me, I just want more money for Peru. I want a free trade agreement with the U.S. Hey, when I was back in Philadelphia at Christmas, I went shopping at a Giant Eagle in Haverford Mills and found fresh Chilean seedless grapes in the produce department."

Despite a leftist boycott, he bought the grapes and the check-out person rang him up without questioning him about it. He fixed a nice Waldorf salad with pecans, currants, and fresh Fuji apples. Chile had good soil and climate for grapes, coastal Peru also had three growing seasons just like California's Central Valley, and with rich volcanic soil could be super-productive where there was water for irrigation.

"Oh, the water's no problem now," Tommy said, tongue in cheek since Peru was experiencing a severe El Niño with torrential rains that had produced landslides and flooding severe enough to overnite create the second largest lake in Peru. "But even as we bail out in hip boots, it's good to imagine the sunny side of the street. Every time you fortune tell, say there will be dark days, but the nation will prosper. It's like a booster lecture at the Chamber of Commerce."

"Hope is the foundation of progress," Jim said. "I think it's just great Tomas is now a licenciado. He could negotiate a trade pact with what you taught him."

"Or defend me if I get locked up for sedition under Plan Tigre 96," said Tommy, who'd not been directly involved in the Mariela Barreto story, but who was digging at the same dung heap of corruption that had eventuated in her murder.

"Take care, man, you know things are clearing up, but it's darkest before dawn," Jim said.

Journalism was a more dangerous business in South America than in the U.S., and reporters did get killed there, often for uncovering the dirty laundry of the Establishment. Peru was a rough territory, had been thus for centuries, for millennia actually since now archaeologist Judy S. had pushed back the date of urban civilization there to 3,000 B.C. with her pioneering work at the Caral citadel ruins, just a hundred miles north of Lima and where cotton was first domesticated in an irrigated valley, and was traded with costal fishermen to make nets. The people of Caral had a diet of fish and gourds and peppers and maize, had a large plaza and ceremonial platform and amphitheater, this right around the same time civilization was developing in Mesopotamia, the Indus, China and Egypt.

These were topics of conversation for Liz's academic friends who had begun stopping by their place in Miraflores now, like they had in Cuzco when they were living together before she began to run. Always the scholars were knocking each other's work, it was like part of the territory, and from the stories they told out of school about each other, there occasionally emerged a diffuse image of truth. Well, the eminent Peruvian archaeologist at Caral, Judy S., said she had experienced the old academic stab in the back while trying to get funding for her research in the U. S, and instead got hardly a byline. She'd approached two top U.S. archaeologists who quickly took credit for the discoveries at Caral, though they had never been to the site Judy had excavated for years, paying grad students out of her own money since there were meager state funds from the Peruvian government, always a burr in the side of Peruvian archaeologists who worked for much less than the Americans. It seemed like backstabbing was a main diversion of archaeologists in particular, delighting in vicious rumor and trashing each other's work and theories, which if it turned out different, they would quickly appropriate and use in their own grand synthesis. He'd always enjoyed the scholars' stories, though he knew from law there were always two sides; however, he was inclined to believe Dra. S. in her denuncia. She was unfortunately shot on her way to the dig at Caral, happily survived, by delincuentes the police said, decrying the general violence that permeated Peru. It was possible it was huaceros, grave-robbers and looters, trying to scare her off from her work. Some of the new huaceros were drug dealers from not around there, less ethical than the locals for whom it was a tradition to dig in the local ruins and supplement the family income with sales to coleccionistas like Frank, who understood that provenance was destroyed by any looting, but did his best to get background on any piece he bought. Jim knew that was several steps up from the 19th century when Peru sold rights to exploit coastal ruins that were mined just for the gold from the jewelry, cutting the mounds like slicing up a cake. That was of course wrong, and the government in Lima had advanced beyond that. The rich tombs at Sipan, for example, the American Tutankamen as it was billed, had first been discovered by huaceros, before the government took control of the situation. Huaceros had in fact excavated and led to major discoveries, and they resented the archaeologists whom they claimed sold items on the black market themselves. This jibed with Jim's experience of Rob Emerson trying to sell the Chimu gold armor in Cordoba in 1974. Rob had gotten taken on that Chimu deal, thanks in part to Jim's conniving with Frank Mathiessen, who was the final buyer at a greatly discounted price.

(Editor: none of the persons above-mentioned or events in Cordoba are real, are fictionalized in The Gate Of Two Snakes by L.H. May, EBook ISBN9781491823392, AuthorHouse 2013, $3.99, to order call 1-888-280-7715 or 1-888-728-8467; Note: this the second novel of "The Tihuantinsuyo Quartet", the first being Riders On The Niño Storms, EBook ISBN9781456764968, AuthorHouse, 2011, $5.99, the third novel is The Coca Bums, ISBN97815049118181, AuthorHouse 2015, and the fourth is what you're reading now, L.H. May, ed.)

Next time they talked, Jim reminded Frank of what had gone down in Cordoba on the Chimu deal, and specified Rob's recent troubles with the American Anthropological Association and Val Davis' untimely decease.

"I have had no contact whatsoever of any kind with the Association for over twenty years, and what would he do if I had?" Frank said. "Why was Rob selling a Chimu armor in the first place, and where did he get it? Why should I be afraid?"

"Because he's somewhat nuts, and has acted like that in the past," Jim said. "He's big time now. Mari may have inherited from her dad. He may not worry about the money you have or that he owes me."

"I don't worry," Frank said. "I leave that to my tax man and my security man, cousin Rico. You may recall he took care of Rob before. And took care of that kraut dealer he was fencing to, delivered him with a pretty bow to Lilah Fein, and her man, Moise. Left his driver tied up in his underwear. Lilah was something. Knowing her was worth all that crazy business in Cordoba."

"She's still hunting down art," Jim said. "I talked to her a couple months ago when I was in Philly. She was excited about a big new find the German tax authorities made, leave it to the tax man, like the IRS got Capone, not the FBI, anyhow one of the old Nazi art capos died and left a Berlin apartment full of looted art, like Matisses and Picassos saved from the stench of the Third Reich, in limbo since then. Yeh, that kraut dealer, Haberman, Rob used to call him his Swiss dealer, he'd sold Picassos to Alois Miedel that now grace the walls of many fine homes in Argentina."

"Seriously, can you picture Rob, who's so deep in hypocritical doo-doo, pitching a new bitch on anything leaning my way?" Frank said. "I don't know what the hell he's up to, and I'm not too worried, but I will tell Rico about it."

"Liz thinks recent untoward events may well stem from her documenting the Ayacucho massacres," Jim said, referring to the line-up of potential Machiavels. "Me, I don't think so. She may be a pain in the ass to them. But they've got more to worry about than her, like where is Montesinos hiding? The rats are starting to abandon the ship of state, as they sense it's going down."

"It sounds chaotic, you really ought to come up here and work for me for a while to see how you like it," Frank said, sounding a familiar theme. "The ship of state is not foundering here because we're landlocked, isolated and now Evo Morales is in. He's the first indio to hold the presidency here, a former coca grower, so he knows Andean economics. If you have any more trouble down there, let me know. I told Benavides to keep an eye on that InterCon shipping agency, and he's been down to the docks to shoot the bull at his old office, which is right across from that of Sr. Ugarte."

In a couple of days Jim got an envelope with photos from Sr. Benavides, taken from his former office across the dock from the InterCon offices. Tommy had been right about Peter Seymour being back in Lima, though he hadn't been around to pay Jim a visit. There were several shots of Pete over a period of two months, dressed in the white cotton suit, no tie, five-o'clock shadow and anodized shades, one on a hot day as he talked to a stevedore working a shipment, so he was sweating like Dan Duryea in a thriller set in a Singapore bar.

Liz was looking at his dockside photos, and said 'Wait a minute.' With her eagle eye, she'd picked out one with Derrick Stephensen, another archaeologist from the 1969 Ayacucho project in the group photo.

"I thought you said Stephensen hadn't been back in Peru since Sendero got bad in the Eighties," Jim said.

"Sorry, it's news to me," Liz said, with an apologetic undertone since she prided herself on being up to speed on the American scholars in the Andes, because she'd worked at so many of their digs. "I thought he was married to a Boston heiress, had tenure and was doing paleo sites in Canada. Maybe he got word through the grapevine about Val Davis."

"This photo is from two weeks before Val's murder," Jim said. "And why would he be talking to Pete Seymour?"

Now it seemed a link between the Larsen and Lenguado murders, suspected from his Eliot dream and acronyms' coincidence, ran through his connection with Helen and Pete and on to Stephenson and maybe Val or others in the Ayacucho Project group photo. Liz knew nothing about Pete or Holly even being in his garden when Larsen was shot there, and Jim didn't feel any compunction about not telling her and worrying her more, when he hadn't yet figured things out himself. She'd brought her own heavy baggage of SIN surveillance when she'd come back to him. He would still have wanted her despite her leftist tendencies, it wasn't like he thought she'd brought down the establishment on him, more likely they might need to look at the old group photo together again and think about it, because there were some twenty people in it, including the Peruvian anthropologist, his grad student assistant, driver and a local liaison, no reason anybody would be going after the Peruvians. There was Mac, as the renowned Andean archaeologist, Dr. MacHenry, preferred to be called by all, dressed in his plaid lumberjack shirt and smiling as if he had imbibed a few Peru Libres soon before, and flanking him on either side, Friedrich, researching in Paraguay now, and Irv Cohen, who knew about Val's death, but hard to think of either of them being a target of some disgruntled student or a rival academic protecting their own reputation in the field.

"Irv would have told Mac about Val, wouldn't he?" Jim said.

"I'm sure he would," Liz said. "I don't know where Mac is now, but maybe I could find out."

"Might not be a bad idea," Jim said. "In case this is some wacko with a gripe against the program. Stephensen's back here, but he's golden and shouldn't be knocking people off. There's Miller beside him. Didn't he drop out of the doctoral program after that summer? He was kind of weird and aggressive. He tried to mug me at the

Colmena. And he made fun of the first fish I caught that summer, a nice footlong cutthroat trout, saying like here's Moby Dick. We just never hit it off."

"He thought you were a narc," Liz said. "You know he was supplying the whole project. He had everything, coke and grass, horse, uppers, downers, sideways, every which ways. Last I heard, he was doing very well in Mexico in that same business."

One side effect of being with Liz again was that the anthropologists were coming by his house out off Avenida Arequipa, some young grad students running on the old 'help a fellow American overseas bit', a few well established to whom Jim gave his card for investment consultation since many had their pensions locked up in conservative investment strategies of university managers who couldn't beat the S&P even in the Reagan-Clinton bull market.

It was like a side benefit having Liz back that those backpackers, climbers, and many scholars dropped by, like being able to audit a course on Recent Developments In Andean Archaeology, the New World Egypt. Now with their Tutankamen, the Sechin Tombs dated back to maybe 1,500 B.C., and Caral back to 3.000 B.C., so as old as the Great Pyramids, with many sites as big as at Giza, north coast Peru was the hottest area, because there were immense ruins that had scarcely been touched, many so extensive and already dilapidated when the Spanish came, they thought they were natural features of the landscape. The archaeologists could describe periods, but it was something else as to larger questions as to why civilization had evolved independently in Peru at the same time as in Egypt, Mesopotamia, the Indus and China. They'd hold back from openly expressing their opinion in print on those, though in informal conversation with a few peru libres under their belts, they'd make claims like he'd heard Dr. MacHenry make, that man had been in the Americas for 30,000 years, when 12,000 was still the conventional wisdom, Clovis and all that. For Jim the reason seemed to reside in the land and the weather patterns. When the Niños came, flooding and landslides resulted. One scholar argued the Moche culture had been wiped out around 900 A.D. as the result of catastrophic flooding followed by extended drought. In the Andes, it was a good idea to plan ahead for what fickle weather brought, not to mention the earthquakes that knocked everything down if you didn't build strong. The agricultural terraces at Machu Picchu relied not only on those massive monolithic granite walls, but also on good drainage and soil engineering, backfilling first with the ashlars from the cut boulders, then with progressively finer soil hauled up from the valley bottoms, all indicating their level of civilization.

Jim had not been back to Machu Picchu since Hugh Thomson found nearby its observatory and sister burg of Llactapata, actually rediscovered it from reports of Bingham and Reinhardt, had told that story masterfully in "A Sacred Landscape", from letting out a whoop on finding its bearings in Bingham's notes in Sterling Library, on down to a modern mule train and machete hacking through mist forest to reveal a grand plaza on a sight line with Machu Picchu, and aligned for the solstice and the rising of the Pleiades for the planting season. The place was a bigger complex than first realized, with monumental building requiring a large population in a hierarchical society. It was hard to see it as a communist society, since the Inca was a divine right absolute ruler as much as any Pharaoh, but he did care for his subjects and filled granaries for the lean years. Yes, Pizarro's sword had brought five hundred years of darkness to the children of the sun.

The sun had shone through to them in the 1960's with Velasco's Gobierno Revolucionario, which instituted agrarian reform, built roads in the sierra and jungle, and made Quechua an official language along with Spanish, back in the late Sixties when Jim first met Liz in Ayacucho. Then in the overwhelming poverty of the sierra, Sendero Luminoso was spawned, in fact they'd been there when Guzman was still lecturing on Kant at the Universidad de Huamanga, before he laid down The Categorical Imperative and took up the Kalashnikov, and brought so much terror, torture and murder to the sierra, and the mirror image of the counter-terrorism and Army reprisals. Ayacucho was an incredible place and Liz wanted him to go back with her, after all that was where they first made love.

Love not war, love not war, give peace a chance. 70,000 dead in the civil war, double the original estimates, and Liz said the new estimate might be low because they kept finding new massacre sites the survivors lead her to. She had photos.

—⟳—

It was at a time Jim was trolling for new clients at an embassy reception that he met Rosa Billups, who had been spurred in her interest in the foreign service by getting on embassy reception lists in Washington, D.C. She was young, attractive, the daughter of a U.S. Air Force captain, a handsome, light-skinned African-American man, and a good-looking German woman, so a self-described Air Force brat, but spoke English and German well, and French too from college, was now learning Spanish during her Lima post. She said that once you got on the reception list at one embassy, and made a good impression, she was an effervescent conversationalist, you'd get on the lists of others. She said she was practically living off the buffets at one time, and eating high off the hog too, caviar, camembert, pheasant, champagne, the whole shebang. They danced together, and she was good at networking and got him a few American clients with the government, who wanted to have something in the stock market, and then when he wanted somebody to cover the office when he went for his extended visits with Helen, he thought of her husband, Ricky Billups, who had a degree in economics from Michigan State, a well-spoken young man of ebony complexion, dark as Rosa was light, as they used to say before it became incorrect to say it, she could have 'passed'. He was teaching English at a private school in Lima, and not especially happy with it, so Jim tried to convince him he should go into the stock business himself and what better place and time to start than here and now, they'd make up an announcement with a curriculum vitae, Hiram is now Hiram & Associates, new associate, Richard Billups. He had a rare combination of good formal education and street smarts. Not that he was from the ghetto, on the contrary, his family was solidly middle-class, maybe even upper middle-class since his Dad was an insurance man with his own agency, so he had an idea of the advantages of being basically one's own boss.

They'd talked over this prospect one afternoon when it was sprinkling, so Jim had put his motorcycle leathers on over his suit to take the cycle downtown to beat Lima traffic during a religious festival. They'd agreed to meet at a German pastry shop they both knew on Avenida Wilson and then go to a bar near there to talk. Ricky must have heard the Harley drive up, but not associating it with Jim, was chowing down on a large creme puff, so Jim came in, stomping his boots and slapping his gloves together.

"Hey buddy, help a fellow American down on his luck?" Jim said.

"Damn, Jimmy, when'd you join up with the Wild Ones?" Ricky Billups said. "You don't have your gang out there, do you?"

"Just give me all your croissants and nobody gets hurt," Jim said, unzipping the jacket and flopping it over the back of the chair. He smoothed his cotton shirt, his sports coat and adjusted his tie. "Feel better now? Clothes do make the man. I remember a sign in a Bolivian guardia station at Desaguadero. It said: 'Man In The Suit and Tie, the Communists are your Enemy.' I happened to be wearing a suit and tie because it was easier than packing them. Customs held our bus up for three hours. There were some French Leftists whose passports they were looking at very carefully. It was around the time they found Klaus Barbie in La Paz. I never saw so many French tourists as I did that summer. I told one of them about the sign and he went in and took a picture of it."

"Damn lucky you weren't on your cycle or they'd have mistaken you for Che Guevara," Ricky said. "Bolivia's where he went down, wasn't it?"

"He's still on the billboards in Havana," Jimmy said. "They let McNamara go there to commemorate the Cuban Missile Crisis, just to get things straight for history. I'm sure the whiz kid covered the main points, though I had a question or two."

"You go asking a bunch of questions, you may get your butt in El Moro," Ricky said.

"Anyway, it's obvious you're aware of the problem of political instability and its downside risks, but it also creates opportunities, --you can sell Treasury notes here to some who just want a no-risk, positive return, and then sell others stocks," Jim said, glad that the Billups lived in a gated community and understood the security problems there. "You're well spoken. Rosa is a natural rainmaker."

"I don't know man, Rosa may be transferred in three, four years," Ricky said. "And she'd like to go back to DC and get a Master's in international affairs. I'm already worried about starting a family. She's not your standard stay-at-home mom. I worry about stability for the kids."

"Kids are pretty flexible, if there's love in the home," Jim said. "And by then, you'd have clients to take with you if you move. State Department people will stay with you if they know you."

They went to a bar and talked about client lists and good will and also about some great Spartan teams, like the one with Mateen Cleaves that beat Florida to take the NCAA hoops title. Ricky needed to learn more soccer because that was the default conversation topic with men down there, and Jim promised to get him his copies of Graham, Dodds, and his dictionary of Spanish legal and securities terms, his copies of the banking regs of Switzerland and the Turks and Caicos, Austria was also a convenient place to put money. They agreed Ricky would come in one evening a week and Saturday mornings to get acquainted with clients and interview them along with Jim as to their investment objectives, to see how he liked the business.

The streets downtown were already jammed with the fiesta as Jim wove slowly behind the procession with a catafalque carrying a painting done by an African slave in Lima of a vision he had of Jesus, a sacred relic of Peru recording a vision in the same realm of spiritual and mythopoeic power as that of the Virgen of Guadeloupe in Mexico. Peru was so Christian Jim could never understand how Sendero could take such a rigid orthodox Marxist stance against religion. It just seemed dumb strategy, like Daniel Ortega having his supporters jeer Pope John Paul II when he was in Managua, yet Sendero was targeting priests and nuns. In just one incident, senderistas shot a nun who was trying to stop them from massacring peasants they'd accused of being police sympathizers in Junin in 1990. She was machine-gunned in the head after praying and blessing each of the victims as they died. It was one of many tragedies in a sad time in a harsh land.

The phone rang and a Lima operator with a pretty voice said, 'A long distance call from a Mister Rad in Chicago, Illinois, of the United States of America. Will you accept charges?'

"I accept, I accept," Jim said quickly. "Hey Rad, what's up?"

"You were right, a month ago your galloping don, Professor Derrick Stephensen, flew from Saskatchewan to O'Hare and on to Miami and Jorge Chavez in Lima, no return as of yet," Rad said. "His wife is at her beach home in the Hamptons. I think they may have separate arrangements if that interests you."

"Not at the moment, though if she's a potential client, keep the file for me, if this latest crap drives me out of Peru, you know things are very up and down here, Helen's back in Philly, but her little brother, Pete, seems to be in Lima now," Jim said.

"Right again, lil' bro Pete has been there for two months, I know you knew about his preference for nose candy, but did you know he's also a compulsive gambler, like he's a familiar figure at Atlantic City casinos," Rad said. "I'd guess they can recognize a fat, zonked sucker. As to Pete's main squeeze, she filed for divorce in Pennsylvania, withdrew proceedings once, reinstituted them recently in Wisconsin, who knows where that's going, but she did go back to Milwaukee."

"I think it's one of the few community property states in the Midwest," Jim said.

"Did you know she was once in a Milwaukee foster home with your deceased Norm Larsen?" Rad said.

"I think I did know that, but tried to forget it since we occasionally see each other at family get-togethers, and the subject of Larsen hasn't come up, nor do I hope for it to do so," Jim said.

"I thought that was a bit odd," Rad said. "Not that I don't have weird in my own family. I screen calls from my sister-in-law because she's delusional. Consciousness is crazy, isn't it? Like in the vast universe man is only a reed, but he is a thinking reed. Is that Sartre?"

"Pascal maybe, though I was just thinking about Sartre, and how the Germans released him from detention, because he spoke German fluently after immersing himself in Husserl and Heidegger," Jim said.

"I imagine they still kept an eye on him after they let him out," Rad said. "Any other philosophical insights tonight?"

"Maybe a quote from Hamlet, there's more than is dreamt of in your philosophy, Horatio," Jim said. "Thanks for all your help, really, send me your bill, I know you're not an eleemosynary institution."

"I'm glad to help gratis, at least thus far, and curious to see how it turns out," Rad said. "It would seem advisable to check up further on Ms. Abbott."

"I agree, especially at your attractive rates," Jim said.

—ᨓ—

Frank had wanted Jim to go to this auction in Miraflores to look at and bid on an Inca silver llama, the same form as those found by Johan Reinhardt in the Ice Princess and other capa cocha burials. This one in its catalogue description noted markings, which were considered a defect, perhaps incised by some huacero or coleccionista, so they didn't estimate it would go for over fifteen hundred or two thousand.

Liz was there in Ayacucho at the time they discovered the silver llama, along with an ichu grass bed where the mummy had lain before a landslide had taken down a semi-conical section of the mountainside, and them along with it. They'd been trout-fishing near Ocros, not far from a disused Inca road, and they'd gotten up to around seventeen thousand feet when they found the site. Frank was of course very excited because he was a doctoral student in Andean archaeology, and this could be the find that made his career. The weather had changed from sunny, to partly cloudy to ominous with freezing rain, a sleet that drove into their eyes. Jim was a law student, and he was telling Frank to hurry, they needed to get back down the mountain. Frank was still walking around the site, had found a silver shawl pin of the same form used by Quechua women today. Then the earth shook and took him down a couple hundred feet in a slide, before Jim got a line down to him and pulled him to a rock outcropping. Frank was pretty banged up and suffering from hypothermia, and thought he'd helped Jim down the path, though it had been the other way around. Neither of them might have gotten out of there, had it not been for a campesino boy who'd been looking for a lost goat, who saw the tarp Jim had thrown over some rocks and the Bunsen burner heating bouillon, and came up to investigate. He led them through a narrow pass to his family's adobe hut, where they rented a donkey and had him guide them toward Vinchos. They stopped at an old hacienda, where the owner, Dona Lucita, a woman of great gentility, but evidently not having many guests and excited at the prospect, offered them her hospitality, hot beef broth with quinoa, and feather beds with down comforters. Frank was still asleep the next afternoon, while Jim had spent the morning perusing the library, conversing with Doña Lucita sipping maté through silver straws on the terrace, sketching the Silver Llama and noting the markings on it, strange because the usual votive form was smooth, though they had seemed cast in, not incised as the current catalogue described.

The Silver Llama was stolen from them in the hospital in Ayacucho or on the way to it, and they both were still so dehydrated and exhausted they slept all the way back. Frank took the loss harder than he did, because it would have boosted his career. Jim thought it would have been nice to discover something, but he'd made other discoveries that summer, including Liz and Peru, so those were pretty fantastic. It might be something to put on your law resumé but on the other hand, firms might take it as evidence of distraction from devotion to the profession.

"I remember him talking about that Silver Llama when he was in rehab back in San Francisco," Liz said. "You think he's still obsessed about it?"

"He said get it for him if I could pick it up for under three thousand," Jim said. "If he were obsessed, he'd have given me carte blanche. I don't like to talk about it because his memory of the Ocros hike is different from mine. It gives me a sense of unreality. If I feel unreal, I start questioning why I'm here. It's like 'no me hallo aqui'. Then I might wish I were back home with three kids and a conventional job."

"Then you know you are out of your mind," Liz said. "Why did you come down here in the first place?"

"Maybe it was my old man," Jim said. "He had a chance to become radio man on a boat to South America, and he used to talk about that when Mom and he would argue."

He'd say he was nothing but a henpecked wage mule, but after kicking at his stall he'd always be at work, because if you went through the Depression you always felt lucky to have a job, forty years with the same company and he died a month after retirement. In his desk, Jim found a clipping with the by-line of his uncle, a well-known East Coast journalist who'd posted a story from Buenos Aires, so maybe that recalled dad's banana boat story. This was the same beloved uncle who had the capuchin monkey that was constantly beside him at his typewriter and became his drinking companion, since booze was the accepted grease for the wheels of journalistic inspiration. The monkey particularly liked that yellow stuff in long bottles. When the old man died, they didn't know what to do with the monkey, which was drinking a lot and was very ill-tempered when it didn't get its hooch. They managed to donate it to the Philadelphia zoo after making sure it was well loaded before it was taken away. It later escaped after biting a keeper, hiding out in nearby trees and ransacking coolers for beer, frisking purses and jackets for flasks. The zoo tried to give it back to them, but fortunately the uncle's estate was closed by then.

After she'd gone to bed, Jim sat up going through some Peru notebooks he'd kept available for writing purposes, to see if he could find the one from the 1969 Ocros hike when they found the Silver Llama, and in which he made sketches of the piece while recovering at the Arcetura ancestral hacienda. Instead he found a poetic fragment he had written sitting at an umbrella table on the veranda of the Pension Inglesa in patches of bright equatorial sun that gave way to a brief shower, then watching an island of dry pavement slowly diminish in size as the drizzle sent a gradually rising line of damp encroaching around it. The dry spot was consciousness, the wet surrounding it was the flux, and the process was like life culminating in absolute nihility. He thought maybe people believed in an afterlife because they thought things would naturally go on as they had in the past, there'd be some consciousness, and how does one think without using words, so the next question was what language would be used in the afterlife. This question had so troubled a 19th century Yale College president that he required not only Latin and Greek, but also Hebrew so that grads could speak with the prophets in the afterlife, though the requirement didn't last, too great an interference with poker and drinking. And why would God chose Latin, if it was a dead language and God wasn't dead. Maybe it would be in English or Spanish, as the final flood surrounded and overwhelmed the last high and dry spot of consciousness, maybe not in those of any other language. It was an uncomfortable unsought unway to unthink an unlanguage, to meditate in the dream of death without any usual means of expression. But why should Eternity so infinite accommodate this fatuous request of a dead soul for a familiar language from a small and distant planet cast away in the infinite reaches of Space. The poem which had begun with such a concrete and abstractly logical concept, almost a neat metaphysical conceit, was fated to remain unfinished, as if the jaws of Death had left its frayed edges to be entombed unrecognized in that dry, dusty packing box. Hemingway was right; poetry was a hard sell, though his sentences had a poetic quality.

It was positionally exotic that night; he'd done the headstand and talked about feeling like an East German about to go over the Wall or like a displaced pied noir. Or maybe it more resembled escaping Devil's Island, have faith, my butterfly, things are changing for the better for us. So they managed to salvage some pleasure, like a nice souvenir from Cayenne—something with a shiny nacre handle to hold on to, a lovely fan—or a lovely fanny, a derriere of superior quality. Hot, hot as Cayenne.

It was a posh auction house in a new glass wall office complex not far away in Miraflores, and he was glad he'd opted for suit and tie rather than tennies, slacks and a pullover, and that Liz had on a black cocktail dress and wore her Monica Vitti turtle shell sunglasses. Frank had set up a line of credit with the house and they were given a paddle to raise in bidding, which started at five hundred, quickly went to a thousand, to fifteen hundred and Jim's last bid of two thousand got raised by someone on the other side, two more bids and it went to the man on the other side for fifty-five hundred, whom they'd been unable to see during the bidding, but toward whom they shuffled as unobtrusively as possible, if only for Liz to get a photo of the piece, that hopefully would show the marks on it.

He and Frank had talked about those markings looking at his sketch and it did seem like an inscription. Frank pointed out that though Pizarro's Conquest was in 1532, it was not until 1571 that Toledo hunted down Tupac Amaru I at Vilcabamba. Forty years was two generations back then, and by then there were already Indian stonemasons and metalsmiths working now on cathedrals to Jesus, not on temples to Inti or heathen huacas, but yet the old Indian beliefs persisted. The idea of a perfect Conquest was never accurate; there was resistance from the first; there were even ghost dances to expel the white devils from their lands, just as there had been among the U.S. Plains native nations. Frank speculated some Inca metalsmith had made up a special Silver Llama, they'd need strong medicine against the Spanish, so perhaps the letters were contras against the magic of writing the oppressors used, also taught to Inca nobles' children. Perhaps this was a special huaca prepared for the old Inca religion. They'd been hiking in the high country near Ocros, and it was backwoods and entirely Indian today as it had been four hundred years ago, a fastness of the Quechua. All this was only Frank's theory of course, and those marks might as easily have been made in the slide that exposed the burial site.

Liz didn't get a chance to get a photo of this auctioned Llama, because when they advanced toward the other side not so hastily as to show too much interest in the piece, a bearded older gentleman was already taking the statuette under his greatcoat, revealing a plaid shirt, and was sweeping toward the exit.

"Isn't that Dr. MacHenry?" Jim said to her when the man turned at the end of the aisle, and she looked surprised and nodded yes in slow motion recognition, so he called out "Hey, Mac", but this only seemed to hurry his departure, and there was another party, a barrel-chested guy with a pompadour in a grey suit, pushing people aside though Jim got to the exit first and inadvertently stepped in front of him. They collided, fell and got up in time to see the taxi pulling away with Mac in the back and the driver punching it. Jim apologized but the big guy had already taken off.

There was nothing more for a couple of days until he got a call from Mac.

"Sorry I couldn't stop at the auction, but I had somebody after me I wanted to avoid," Mac said.

"Somebody like who?" Jim said.

"Now that is an interesting question, and one I'd prefer to discuss in private," Mac said. "You know the chifa a couple blocks from the Pension Inglesa? Can you meet around seven-thirty?"

"Sure, should I bring Liz Teris with me?" Jim said.

"Lizzy's a great gal, but I'd prefer just you," Mac said. "It's a somewhat sensitive matter. You lawyers talk about privileged communication. Listen, just give your name to Song Li or Hop Sing at the bar."

When he heard Mac mention 'you lawyers', Jim thought 'uh, oh, trouble, which is why I ran from the law, had enough troubles of my own without having to deal with other people's. With this on his mind and the man who'd been following Mac at the auction, Jim went to the chifa with some trepidation, but it was no problem, Song Li led him into a back room where five Chinese men were gambling at mah jong, through a passageway and into another bar where Mac was putting down Peru Libres, pisco brandy and Coca Cola, and they were then ushered into a private room for dinner.

"I did want to ask your legal advice on this, because there may be some liability on my part, since I'd like this kept as quiet as is reasonably possible given the ethical dimensions, and I know there's attorney-client privilege, so can I retain you?" Mac said.

"I'm in stocks and bonds now, Mac," Jim said. "But that doesn't mean I can't keep a secret. I mean, are we talking about black market art or murder here?"

"Oh Lord, who knows, you've heard about poor Val Davis, and the group photo from Vinchos they found with him circled," Mac said. "I hope it's not related, but Val was in with them back then."

"Them?" Jim said.

"With Stephensen and Emerson for sure, you must understand I didn't discover this until much later," Mac said, recounting that after Frank's motorcycle accident that sent him home in '69, those two had evidently tracked down that site in Ocros. As Frank found when he hiked back there a year later, not much was left of the upper site after the slides. But the slides had not been the only factor. His fellow young archaeologists knew the Incas would build on a slope with a hanan, an upper sector, and a hurin, a lower sector, which they later that summer claimed to have found at a bridgehead near Ocros, but they were actually salting the site with finds from above, including pieces from an altar near the capa cocha burial. Jim remembered hiking past the bridgehead when fishing upstream from Vinchos, up a rock knoll with thorn trees, past an old plum grove in the river bottom, the quixotic hope of some hacendero given the sierra freezes, unpruned, woody and witchy with mummies fallen in the old irrigation channel. It was years later before Mac heard anything about this, from a disaffected former grad student of Emerson, who was by then a recognized scholar, and he had to wonder how much to believe in a case involving a clash of personalities. Frank was long gone from the program and it was no longer safe to check out the physical evidence in rural Ayacucho Province, the birthplace and a stronghold of Sendero insurgency. Jim was once again reminded that a hazard of being an Andean scholar often more serious than terrain, climate or even guerrillas, was professional, recalling, ah the venerable Maria Reiche, considered a saint by local townspeople for creating a hundred thousand dollar a year tourist industry of the Nasca Lines, acted like she owned the place, once got a denuncia against Urton and Aveni, two of the best young archaeo-astronomers, it didn't help they disagreed with her belief that the lines were for astronomical observation, or that they were dressed like hippies, the grande dame nearly getting them thrown in jail, after their air balloon crashed while photographing the lines, sending their jeep up the pampa, before being saved by the evidence of the noted Dr. Z, who gave assurance that these hippy gringos were in fact serious scholars. It was always best not to go stepping on toes when you might be the next to have some spurious denuncia registered with the authorities because of a vendetta, and the scholars could be venal and petty, ran their departments like feudal fiefdoms.

Mac's interest was in pre-history, and he'd been busy at an ancient site in the Brazilian Amazon while the Peruvian sierra was under martial law during the Sendero terror. But he got back to Ayacucho in '93, managed to find a local who confirmed that Emerson and

Stephensen had hired arrieros to take the same route Frank and Jim took to the Ocros site. Mac then went to Trujillo and questioned Val Davis, who said he knew about it but wasn't in on it, claimed it was only some run of the mill utilitarian objects, but even this was heresy to a good archaeologist.

"You think Emerson killed Val Davis?" Jim said.

"I don't know if he's homicidal," Mac said. "He went after you once with a knife in Cuzco, didn't he? I heard you were involved with his wife?"

"That was after he stabbed me and ran off with Liz, Mari came around to console me," Jim said. "I assume he told his side of the story."

"In technicolor," Mac said. "You weren't in the loop to defend yourself, just like Frank was no longer around when they were mining his site. You see, he is the one I feel worst about because I was his doctoral advisor. He was a promising student. It changed his life. When I saw this Silver Llama on auction, I remembered how you described it with the markings, which at the time prompted more than a scintilla of doubt on my part, since every other one found was completely smooth. I went to the auction thinking Emerson might be unloading some old goods if he thought Frank was behind this ethics thing. However, when I saw that big fellow with the pompadour, it occurred to me it was bait for the next sucker after Val. That's why I took off in such a hurry. Anyway, I feel kind of compelled to give this thing to Frank and tell him the whole damn sad story."

"You might reconsider that," Jim said. "Frank's been very successful in business in La Paz. The people skills he learned in fieldwork, he used to good advantage. He has a lovely wife and three children. Why reopen an old wound and rub salt in it? If we do, he might just chime in on this ethics inquiry. He only talks about it when he's loaded, and anyway we don't even know that what you bought is the same Silver Llama we found at Ocros."

"I have it back at the Pension," Mac said. "I'm staying there because it's out of the way. I've hidden it in the garden in case anyone finds me. Why don't we go have a look-see?"

"I'd love to see Dona Olga but I haven't visited in a year and she'd talk my ear off," Jim said. "You mind if I eat dinner here while you go get it."

"Not at all," Mac said. "I can be back with it in half an hour if the old girl's watching her TV programs. And your advice is not to tell Frank about Ocros? It's important to me that you're his friend."

"That's my best advice," Jim said. "Do not wake the sleeping tiger. You can sell me the thing, I'll tell him I got it at the auction, and leave the rest of the story out. Maybe I can get him to donate it to a museum here. That's really where it belongs."

—⁂—

It was a well-stocked bar at the chifa, with a full wall mirror behind it and bottles with all different color liquors and a color TV that had on a soccer match Jim went out to watch while he waited for his food to come. He had a gin and tonic and then proceeded to a dinner of duck in oyster sauce in the private room, thinking he'd share drinks and an order of appetizers with Mac when he came back. A half-hour went past, then forty-five minutes and at an hour Jim paid the tab, took the extra food in carry-out cartons, and walked the six blocks to the Pension Inglesa. A police car was parked outside with lights flashing, the gate was open, and the officer was speaking with Dona Olga when he came in. She greeted Jim, who explained he was there to see Dr. MacHenry, who it appeared had either been spirited away by intruders or had escaped them, there was a bloody plaid shirt in his room that didn't bode well for him, and the intruders had torn up the room completely.

The men had also knocked out Vicente, the mayor d'omo, when he confronted them. He was laid out on the floor of the entryway by the pantry, looked after by another cop and Pacha, the Egyptian silver cat with whom he waged a running battle with his broom to keep him off the credenza and the sofa which was a perfect scratching post. Pacha, as if in honor of his worthy adversary, had come to perch on the steps right above Vicente and stayed guard until the medics arrived. It was not a convenient time for Jim to check the garden for the Silver Llama, though he did call Capt. Fregosco, who lived near enough that he came by, saw the photocopy of the group picture of the Ayacucho project, this one with Mac's picture circled, the same modus as had been the case in the killing of Val Davis in Trujillo. Fregosco of course did not see any relation to the prior Lenguado murder, and Jim didn't mention anything about Larsen's disappearance or about the Silver Llama. They shared the rest of the Chinese carry-out, the captain especially fond of the dumplings with plum sauce and crisp golden shrimp petites croissants with hot mustard, nice to wash down with a fine pilsener like Cristal. It gave Olga an audience for a favorite story of when she was on her grand tour of Europe as a young lady and they got stopped by Spanish Customs and strip-searched, since the Republican government was looking for any funds to fight Franco, so the only way to get the gems through was to take them out of the settings, swallow them and fish them out of the chamber pot on the steamer back to Peru.

Nothing of value had been taken that break-in at the Pension Inglesa and to avoid any insurance rate increases, no police report was filed, though Fregosco did put out a notice about Mac. It did not say that he was kidnapped or injured, but simply that he was a possible witness to breaking and entering resulting in the assault on and injury of a domestic employee. The mattresses had been turned upside-down, the closets and chest of drawers ransacked, of course the bloodied plaid shirt, a broken ceramic base jar which had a bloodstain on one of the shards, so somebody got konked and then was taken or ran away. In the back of the drawer of the writing desk he noticed a small ceramic frog, on an Inca model if not an original. The Incas loved animals and found meaning in them, snails for example were good luck because they carried their house on their back and so were always at home wherever they were; for them the condor was a sign and symbol of God above.

The icing on a bad night was when they heard water running in the upstairs bathroom, and Fregosco with his gun drawn crept up the stairs, Jimmy behind him carrying a good solid cleaver from the kitchen.

"Venga afuera con manos arriba," the captain shouted, positioning his portly frame outside the door, but there was no answer from within and after another try, swung the door open, then let out a groan of disgust with an undertone of terror.

The place was a horrible mess. The intruders had dragged there a huge Paracas chumba, a ceramic funerary vase five feet tall, which some archaeologist had left there years before and never reclaimed. They'd cracked open the chumba, not especially rare since there were thousands of them down the coast, had removed the mummy from it and set it on the commode. Jim volunteered to clean it up. He'd always wanted a chumba for his place and knew how to use Epoxy and Super Glue. He put the big shards at the curb to go in the trunk of the taxi, though the mummy presented a more complex problem because the cabbie probably wouldn't want it unwinding in his cab. So he wrapped it in his London Fog and wool scarf, set his pork pie atop the skull and carried it to the back seat, saying his friend was passed out drunk. The cabbie was chatty and offered a pharmacopeia of hang-over cures.

"Hair of the dog that bit you works," the cabbie said. "A raw egg and picante sauce. Your friend's not very sociable. Bien borracho, eh?"

"Some it makes talk, others it makes silent," Jim said.

"Probably a woman," the cabbie said.

"Now that you mention, it might be a woman," Jim said, turning to his new friend. "What about that?"

"The real silent type," the cabbie said. "He refuses to answer."

"He's been out of it for a while," Jim said. "We're both half gone."

"A fog like this gets into your bones," the cabbie said. "I think you'll be my last fare tonight."

"It's no surprise he's feeling no pain," Jim said. "He was dead tired before his first drink."

—⟋⟋⟍—

Jim did go to the Pension a couple days later to help Olga with the damage claim and found she'd been sitting on an insurance bill while contemplating raising the deductible to save some money, because Lima is an expensive city for a pensioner on a fixed income in an inflationary economy. Fortunately he got the bill in the mail before the expiration deadline, extending the existing lower deductible, and the claim later went through good. It gave him satisfaction to collect on a her claim, because insurers believed in science and employed statisticians and actuaries, so it was like winning at a casino when you knew the house always won or it wouldn't be there. In appreciation, Olga gave him some Arcetura documents and stock certificates from the old mine her father used to manage, which hadn't been worked in years. They had a Goddess of Progress etched in diazo presiding with outstretched arms over the rail lines, the cables, the hoppers and ore crushers, with a series of modern buildings which were where the stables actually were, 'those burros, we had to ride them down to the coast to catch the steamer to Europe, because the paths were too narrow for horses. One false step and it was over the side'. And speaking of progress, she had found a photo of her great-uncle, Don Pedro, known as El Progesivo because he had instituted some reforms like not using child miners, and safety measures such as protection against poisoning from mercury, which was used in gold refining. The photo was taken in the early 1900's at a hotel on the Costa del Sol, where he had spent his later years far from the harsh rigors of the sierra, and had written his memoirs, published in Madrid, which she loaned Jim to read because he had met one of her Arcetura cousins at an ancient hacienda near Vinchos after the hike at Ocros. The book included a family tree and she also gave him a packet of old deeds to look at. She said she doubted if the certificates or deeds had any value, since Velasco's agrarian reform had split up much of the family estate in the sierra, and he could use them to line cabinets, since they were printed on high quality paper.

—⟋⟍—

When Jim called Frank to tell him what had happened with Mac, of course omitting the part about Emerson and Stephensen robbing his site at Ocros 25 year ago, which would really have set him off, Frank was still excited and more convinced than ever that this might well be 'their Silver Llama' with a unique historical value. Frank knew a historian who'd researched the forty years from Pizarro's 1532 conquest to when they killed off the last Inca pretender to the native throne, Tupac Amaru I, at Vilcabamba in 1571. In those two generations, Inca artisans were building cathedrals to the Christian god, oh, right after they were metal smiths smelting gold from heathen ornament to send back to the mother country, next to create chalices and crucifixes and monstrances to ornament the churches and mansions of the new rulers. The Spanish colonials kept great records, and some Indians had done well under the new regime. After all, Pizarro had been savvy in copying Cortez's modus of getting subject tribes of the empire to revolt, in fact it was troops from the kingdom his mistress, a Huancayo princess, who won the Seige of Lima for him against the resurgent Incas, as the Crown pointed out in denying his suit for reimbursement, so not quite the Tarzan myth of the Conquistador. The indios who did all right under the new order went the gamut from arriero muleteers hauling goods over a disrupted road system, to the many Inca princes like the commentator Garcilaso who was sent to Spain to be converted and educated, was literate and wrote chronicles that retained an underlying sympathy for his subjected people. One could imagine a Quechua silversmith of that era, who had been exposed to the new ruler's methods, who'd seen their writing supplant the quipu, who had also seen the sword and fire of the conquistadores and decided their real god was gold, who was still loyal to the old gods in support of a native uprising, and to include in a sacrifice to them might have crafted a silver llama huaca with a contra (a counter-spell) on it in the letters, TASA, was what it had looked like at first, perhaps Tupac Amaru Sapa Inca (the 'high Inca' since he was the hereditary successor to Atahualpa, whom Pizarro murdered after a show trial).

Jim didn't doubt that if you ever really want to see something, sketch it and you'll see details you didn't notice before. But it was hard to see, fuzzy in the glaring sierra sun when he'd been sketching it on the terrace of the old Arcetura hacienda and he didn't want to pick off much of the patina, spots on it had already been scoured in the slide, and the archaeologists cautioned against removing coatings which could be used to carbon date pieces, or to tell if they had been in touch with cochineal red dye used in funeral garments. Frank and he had theorized a lot about this Llama, when they thought the piece might have been temporarily misplaced; but since it became clear they had lost the actual piece, the others tended to think they were just fantasizing and still zonked out from soroche and hypothermia, though they knew what they'd seen.

For Frank, after he heard Mac might have taken off with the Silver Llama of Ocros after an incident at the Pension Inglesa, it was like he was thrown back into a confrontation mode, why for God's sake did Frank care so much when he had it made, was it related to empty nest syndrome, needing something to replace what you lost, Jim didn't know, he was just trying to swim and not sink. The markets had for the most part been good to him recently, and now that Liz was back with him, he thought maybe he could slide by and stay longer in his happy garden in Lima. It was two years since Helen had gone back to Philly. The idea that his brother-in-law was now back in Lima and was in contact with Stephenson was quite disconcerting in light of the recent murders. He needed to check that out, but wasn't about to invite Pete over for a convivial family dinner with Liz now in residence and feeling like his main squeeze. He was so happy he was back in a relationship and having regular heterosexual relations, and just felt too tired to dissemble it.

—⚏—

One, two, buckle my shoe.

"Hello Jim, hope I'm not disturbing your sleep," it was the voice of Vince Scarlatti on the answering machine.

"Hi, Vince, just finishing supper, Lima's the same time zone as Philly," Jim said, picking up the receiver.

"Yo man, what's shakin' in the Ring of Fire," Vince Scarlatti said.

"Not much, what's goin' on in the City of Brotherly Love," Jim said.

"Funny you should say brotherly," Vince said. "I just got word about your brother-in-law, Pete, from Dev Smith. He's trying to get in touch with him. Holly's sued him for divorce and she's asking for an incredible amount in alimony or property division. It's enough it's going to affect the company. Helen doesn't know where he is. I have an old frat buddy from Penn State who manages a casino in Atlantic City. The skinny on the street there is that he went to Lima. You know anything about our boy?"

"Yeh, I had somebody checking up on a shipper down here for a client, so I'm looking through the photos in his file, and bingo, in one of the photos there's Pete," Jim said. "What the heck is he doing down here, I said to myself. He knows I'm in Lima so I figure he hasn't dropped by for a family visit for his own reasons. I do know ten years ago when I first found him in Tingo Maria, somebody said he was peripherally associated with the coke trade."

"Peripherally associated, I like that," Vince said. "You still have a lawyer's way with words. Are you sure you're not representing him now? Dev said Pete thought he could dodge process servers and get away with it, but Holly can just publish if he doesn't answer. Dev needs to talk to him."

"Haven't spoken with him myself, am not sure whether he was just passing through, but I'd be happy to look him up for Dev, though Pete may want to stay in hiding and claim no service, or sewer service," Jim said, using the term from the days when process servers who couldn't find a party would just drop the summons down a sewer and affirm it had been served. "Dev may be better off not filing an appearance as his lawyer of record, since then they can serve him. And a domestic relations court is gonna be slow to give million dollar judgments on publication service. Pete can come in later, claim bad service and no assets, working on the docks just to make ends meet, aw man, even the judges will be crying for this prince on the waterfront. But Dev's been gold for us, so I'll find the man."

"Anything you can do," Vince said. "There's a proxy fight pending, and Dev says that could result in big changes, like for Helen's preferred dividends, not for Pete's because he already pledged those out as far as he could, but other things like retiree pensions are in play, and you know I'm teetering on the edge of early retirement. Like my uncle Vic used to say, always work hard and save your money, they serve thin soup at the poor house."

"I'll do what I can, Lima's as big as New York now, --heh, what would you say if somebody asked you to find your long-lost brother-in-law in New York?" Jim said, remembering the Scarlatti worthless brother-in-law theory for everything from the decay of modern society to the downfall of communism, since everybody has a lazy, drunken relative, not necessarily a brother-in-law though that was his pick, whose main aim in life was gaming the system for a free ride with as little effort as possible.

"I'd say I haven't seen him in seven years, what's he wanted for, officer?" Vince said.

"So Holly's finally cutting loose," Jim said. "Well, at least they didn't have kids to get messed up by this."

"Or to have Pete pay child support in addition to the twenty million she wants in alimony," Vince said. "It'd be nice if he could show up for long enough to sign the proxies supporting our directors whose plan retains the pension system."

"I know a guy down on the docks," Jim said. "I'll see if I can't track the Prodigal. I'd like to know what he's doing here too."

Three four, open the door. Lost films and Liz on the sierra road again.

When Liz came in from Ayacucho this most recent time, she brought duplicate rolls of film from her recent trip because of concerns about losing them. He'd taken one set of rolls to his basement for safekeeping behind his big oak door with the interior steel plate, and Liz had been so relieved she had a back-up set after her lab informed her that all the negatives of her first set were fuzzed. After she found the back-up negatives were also spoiled, she was down and depressed. Liz thought the airport detector at Jorge Chavez might have ruined the first set in her carry-on bag with its x-rays, but she didn't expect they would have gotten the second set, wrapped in tin foil in the seams of her luggage. They might even have gotten it in Ayacucho, where there was a large Army base. She was only down for a while before declaring she would be going right back up to Ayacucho to get more film. Oh please don't go back so soon, Jim pleaded, you know Sendero is defeated but not deracinated, nor is the Army pleasant when it comes to documenting massacres, or commemorative ceremonies like that one with the survivors of the village all in their finest brightly colored sierra fare, parading up an incline in a denuded moonscape, remembering people they had known who had died in the Sendero civil war. Please don't go, not for nothing do they call it the Corner of the Dead, I don't know if I've told you lately how much you mean to me, and she said, 'Gonna go, can't stop me. You'll love me more when you miss me. And that was that.'

It was so different from what Helen's reaction would have been. One of Jim's first mistakes with her was when he had wanted to take her to the sierra because, though Lima was like the NYC of old Spanish America, the sierra was the Indian heart of Peru, some said like two different countries, but not to push that too far—Lima was clearly the center of power. E.g., public school teachers in far south Arequipa had to go to the capital to get their paychecks, if that wasn't debilitating centralization, what was? This trip was back before Sendero had gotten going good, was doing some raid operations, provincial bank jobs for money, indoctrinating cadres for la lucha armada to come, ramping up munitions and there were as yet no U.S. State Department travel advisories. So Jim had had his Satellite tuned up and had scheduled two weeks out from the office for them to tour the Peruvian sierra and give her a feel for the resinous indio heart of the nation.

It hadn't been a good trip to say the least. He'd planned for them to arrive at Huanta by three p.m. in the afternoon sun to catch the red cliffs that recalled the blood shed there in the final defeat of the Spanish Empire a hundred and seventy-five years before. It was their Yorktown, won by Bolivar's General Sucre after a disillusioned San Martin had left for Europe, a victory for freedom on that high cactus plain, though in the dusty unpaved plaza there had been erected only a small concrete memorial tholon with a brass plaque. The criollos blancos feared too much freedom might unleash an Indian revolt like Tupac Amaru II led thirty years before Independence, when the Spanish and white criollos had been indiscriminately murdered by his Indian followers during that uprising, despite their leader's instructions and his alliance with the criollos. Jim had envisaged himself as the guide of the trip, but auto glitches had intruded on his tour of the grand panorama of History. They'd made it driving up to a pass at around eleven thousand feet, to where there was a high, short but deep, intra-montane lake the Army engineers had constructed, a gem of lake with trout big as the lunker Dolly Vardens in Lake Mead and Lac Pend Oreille, but with the water crystal clear and no cover, the big fish saw them on the banks and swam right by their lines and lures. He wished he could abandon the car after they encountered carburetor problems, just hike away and fish for the big trout, but now he had Helen along to consider. He took off the air filter, held the circular carburetor disk open to air it out, before he had her try to start it. No dice. He lowered the idle on it and tweaked the mixture screws. Again no dice. There was no triple A to call in the Andes, so they stood thumbing by the side of the road until a passing two ton truck with an open back picked them up and took them into Huanta. Helen was wearing a light brown alpaca poncho, but she still reminded him of a Gay Nineties photo he'd seen of New York debutantes palavering with Blackfoot braves at the Great Northern stop at East Glacier, Montana.

The sun had gone down and the temperature fell like a brick and they were all huddling from the wind like a load of cattle. Helen was already nauseated by the altitude, and the scent of rancid sweat intensified that, before nausea gradually turned to terror. As people got off at a stop, she saw that the campesino man at their feet, whom they had assumed was just sleeping off a drunk, was unresponsive when others tried to wake him. He lay slumped in a corner with his soiled, curling coarse felt cap pushed down and partially obscuring his face, a thin rivulet stain of coca juice at the corner of his mouth. He was probably an itinerant agricultural worker, his knee breeches ragged at the edges, his uputu sandals cut from used tires. He seemed to have been alone; no one remembered when he had gotten on, and no one stepped forward to claim the body. Every detail of the man's appearance bespoke extreme poverty, and his sad and lonely end really depressed Helen. She had Jim take care of his burial at the next stop, which happened to be Huanta, the site of the actual final victory over Spain in South America, but it was already dark and impossible to see the sublime beauty of the red cliffs there. Natural beauty combined with human tragedy. A poor dead cholo, a soltero gone from his family and finding no luck anywhere in his harsh world, it didn't work out to introduce Helen to the sierra, but for him it helped confirm his career there, since it clarified what this country needs is mo' money.

It was clearly not a good trip, and after that the sierra was a hard sell for Helen. Lima is a very cosmopolitan city, one can find anything there, and one can live in the wealthy south suburb of Miraflores and walk to the park where the food stand wafts good smells and pretty balloons tied there stutter and dive in the Pacific breeze. Helen was somewhat quietist, could accept bad fate, but Liz was just the opposite. He would have taken off for Ayacucho with her, but he still had a business to run and he had his bi-monthly stock newsletter with another deadline coming up, and not having had time to read his stock papers because of the hoopla over Davis and Mac and the Silver Llama. He'd include an answer to a question about gold a letter from a geologist he met in Bolivia; yeh, in Peru, the gold was in the north, the silver in the south, that's from the archaeologists' books, not the geological surveys. And what is this in my briefcase, the Comercio I picked up from the basket on the second floor near Mac's room, to check the market for fishmeal and copper and other commodity prices and futures. The oldest and most staid of Peru's papers, it had survived the collectivization of the press under Velasco, whose reforms Jim generally supported, but not government press control. It was, after all, a military government with whose program not everybody agreed. Jim was perusing the Business section when he noticed in the shipping news, the arrival of the freighter, "The General Ordoñez", was underlined, Tuesday, 8 P.M., Callao.

—m—

The docks at Callao were extensive, probably the biggest port on the west coast of South America, though Chile was coming back after its flirtation with communism and veering into a dark age of fascism. 'El Aguante' from Calle Trece, a Puerto Rico rap orchestral group, was a catalogue of all the things we'd survived, including Aguantamos a Pinochet. Finding addresses was not always easy in Lima, and he'd hoped to have Tommy with him to show him the way, but he was very busy with a big story. Calling on his rat-maze memory, he took the turns that had led him to the dock with the InterCon offices twenty years before. The fire was visible from the police line and an ambulance came racing out over the fire hoses distended like anacondas. He had a press card from his old days as a free-lance foreign correspondent, which he showed to the fire marshal to get the story. It was the freighter, El General Ordoñez, that was burning. It was a ship of Panamanian registry, contracted through InterCon shippers to carry arena de pescado, fishmeal of dried anchovies used as excellent fertilizer in Europe and the U.S., which accounted for the dank odour, like an Amazonian taboo hut was burning. It had enough ammonium nitrate that the concern was that if it blew, it could spread to the other freighters and the big oil tankers creating a Pearl Harbor effect, so the firemen were pouring water onto the burning ship, which produced a big black cloud. The air, redolent with fish stink and petrochemical stench, kept billowing like a huge brown moth hovering above the gates of Hell, as the demons shuffled below. The ambulance had carried two out, the fire marshal said, one of them an older gringo but he didn't have names, so Jim surmised Mac had come to some rendez-vous and escaped with his life, he'd need to pick up flowers on his way to the hospital, and find out what happened back at the Pension Inglesa when he disappeared after their meeting at the chifa.

Things were further put in question when he slipped around the fire marshal and down the dock toward the ship after the fire was under control and found a copy of the Ayacucho group photo smack wet beside the gangplank, the same one that had been on Val Davis's body. The water had saturated it, and the lighting was weak spots for the retreating firemen, Jim couldn't see it well and folded it carefully to dry out later.

It wasn't until he got to the emergency room at the hospital, waiting to talk to the physician that he unfolded the group photo again, and was surprised to see it was not Mac's photo that was circled. It was that of Derrick Stephensen, the Ivy professor who'd not been in Peru in thirty years, who was supposed to be doing fieldwork at Saskatchewan or north Ontario sites, but had hopped a shuttle to O'Hare and through Miami and on to Jorge Chavez in Lima, his Chicago detective, Rad Ratko, had informed him, while his heiress wife was at the place in the Hamptons. Tommy had caught Derrick in a photo with Pete Seymour in front of the InterCon. So maybe Mac had come to the docks to warn Rick.

At the hospital, Jim was still hoping he'd find Mac in good shape with minor abrasions, but when he slipped the head nurse to check the emergency room, it wasn't Mac in there, it was Stephensen and the other man they'd brought in wasn't Mac either, some innocent crew member who suffered burns. He left the hospital soon after giving the desk three hundred bucks to make sure those two were well taken care of, and a guard posted outside private Derrick's room, Jim lied that the patient was a relative of W.R. Grace, and that name was big in Peru, shipped high yield fishmeal fertilizer to the U.S. and Europe, he'd seen their signs alongside Ohio cornfields. He didn't want to hang around the hospital long, he might find yet another photo with his own head circled in it.

After he saw it was Derrick in the ER, Jim slid on home, because he had to think things through after having seen the photo of Derrick with Pete Seymour in front of InterCon Shippers.

It was quiet in his office, Liz had taken off for Ayacucho in her irresistible quest for truth, Jim got himself an Irish coffee, and put in another call to Rad Ratko in Chicago, who got quick results now that he'd brought his detective agency into the era of cyber-research. Rad had already alerted him that Stephensen had returned to Peru that summer, evidently surreptitiously, and Jim now wondered whether he should contact his wife about the hospitalization, but demurred since she was enjoying the Hamptons and her hubby was not in extremis at the American Hospital. The salacious banger on the side from the last report was that old Derrick had improvised on the standard 20th century alpha male model of corporate CEOs periodically trading in for a new, younger trophy wife, having taken up with an attractive grad student half his age, though he hadn't dumped his old lady, Sylvia, who was quite wealthy. Since '76 Jim had been happy with Helen, in her mid-forties now, and Liz was almost his own age, Pocha had been twenty years younger, oh she was sweet as fresh honey from a new beehive, though the attraction ultimately came down to personality for him, not chronological numbers.

Rad called back later that evening when Jim was still in his study. The news wasn't about the recently hospitalized Derrick, it was about Holly Abbott, and about the foster-mother who'd had both Holly and Norm Larson in her care when they were wards of the court assigned to the same foster home. Their foster-mother,

Gertrude Pinaro, Momma Gertie, had reached a settlement with the insurance company on a life policy as a beneficiary of Norm Larsen, who'd disappeared ten years before. The face value of the policy was around thirty-five million, and their agents had offered the woman a half-million, citing all kinds of evidence Norm had absconded before going into hiding. The settlement was like the Second City send-up of the Sixties TV series 'The Millionaire', making fun of the old days when a million was a million, versus now when it'd take a chunk of that after taxes to fix your luxury car door at the body shop. A half million hadn't looked bad to a woman who'd been taking in foster kids for a living, and Gertie had not consulted an attorney before she signed off on the deal, but that made it easier to set aside when guess who had gone to court to stop Momma G. from taking it. It was Holly, who knew a couple of Chicago lawyers who had already filed motions to set aside the deal on the basis of fraud in the inducement. Of course the insurance company attorneys noted in its motion for summary judgment and dismissal of the contest of the settlement that the beneficiary had signed a fifty page release that covered everything from nuclear winter to global warming, but Moms Gertie liked to hit the bottle and was kind of crazy in her own right, though her kids did love her obviously.

Jim was fairly sure he knew why Pete was back, he was a cocaine addict and a spendthrift even beyond the ample limits of the Seymour Dynasty Trust, but Jim was clueless as to why Derrick, who was in Fat City, had come back to Lima. Rad told him, I think Derrick and his wife may have separate arrangements, if that interests you.

"Hell, if she's a potential client, I'll put her in the hopper," Jim said, "On a personal level, I'm in a relationship now. Helen's been back home a while and now it seems her brother's here in Lima. Look, I survived Sendero, I can't believe this new old crap, what is a Wisconsin probate case about to drive me out of Peru?"

"Speaking of new crap on old people, ever heard of the Sinaloa Cartel?" Rad said, giving him the run-down of others he'd asked about, including from the old Ayacucho gang because he wanted to check out everyone in that 1969 group photo, so he heard what he already knew about Emerson near Chan Chan, and his wife Marilyn whom Jim knew well from 1976 when they became friendly, well, Rob Emerson had been running around on her with those grad students to where she went with Jim. It was a good diversion for him, since her father was in stocks in Chicago and gave him a shot at making money in commodity markets after which he put things together and went back to Lima to invest in NYSE & NASDAQ for Lima new wealthy, and a few American friends like Frank, not as Rob claimed, to do money-laundering for dealers in cocaine at least not knowingly, not that it was hard to find its current quote in the Amsterdam market and the profit margin on it was better by a damn sight than for fish meal.

Drugs was a volatile business, big business because everyone was trying to make money and escape at the same time. Jim liked things clean. He was even ashamed about some old views inherited from Victorian Cincinnati that he hadn't shaken til he got away to college, especially ethnic and sexual stereotypes. In Peru, he was glad he wasn't gay. You could be a great athlete, a great soldier or statesman, and if you were a maricon, it was like you weren't really a man. Oh, and machoras weren't widely respected either. Jim didn't believe any of the old bullshit now, and it was so much easier not to lug along that mental baggage. The main racial thing in Peru was the blanco-indio split. He'd always identified with the underdog, the Indians, though he never shortchanged the Spanish whatever their ancestors' exploitation and oppression had been, because they connected Peru with the wider world through their Empire and their language, yeh, about fifteen million Quechua speakers, compared to Spanish, in Latin America and the Philippines, Spain and Ifni, and the U.S. Southwest, many more millions to talk to.

"I do remember Miller, because he punked me at the Colmena Bar in Ayacucho," Jim said. "He could be a mean dude when he was drunk or stoned, and he usually was."

Oh, yes, Jim was aware that Sinaloa was the center of a Mexican drug-smuggling operation with a very nasty edge, like for its reputation of decapitating the bodies of its cartel rivals and dumping them in mass graves in the desert. Because it was big money and they could kill little people without fear of prosecution since most were in it as underlings because of their need. And north of the border there was hypocrisy because that's where the demand was and that's where the dollars were. Hell, Jimmy liked a toke of Mexican yerba for transcendence after a long day trading and trying to understand Wall Street, which so often seemed counterintuitive in reaction and also to mirror herd behavior, so hedge fund traders could make money sending stocks down as well as up, like devilish vaqueros driving them down with their shorting, moo moo. He believed those companies could rise through their research, create a New America by Microsoft and a new world in the process. Always trying to get ahead of the Curve, because always Change was coming.

As Time and Tide were defined by change today, Jim enjoyed the time to observe changes from his Lima study, liked to track weather from Sydney and Manila about western Pacific ocean temperatures where El Niño's were born, because they not only tore up Peru, they also had a direct correlation with U.S.climate and ag production. He'd send weather reports back to Stan Lucca's brokerage in Chicago because Stan still did commodities like corn, soybeans and grain futures from his early days in the pits, after he left the Ivory Tower at Northwestern. Stan had basically given Jim a paid internship even though his relationship with his daughter, Mari Emerson nee Lucca, had already gone south when she went back to her husband, Rob Emerson, yeh, the same prof who was now a world authority, who'd been with the anthro/archaeo team in Ayacucho in '69, and of course all the leftist Californians thought the Aerospace Program was a colossal waste when the money could have been used to relieve urban poverty. Oh yeh, he knew Rob from previous encounters from 2 decades ago at the Bolivar, like Coriolanus knew his warrior rival, Aufidius, the post-new critics were kept busy speculating on homosexual themes.

Rob was a very smart guy, and Jim thought he had set up a good roadblock and substantial impediment to the re-incursion of him into his life, namely the promissory note for $25,000 that Jim advanced out of his own money to pay off Rob's Colombian creditors in his drug deals. It was most of his savings at a time when Jim was still trying to make it as a foreign correspondent with Liz as his photographer, and she argued against giving it to him, but Jim wanted closure that night. It had been a bad night with the killings of Doc Penny and Haberman's driver, Otto, neither of which Jim had committed, though he witnessed them, more in fact than Rob who was hidden in a utility closet, but could have presumed and accused, though unlikely since he was responsible ab initio for the deaths because of his black market and drug trade activity.

That $25K note had an interest provision based on US APR, and that was around 18% per annum during the Carter Years, another reason Jimmy went down to Reagan besides the Iranian Hostage Crisis. Jim typed the note out himself on his Olivetti portable at the Pension Inglesa with a daguerreotype of Sancho Panza counseling him with peasant wisdom, 'If you don't want to see a man for a while, loan him money.' Rule of thumb with 6% average interest compounding semi-annually, doubling twice over twenty years, the total could now be pushing $100,000. Their tacit understanding was that Rob would not mess with Jim, who in return would not collect on the note. Now if someone were using the events of that night to discredit Rob academically, that might account for Jim being brought into this recent vortex of unexplained violence.

It seemed like a more dangerous world from close up to far away, this after investigations pointed to the involvement of Iranian agents in the '94 bombing of a Buenos Aires synagogue and community center, 85 killed, more wounded in the worst terrorist incident in Argentine history, in a nation that let in more Jewish refugees from WWII Europe than any other Latin American nation. So Tehran revolutionary theocrat Ayatolas' petrodollars at work to aid murdering zealots to project terror onto people who had suffered much, like wolves descending on unsuspecting flocks from half a world away.

—⦿—

"Tommy, could you help me out?" Jim said. "I need you to go back to that InterCon Shipping office."

"Sure, I'm just editing a couple of long pieces, when are you talking about?" Tommy said.

"I'll call you when I get a call from Benavides when he sees Pete there," Jim said. "If you're free then, you can go. If not, we'll try another time. It's not super urgent. Just keep it on your radar, okay?"

The plan was for Tommy to strike up a conversation with Pete, and in the process discover this Sr. Pete Seymour was Helen's brother, how is she, Jim told me your mother had been ill, et cetera, I'll tell Jim I met you, which would then give Jim a colorable pretext for calling Pete, whom he really wanted to talk to. He was especially curious as to why Rick Stephenson would have been talking to Pete a couple weeks before then, and why Rick might have been on board a Seymour ship the General Ordoñez the night it burned. A dockhand Benavides talked to after the fire said it was a bearded old gringo who had carried Derrick down the gangplank and then disappeared. If this was Mac, it was good news, and he had perhaps been trying to warn Rick of the danger since Rick was the next one circled in the Ayacucho group photo. Shades of 'The List Of Adrian Messenger' or 'Charade', big help from Hollywood, his antagonist might know

Classic American Cinema in addition to T.S. Eliot, really quite different streams in American culture, oh that olde Shakespearean Rag, TS fled to a Europe about to descend into barbarism.

Oh Rob looked like the prime suspect and right for the rap, what was $100K to Rob if he got current Great Scholar salaries at Olde Ivy, they were paying big time for truth and big reputations and let the great profs have cottage industries on the side. The Ivory Tower could have been a good life, Jim pictured himself as an eminent authority on Elizabethan drama, Marlowe done in at Deptford Inn by agents of the Crown, like Yorick a man of infinite jest, or gestae beyond the bounds, the marl dusted from the skull, there was a common saying, Death Pays All Debts, what was it Marl owed at the Debtford Inn, his life, it was only five years after the Armada and he of the Oxford Catholic underground, certainly an object lesson to Sweet William. But you couldn't prove anything, which was as both the Crown and the elegist would have wanted it, and to put it into a monograph would just be bad form, today the big guns needed a grand theory, like this Derrida whose 'Plato's Pharmacy' Rad had sent him, with the dichotomy of writing versus speech in the myth of Thoth, had a lot of anthropology in there too, though the anthro people who dropped by the house weren't into Deconstructionism yet, though Structuralism had been declared dead by the master, and he'd taken on Levi-Strauss on the issue. He loved to hear them talk and had learned a lot about the vast cultural background there besides the Incas. Most of the scholars had their money in their university pension funds with managers who controlled huge sums, could move markets such that little guys like Jim had to watch the elephants. He'd gotten a couple of clients from the academics, and of course Frank was an ex-academic so had personal IRAs and stock accounts with substantial funds that Jim advised him on. He hadn't done really great like Frank, but he could still afford wine with corks instead of twist-off caps. Though sometimes he imagined it would have been nice to be in the Ivory Tower, when markets were turbulent, and the scholars didn't have to hassle the IRS or DEA or have bodies lobbed over their garden walls. And they couldn't get fired except for moral turpitude, though murder might qualify, if Rob had done in Val Davis. He had shown a violent streak in '69 when he beat up another grad student who was making time with a female grad student he'd set his cap on. And then he sliced Jimmy up with a knife in Cuzco, and he might know Eliot though he knew things like New Wave films but not modern poetry.

To escape all the dithering and present stress he snagged a couple of books to read in bed, Pike's "History of Peru" on the mita, or the communal work contribution the Inca exacted, and how the Spanish used it and stepped up the amount of work required so that the Quechua peasants became virtual slaves. The mortality rate in the mines was high, including for small boys used because they could fit into tight spaces, which pinched his claustrophobia. He was dreaming of going down a long tunnel to find the Silver Llama, like a spelunker squeezing through tight spaces until there was no way out and it was the end of the game. He screamed out Jesu, because he was surrounded by dense matter in narrow spaces far below the surface of the earth.

'Oh Christ, forgive us our greed,' Jim was trying to express, even as he was attempting to wake up from his nightmare, trying to scream but nothing came out of the voice box. It was one of those bad dreams that tried to pull one into the medieval time frame of the provincial sierra, a past from which it seemed he could never awake, and even after he had, it was like he could never escape the experience of tightness and demise in an unmarked tomb from the avarice of greedy fools. Happy Days, Boola Boola, Moola Moola, wasn't it in New Haven I learned not to be incorrect. If you bombed in New Haven, you were sure to not make it to Broadway.

He was sweating when he woke up. There was enough moonlight that he could see the waves coming to the shore. The darkness held the air. The air was still. He could believe there was some relief. When the morning came, the light would chase the terrible dream away. He would run all the way North to downtown Lima. He'd run all the way South to Ica. He'd breath deep and go wherever he wanted, no matter what the lord of the manor said. The dream was fresh enough that he could feel the converging angles of the tunnel, the force of the rock on his shoulders and the sense of diminishing personal space. It made the sweat rise on his brow and he had to get up and walk around. It was horrible to think of being buried alive, but he was out of the claustrophobic grip now, able to sit and read. He picked up the first thing in easy reach and opened to a page of Don Pedro's journals, a narration of the Andean mines in the 1880's and 1890's. There was a photo of Don Pedro tucked in to those pages, a photo of him smiling, a handsome, dapper man in his middle years smiling because of his personal success and perhaps because of some reforms he'd been able to institute at the mines. They called him El Progresivo and though now it seemed little enough that he'd done. At least it was better than what had gone before, and that was something.

—\m/—

Rad called back again and confirmed the burned ship had been insured under a rider to Seymour Industries' policy, but that was not the biggest news. The real insurance news concerned the $35 million policy on Norman Larson, and the recent settlement of Gertrude Pinaro which Holly Abbott had filed to have set aside. An appellate court had ruled it invalid and remanded it to the trial court for retrial. Rad had seen the witness list and noticed Jim's name on it, along with Helen, Pete, their mother, and Norman A. Larsen, address unknown. By phoning the attorney, he also found notices of deposition were being sent, with one to Jim at the Haverford Mills address.

"They're going to have to come here to depose me," Jim said. "By the way, you never told me this. I haven't seen it in writing, so it doesn't exist for me."

"I never said it, I never saw it, no way," Rad said.

That again reminded Rad of "Plato's Pharmacy" by Derrida, who argues that in Western philosophy, Logos or the spoken word is primary, and the written word is secondary and subject to sophist charlatanism and mere rote memorization, saying Socrates' telling of the myth of Theuth is an explicit expression of this opposition and valuation. Like the bastard outré contra the legitimate heir, the golden boy. Thing though was, Plato was a writer himself, and writing had a higher status in many legal fields like real estate and probate, though it was true that trial evidence did give importance to testimony in court where the witness's demeanor and memory could be tested. But 'get it in writing' was an important point in complex business deals, because obviously you couldn't have CEOs remembering everything, even if they wanted to. And like Jimmy Durante used to sing, Inka Dinka Do, though the Inca didn't use ink.

"Well, the Incas had a high civilization without writing, so I guess that tends to prove Plato's point," Jim said.

Though that wasn't completely clear now with new research on their quipu, their multi-stringed counting and mnemonic device. At an old hacienda south near Tambo Colorado, a gentleman had shown Liz and him a collection of quipus he had from colonial times because they preserved well in the dry southern desert, and though they were faded and dusty, still were visible the colors of the different strings, to be knotted to count crops, mita days, troops, the reigns of the Inca emperors and their great victories or perhaps also to recall the main points of speech. Visualize a necklace with strings of various lengths and colors hanging down from the central circular loop. If Rimbaud could assign different colors to the various vowels, why could not the Inca use a similar system inversely? The Spaniards came with fire and sword, but it was fascinating all those Inca things that survived. Sendero had communicated with fireworks with messages in the colors. The mafia didn't write all things down, some business was better done without records.

Back when Tommy was researching the Banchero murder case as a conspiracy story, Jim mentioned an Argentinian union leader who was assassinated right around the time Peron arrived for his Second Coming. It was a story Harry Stein gave him to show him how things went down there. Not such polished police work, more like from the bowels of the earth run these rats from their ratzskellar. Even if you can't write what you know, you can still know it. So Socrates had something with the myth of Thoth.

—⋙—

This news from Rad of a pending deposition on Norm's big policy, made Jim reluctant to call Helen and all the more anxious to talk to her brother. Pete had been sighted at the InterCon office by Benavides across the way on the day after the fire, but Tommy was busy and Pete didn't stay long. That was the last time he saw Pete on the docks for a couple of weeks, but it was not the last of the problems involving him or his.

The cab pulled up outside his garden wall, its exhaust rising in the garua fog pouring in, thick as anything London had. He heard the trunk slam and the front bell ring, and thought it was probably Liz coming back from Ayacucho without calling beforehand, to surprise him. When he opened the door and saw it was Holly Abbott Seymour, his astonished expression made her emit a small laugh which she turned into a smile before she apologized for not calling him first, but all the phones at Jorge Chavez were busy or malogrado.

"Hi, Jim, I'm sorry to bust in on you like this," Holly said. "I need to talk to you."

"Sure, come in, what a surprise, sweetheart, it's good to see you," Jim said, giving her a brother-in-lawly hug and looking at the cabbie who then waved and drove off. "I was sorry to hear about you and Pete, the divorce."

"We haven't been a couple for a while," Holly said. "The divorce is hung up because he's down here, and typical Pete behavior, he's not answering summons and service. He's like an ostrich. He thinks if he hides long enough, it'll all go away."

"You need help finding him so you can get personal service?" Jim said. "That could put me in a bad position."

"To put you in a bad position, you know that's not what I want," Holly said. "I just need your advice. You know so much. You know the law, you know things about the past, mine, yours, all of ours."

"What's up with that?" Jim said. "Come on in, get you a snack or a drink?"

"A gin and tonic sounds good right about now," Holly said.

She sat on a stool in the kitchen and he set her g and t on the counter.

"So what is it that brings you to Lima?" Jim said.

"It's not as much about Pete as about Norm Larsen, the man shot right over there ten years ago," Holly said. "You remember that night?"

"Somewhat," Jim said, looking up at the ceiling fan. "Enough that I'm wondering why you want to remember it."

"Does thirty-five million dollars sound like a good reason?" Holly said. "I've filed an action to have Norman declared dead."

"That shouldn't be a problem," Jim said. "Most states have a seven year, missing presumed dead statute."

"It's only a presumption though," Holly said, recounting then what could have been a checklist for the opposing insurance counsel, that

Larsen was on the passenger list of a flight for Chile that same night, another passenger remembered Norm as saying he was a lawyer in mergers and acquisitions in Philadelphia, originally from Chicago, that evidence existed he made bank withdrawals in Valparaiso from an account with funds siphoned off from Seymour Industries, was seen at a bar restaurant there, planted evidence of his death on a nearby beach, in an attempt to stop pursuit when he absconded, or to facilitate insurance fraud, admissible as showing a pattern of deceit, is now probably sitting on another beach sipping a margarita with an umbrella swizzle stick, while a pretty woman is fanning his brow with a palm frond, and with that crap the chances of proving Norman dead were not so certain. "My attorney says we have less than a fifty-fifty chance on the facts, unless there's something else we dig up."

"Why don't we take this discussion to the wine cellar?" Jim said. "I've had some recent incidents that had me call my electrician."

He mentioned that somebody had thrown a body over his garden wall not that long ago and that the case was still unsolved. NAL and the acronym match he didn't mention at the moment. He'd just had his monthly debugging sweep, office and home for a reasonable package rate, but he just trusted the basement best. It had no electricity inside except flashlight and candles, had an oak door that would have stopped a battering ram, and through which the trumpeting of Hannibal's elephants would have sounded like but mousy squeaks. The walls and ceiling were all white-painted hard-parged mortar and stucco, and two inches of hard cement poured in the floor. They said a Colombian drug lord had killed the carpenters who built his bunker safe house, just like those who built the Pharaohs' tombs were killed to protect the secrecy of their divine master. Jimmy was more on the democratic vibe and said he'd match anybody who asked around about doing a job at his place. He'd also put in fresh basement steps, so Holly descending right past where Norm Larsen had gone down in a gunfight, looked around but the only stains were sepia wave patterns from the drains in his planting beds above where the old salvia had tan dry petals low on the stalks.

"Come on in," Jim said, entering the security code, throwing the bolt open and unlocking the basement door. "It's safer to talk in here."

Though he kept it smooth and uncluttered, it wasn't totally ascetic, with a Danish modern couch and a sturdy cherry coffee table, an open three shelf cabinet with wine glasses and his hydraulic opener, a can of ravioli, in case he went down to write, which he never did anymore since his creative juices had dried up like a Serengeti waterhole in drought, and a square black table like the one in Cezanne's "The Card Players" and three straight back chairs, two long-necked floor lamps with the new long-lasting bulbs, battery powered got them from China out of a catalogue.

"Come on in," Jim said, entering the security code, throwing the bolt open and unlocking the basement door. "It's safer to talk in here. Nothing alive but us and the wine and it can't hear us. Would you like Mendoza Riesling, or a taste of Madeira, m' dear?"

"You choose, you know the wine list," Holly said, sitting on the low couch where Helen used to sit and show her pretty long legs, so that was kind of like exterior déjà vu. "You have an amontillado?"

"How about an Ocucaje cabernet?" Jim said. "It has a nice body."

"Like the host," Holly said.

"And like the guest, mi cuñadita," Jim said. "I toast you, because I told you to keep this under your hat back then on that night, and you have done so. Tell me how much you want to dig around now, it's like careful what you find, it may not be everything you wished for. I know it's big money, but you may be exposing yourself. And how do you benefit from that?"

"What happened was that in year five after Norm died, the insurance man came in with a settlement offer of five hundred thousand to the primary beneficiary, who wasn't competent to accept it," Holly said.

That beneficiary as he knew was one Gertrude Pinaro, Moms Gertie as she had been known when she was their foster mom after the parents of both had died. Both kids had been in a lot of trouble before they ended up with her, and Moms gave them not only bacon and eggs at breakfast and Fruit Loops and all the peanut butter and jelly sandwiches for lunch and Eskimo pies and didn't keep her refrigerator locked up with a chain and padlock like some of the foster parents, and maybe that explained why Norm, who had been her shining star of all the displaced kids who had gone through under her care, why Norm had put her as prime beneficiary on that $35 million policy that was now in litigation.

"I'm legal guardian for Gertrude Pinaro," Holly said. "She was a mother to me when I was a very troubled teen, as she was to Norman. She called him her shining star, and was a good foster mother to him, or he would have never put her as a beneficiary. She's in the nursing unit of a good retirement home. I made sure of that. None of that comes from the insurance. I'm paying for all Moms Gert's care now. I stepped in to keep her from getting ripped off by the insurance company. Poor dear was living on sardines, canned ravioli and booze. Moms Gerts hit the bottle hard and any money looked good to her."

"It's great looking out for somebody who helped you in the past," Jim said.

"It's not without compensation," Holly said. "Before she got so nuts she was seeing pink elephants, she executed a will to me as her sole beneficiary, also a power of attorney with the right to bring lawsuits."

"So you've come down to see if you can help your case," Jim said.

"You know that insurance man, Pirasini, asked me if I thought Norman might be buried in your garden," Holly said. "Is he here, Jimmy, because there are a lot of ways we can play this."

"No, Norm's body is not in my garden, and I don't know where on earth it is," Jim said, mixing truth and untruth which was literally metaphoric truth since Norm was not on earth, but in Davey Jones' locker. "Hey, if you don't believe me, I'll give you and the insurance company the right to dig up my garden, as long as you put everything back, every stick, stone and stem just like it was. Might be good for aeration, but that big fig's gonna be a bitch to uproot."

"Okay, just say if Norm were here in your garden, he could be exhumed and put somewhere else, and discovered there from some new records, and all we'd need is dental records and a DNA sample," Holly said. "How would you like half of thirty-five million? You wouldn't have to read any more stock charts, or worry about Helen's analyst's bills."

"Half, hey, your attorney's going to get at least a third plus expenses off the top," Jim said. "You might be well advised to roll the dice with him, since if the body were found, it'd raise questions as to the cause of death."

"I'm not worried because Norm was firing first and that's self-defense," Holly said. "By the way, I just hired an attorney to file the motions. I said I knew someone else I wanted as my attorney. You can have a third, you can have a half, you can have what you want, Jimmy. It's a slam dunk if you can get the body."

"Or a ticket to the slammer," Jim said. "Were those firecrackers or gunshots? Who might have shot first? I couldn't tell. I was behind this big oak door. Norm was slumped in the stair-well when I ran upstairs to see if you guys were all right. I think I told you to take off and I'd take care of everything. When I went back to call the medics, Norm was gone. Maybe he hit his head dodging the bullets, recovered and took off. They traced him to Chile. And didn't that Pirisini say he'd been treated for abrasions at a nearby hospital and returned his rental car at the airport?"

"I saw Norm jump and fall, Jimmy," Holly said. "He wasn't driving anywhere after that, except on a highway to Hell, which was where he belonged, by the way. Besides, I won't have to say it was Pete who shot him, because of marital privilege, and whatever you did, we'll have attorney-client privilege."

"I'm not going to be your lawyer, sweetheart," Jim said. "I know a good man in probate litigation in Oak Park I can refer you to. It's better to roll that way. If you lose, you can always reopen the case with newly discovered evidence."

"So you do know something more?" Holly said. "Don't be afraid. I won't sell you down the river. You covered for me, but now we can make it work for us. I have bad memories of Norman, enough to flood any jury box. I have scars to show, physical scars in addition to the mental abuse. You know he killed Harry and intended to kill you? We both owe each other, don't we? Isn't that the basis of something for us?"

"Thirty-five million sounds great," Jim said. "Money talks, and big money has a siren call. I've got an ongoing business for which a homicide investigation would not be a drawing card, not to mention tampering with evidence charges, if I did have to repatriate and go back in practice. I've survived Sendero and Fujimori, I don't mind working, keeps me off the streets."

"Well, I was on the streets at fifteen," Holly said. "I want to win this case. I'm through with Pete. You know what he said when I filed for divorce. He said get in line, baby. Because his silver spoon has been busy cooking dope. He's pledged everything he's in line to receive from the Seymour trust for the next five years, to pay his gambling debts and his drug habit. And if the company goes into bankruptcy, the stock won't be worth much. The Seymour's are aristocrats who think the world revolves around them. Commoners like us can be such nuisances."

"Helen's pretty considerate," Jim said.

"I know she's been away for two years taking care of Mom while you're here working your tail off," Holly said. "It must get lonely for you."

"It does, but I've got my reading, my gardening, bridge night with the Brits at the Bolivar, where occasionally some drunken embassy wife falls into my arms," Jim said. "Let me think about this. I could maybe help you find Pete if you need to serve him. He shouldn't be able to stiff you."

"I heard he's working for a Seymour shipper here," Holly said. "I need him to make a serious settlement offer, and I'd like to talk about the insurance case, since he was here that night, and I don't want him screwing it up. We need to get our stories straight, you know, straight."

"Let me make a couple calls," Jim said, not telling her that Benavides had been watching the InterCon offices for some time, but explaining in a general way there had been a body in his garden recently, police were also investigating the murder of Val, one of the old '69 Ayacucho gang, and with thirty-five million bucks on Norm's policy, well, of course, a reputable big cap North American life insurance company would not be involved such shenanigans. They'd have a bank of Ivy League lawyers to warn them off. "You wouldn't know if anyone were trying to lean on me?"

"It wasn't me, honest," Holly said. "And if you're all worried, why not throw in with me and get the money? Look, Norm was going to kill you that night. He wouldn't have killed Pete because he was his golden goose. And me, he thought he had me under his thumb blackmailing me about my past. But you, if I hadn't shown up with a gun, you'd be dead. You know that and you know more."

"See, the thing about suppression of evidence, once things start coming out it's hard to be selective," Jim said. "I can almost hear the questions of opposing counsel. There was a shooting, well, where is the weapon? Did you throw it in Lima bay? I think you need to think this over. I need time to think it over."

"I'm not giving up," Holly said, lying back with her legs up on the rung so he was seeing London, France and her underpants, and she gave him an odalisque frank smile. "You know what Norm gave me when I said I wasn't hitting the streets again for him. This was after we'd both been whipped in the previous home. He made a special cat o' nines for my butt. Come over here."

"The view's just fine from here," Jim said, as the delta of Venus appeared as she hitched her skirt.

"No, I want you to know it's not just greed," Holly said, getting up from the couch and coming up beside him at the table where he was sitting with his glass of wine. She put one foot up on another chair and lifted her skirt up high on the thigh, and slid her panties down over her derriere. "Pete thinks those are stretch lines from when I was fat. I was never fat. I was always hungry. You can still feel the ridges of the welts even though I had corrective surgery. Don't you want to feel that?" she said taking his hand, and placing it where he could feel the scars. "Does it disgust you? Do you know how long he used me after that? You think it's weird I think he owes me even if he's dead?"

"No, I feel sorry it happened to you, but you're a beautiful woman, and hate can eat away at you," Jim said, taking her hand and holding it. "I don't go to church much, but if you can find a way to forgive, I mean, the s.o.b. is not around, you're just hurting yourself, unless you simply can't let it go, maybe now you hate all men."

"Not all of you," Holly said, taking the hand he had offered in compassion and raising it toward passion fruits with stems to pick. "An Iowa insurance man out on the town to have some fun, told corny jokes, I didn't hate him because he paid well and didn't smack me around, in fact, I felt kind of sorry for him when he got drunk and told about his prairie prude wife, a real Frigidaire. But he wasn't a man I could fall for, like you."

"Oh, mi cuñadita, tan cariñosa," Jim said, getting up out of his chair and dancing around to the song, mi cuñadita, tan cariñosa, mas cariñosa que mi esposa, (my sister-in-law, so affectionate, more affectionate than my wife), a little ditty like the Cuban, La Negra Tomasa, as if she might realize the silliness of their liaison by a little dance, sit back down and be a good girl again, as social propriety would by weight of custom put off her come-on. But she picked up on the tune, knew Spanish well enough to know the meaning of the verses, also knew the cumbia from her time in Peru, and started to dance a close cumbia with him, a highly rhythmic dance which he absorbed and slowed not without a ray of reaction. "Whoa, I think I was maybe giving the wrong signals."

"I know what it means, Jimmy, it means 'my sister-in-law, so loving, more loving than my wife'," Holly said, or rather half-sang in a childish voice she maybe used back in the life, and made him momentarily feel the role of a drunk Midwestern salesman on a convention spree. On the other hand, it had occurred to Jim, that though his own bomb shelter was bug-free, she could be wearing a wire, she obviously had an agenda to win the big insurance case. As far as her wearing a bug, he'd already had an opportunity for a look around her basement, and thought he might as well check upstairs, and of course, this prompted her to think he was saying no, even as his hands were saying yes, but he was thinking, find yourself in the thick of it, help yourself to a bit of it, he could always tell her later he was drunk and felt guilty, would she please not tell Helen, because that was the last thing a forty-three year old woman needed to hear was that her man left her for a younger woman, her ex-sister-in-law no less, a bad scene.

"It does happen, some men want to start another love life at forty or fifty, I know Helen was so depressed after she miscarried," Holly said, now stepping back patting at her disarranged bodice. "She told me the thing that made her most sad was how much you wanted a child. She said she'd never try again, because the biological clock had run out."

"You gals do talk," Jim said.

"Maybe she felt guilty she couldn't give you a child," Holly said, approaching him again and putting one hand on his chest, and with the other twirling a curl of his hair. "You know they have surrogate mothers now, they impregnate the father's sperm. But that seems so impersonal, why not do it the old fashioned way? If you want a child, I'd just like for Aunt Holly to have a chance to visit every so often, but you might find you like me, if you try me. I'm not bad. It's not like I'm inexperienced, and I know you must be lonely after two years. I can feel it."

"Promise you won't tell Helen or Pete, I'm in a new relationship," Jim said.

"Who is it?" Holly said.

"It's Liz Teris, an old friend of Helen's, she's working down here and we're living together now," Jim said.

"Hell, Liz is older than Helen, she's not going to have your child either, don't you want me, because I want you, and we could be such good partners," Holly said.

"Under other circumstances, yes, you're incredibly beautiful, a perfect partner, but all this is so new, it's like a dream of wealth and good sex," Jim said, putting his arm around her and going toward the oak door. "Why don't we go upstairs and have some gazpacho and barbecued ribs? Desire makes me hungry. And let's just talk about us, not about Norman or that case, okay? You say you want me to be your lawyer? No hassles the last ten years for you or Pete on this. Now you want to go a different direction. It's not like I don't want you, but you're what, like seventeen years younger than me, and I never pictured myself a degenerate sexist sugar daddy, to tell the truth I feel more at ease with a woman my own age, because it's like we always have something to talk about."

"Okay, I know you had my back, why do you think I'd open up to you like this?" Holly said.

"Just give me a minute to think," Jim said, giving her a pat on her pretty fanny and sitting back down at the table, after which she naturally sat on his lap, prompting him to say, "No, you're only making it harder."

"Isn't that the point?" she said, mussing his hair.

He had to get her back to her chair with a good tickle on the ribs. She was beautiful, the closest thumb-nail physical description for him was the work of the super realist sculptor Della Andrea, 'Freckled Woman', a five ten, modern Venus de Milo except she had arms, and she had hair, above and below, drapes and rug matching, though no freckles, and not a milk-fed vacuous co-ed expression like some art critic had written about the exhibit, more focused than that, so the knowledge of her naked beauty gave her eyes a squint in his direction. At that moment, he had a vision of Liz sitting in that very same basement chair across from him when she realized her backup negatives of Ayacucho massacre photos had been fuzzed by airport security or Montesinos' people, had declared in the bomb shelter that she was going straight back up to the sierra and getting the same and better, though she was depressed and bent over her glass of wine thinking of all the crap, and he'd chucked her and said, 'Absinthe makes the heart grow fonder'. She'd called once from Ayacucho, the Corner of the Dead, to tell him she was alive and was hiking out into the hinterlands. That was Lizzy. He never tried to hold her back. Though he was kind of glad she wasn't back yet, because it made things easier to resolve with Holly.

"I just went down to the docks at Callao," Jim said, telling her about the recent fire that destroyed the Seymour-leased freighter, El General Ordoñez. On the plus side, Holly didn't seem to know anything about InterCon shippers at all, nor about them having sent down one of their own ships ten years ago. The first insurance man down thought it was a rumor Jim had started, so evidently hadn't mentioned that to Holly, so there were some gaps in her knowledge of things that had gone down back then.

"I don't know a thing about that," Holly said.

"This fire down on the docks injured another old buddy of mine," Jim said, telling her that this was another of his old gringo compadres from 1969 like this was part of a pattern.

"Why would I do arson? To spite Pete? To lean on you? You're way off on that," Holly said, and he believed her because she knew it would be counter-productive to getting him involved in her scheme.

"Did Pete ever mention a Derrick Stephensen?" Jim said. "He's the professor that fire sent to the hospital."

"I don't think so, there were musicians and dope dealers, no professors, but see, a lot of the people an addict pusher meets don't give names and occupations," Holly said, as they sat there at the table in the basement, not far from his cache of c.y.a. evidence from that shooting in his garden ten years before, yes, he'd bagged in a ziplok the handgun used to bring down her bête noir in his garden. His recollection was, after he peeked out the basement door he'd ducked behind when Holly told Norm to hold it right there, and when he heard the shots and saw Larsen was down, he ran past him to the top of the stairs and Pete was holding the gun in his left hand, with his other arm around a tearful Holly comforting her, but he could have shot and switched hands. In any case, both of their prints would be on the gun. Jim's problem was he'd covered it up, from several motives: he'd fallen in love with Helen and wanted to save her and her mother from a lengthy and costly inquest in Peru after her father's death in the sierra, having obtained a toxicology report. The Lima bureaucracy was ossified and entrenched from the days when all the paperwork of Spanish South America had to go through there, it continued after Independence and Moby Dick refers to it as the most corrupt Customs of any port in the world. Recently a Sr. DeSoto, a businessman of Peruvian background, who'd grown up in Switzerland and was appalled by the poverty when he came back, did a survey of the andantes, the street sellers who carried their wares on their backs, spread them out on tarps on the sidewalks, had their hibachi grills on street corners. He found most wanted to have shops but to open a shop it took licenses from eleven different ministries, all charging fees and having long lines, nine of which solicited bribes, two of them were paid, and the whole process took over a year. So the andantes didn't even try, and that limited access to capital. Yeh, this country needs mo' money, the same insight he had in Huanta, Ayacucho. Not only did the bureaucracy not appreciate this research; Sendero didn't much like this capitalism for the people, so they bombed DeSoto's office and killed two of his employees. Jim could imagine what would happen after Helen's father died in the sierra, if it became a murder trial there—kind of like the sharks stripping the whale hung portside. And he was left with the task of disposing of the victim's body, i.e., Norm Larsen, whom he didn't doubt had also planned to kill him. True, it wasn't all love: there was also a personal monetary incentive also for his deception: he didn't want a homicide investigation that would send clients fleeing from him when he was finally making good money getting Limenos into MicroSoft, Intel, Sun Microsystems, Dell, all riding the wave of the computer revolution. And there were fear and anger: Holly was right, Norm was marching him down those very basement stairs with the idea Jim would not be coming back up to cause him any more problems. So he rode Norm's ticket from Lima down to Santiago, his thinking at the time being that fascist Chile would be a superior site to confuse the question of the whereabouts of Larsen, who'd been skimming off profits from Seymour Inc., who had shown ample motive to fake his own death there, defalcate and not be found from there to ever after.

"If Pete's here, we ought to get him in the conversation," Jim said, leaning over and kissing her ear, putting his hand on her gam, running it up high on her thigh, patting it and giving her a squeeze. "We ought to cool it til we get him in on the deal. You know he's emotional, and it would be salt in a wound if he knew I took you. He could screw things up big time if he went ballistic in the divorce. You know a beneficiary can't take if they kill the insured. That probably applies to conspiracy to murder. Why risk it? Why not do it smooth? It's easier playing innocent when you actually are. Have I let you down before? You know I am seriously attracted to you. I've used up all my resistance just not to tumble on the couch. But let me handle it my way, will you?"

"Whatever you say, Jimmy," Holly said, and he escorted her upstairs to the kitchen, making sure the basement door was triple locked behind him, then went on up to his study to make those calls.

He was giving Holly the royal treatment, had grilled a couple of T-bone steaks, had brought fresh linen to her in the guest bedroom, was caressing her lightly, saying poor darling child, when the phone rang and it was Benavides calling from Callao.

"Your man, Peter Seymour, just showed up at the docks," Benavides said.

When Jim told Holly he had to go out to check out a lead on Pete, he showed her the periphery security system and alarm, let it beep whoop whoop a couple times, locked everything up and tucked her in with hot chocolate and scones and a good movie to watch, The Postman Always Rings Twice, so she recalled it was important to get the stories of all the principals to jibe before the cops put you in separate interview rooms.

He told Holly he'd be back in an hour, maybe with some news about Peter. There was no time to call Tommy, who was probably busy anyway, so he got in his car and drove like the wind to Callao. He parked at the end of the dock and went the back way to the office where Benavides had been keeping watch. Just as he got to the window, Peter came out of the InterContinental offices across the way, and went down the dock toward the parking lot. Jim followed at a good clip and thought he was going to catch him, but Pete got in a green and yellow cab with a checker bar on the top.

"Pete, wait," Jim yelled, but he got in the cab and it took off.

Fortunately, Jim was parked right there, burned rubber out of the lot and managed to catch up with the cab at the next light. The cab went south and then caught the Pan-American highway along the coast. Lima was so big now they were driving through urbanized areas for almost an hour, when the cab sped up as traffic thinned, went for another half-hour before it turned off at a roadhouse on the coast, made a stop and Pete got out. He started jogging along the shore, and it was another fifteen minutes after Jim had parked, and caught up with him by seaside.

"Pete, I need to talk to you," Jim called over the screech of the gulls.

He turned around and waited for Jim to jog up out of breath.

"Señor?" the man said. He was tall, blond, with a five o'clock shadow and shades, the same build as Pete, in a white cotton suit and a light blue shirt.

After Jim apologized for the mistake, the man shrugged, smiled and jogged away. That was only Act One of Jim feeling dumb. On his way back to his car, he recognized this was the place he and the gang had gone when violence in Ayacucho had held them back in Lima that first summer. They could get cold beer and buckets of shrimp fresh off the boats, play beach volleyball and grill out. Jim had called it Bimbo's because of the neon sign, at a time when he thought bimbo was a blond bombshell and didn't know it was a big brand name like Coca Cola. Act Two of Jim feeling dumb was when he got back to his car and found it up on jacks, stripped of the wheels, the stereo and his seat cushion.

The last act of Jim feeling dumb was when he arrived home two hours later after two bus transfers and a cab. The first bus was the local; campesinas in full skirts boarded with live chickens. At last arriving home like a drug rat, he found the carved front trellis that spanned his gateposts, that had such a verdant mélange of grapevine, fuchsia and wisteria, had been removed. The double gates were open and dirt ridges from the backhoe tracks led right to his garden, which was a fresh crater with the big fig tree sitting on a walk like a beached whale. Sra. Sanchez's gardener, Lorenzo, who was always interested in his garden, told him he'd come down when the new landscaper arrived with the big truck and the backhoe. They had a dog too, which had left a gift near the blood meal pile Jim got from the slaughterhouse at bulk rate because it was great organic fertilizer. His take on it was that they'd brought in a dog trained to sniff human remains to supplement the digging efforts, which revealed nothing since there were no bodies buried in Jim's garden despite rumor and frame-up. The backhoe had gone down ten feet to his sewer line, and he remembered after the insurance investigator, Pirisini, had interviewed him about Norm's disappearance, a municipal crew had been excavating to the curb outside his door. He wasn't worried if they tunneled under his wall, or had high-tech probe sensors, because nobody was there.

"Carambas, you finally decided to get rid of that big fig," Lorenzo said.

"It was shading the flowers," Jim said. "You want a fig tree?"

"The senora would say that was too much," Lorenzo said.

"I'll get my chainsaw in the morning," Jim said.

Holly and her pretty self were nowhere around of course, it seemed clear it was a set-up to get Jim away for the afternoon for the excavation. Though he wasn't a big winner in the last act, at least it showed her he wasn't lying to her about Norman not being there, and she'd kind of played her last card with him. As he was standing looking at the big ditch dug in his back yard, thinking big help from 'ma' fallow 'Mericans', like what's that anagram, 'A Man A Plan, A Canal, Panama', money men in the Colossus of the North, where this bullshit started and came here, mud in your eye from a big case. While he was standing there surveying the open pit, a cab rolled up and Liz got out.

"Holy shit, you really tore up your garden," Liz said.

"It wasn't exactly me," Jim said. "Now I can put in a moat with piranhas. We'd have enhanced security and fresh fish."

"On the plus side, I got good photos, some even better than before," Liz said.

"That's good, I need a win for us now," Jim said. "It hasn't been a great day for me. But I missed you a lot."

"I missed you too, baby," Liz said. "I went back to that park where we first made out."

"Oh yeh, the one with the Grecian columns commemorating the Battle of Ayacucho," Jim said. "A shrine to freedom. Peru from Spain. You from Frank."

"The town's much bigger now, over two hundred thousand with all those who fled the war in Manchay Tiempo," Liz said.

Manchay, from 'fear' in Quechua, the tongue of the Incas, Tiempo, 'Time' from the Spanish of those bold Conquistadors, who had willed to the Indios enslavement, chaos and poverty, their inheritance four and a half centuries from then to present eventuating in another bloody sierra uprising and civil war, now again Hope after internecine violence, almost like it hurt to entertain Hope budding after so much painful disappointment.

—∿—

'Besos de Lejos', or 'Kisses from Afar', a joint effort from Carlos Santana and Christina Aguilera, was on the same track that included 'Ludmila', Argentine hispanorock, Uzi with Brown Out, some hard core Latin funk from Austin, TX, Joan Jett and the Blackhearts with 'Nag, Nag, Nag', the Cobra's 'Nothing But Heartaches', and 'My Baby Left Me At the Liquor Store', playing on the recent tape his old buddy, Milt Takita, had sent him, as Liz and he lay in bed after homecoming intercourse. She had given this 'uh' when she had it or like she had it if she was so tired she wanted it over, she exhausted herself in the sierra, and he had it because after being hoodwinked for a sugar daddy that afternoon, he was happy for real love. His dreams were not entirely calm, must have been from back in Neanderthal Cincy teen years somebody pissing with his pooh bear, don't need your bully ass shining on me, woke up ready to fight but she pulled down his pants and wouldn't let him out of the car to go after the jerk. The phone was ringing, kept ringing so he looked outside and it was dark, Liz was snoring like she had a kazoo in her nose, so great to have her back even though it was irritating, like the ringing phone that kept ringing and at last the call went to the answering machine, and he recognized the concerned voice of Professor MacHenry leaving a long message, so he picked up.

"Can you meet me at the chifa near the Pension Inglesa in a half an hour?" Mac said.

"You're all right, thank God, I thought you might be dead after I found your shirt with blood on it," Jim said.

"It wasn't my blood," Mac said. "I clocked one of the sons of bitches. I got away before I had a chance to get the Silver Llama. I'm thinking we have supper at the chifa, and I'll tell you everything. Then we walk over to the pension when it's dark, this time together. If you could just distract Olga, while I slip out to the garden, I'll get it for you, as I promised. For you and Frank, you discovered it. I was lax in my oversight of Emerson."

"Was he behind that attack? And what about the General Ordoñez, you know that fire on the docks sent Stephensen to the hospital," Jim said. "Has Rob gone postal?"

"I don't think it's Rob behind it," Mac said. "He may have done high jinks in the past, but he's done great work near Chan Chan and has a solid reputation. Derrick is actually more of a question now. You know he married that heiress. Then she found out he was having an affair with a grad student. She cut him off, and he came down to make some money on the side, evidently doing some of what Rob had done when he was in the Gang of Four."

"Gang of Four?" Jim said.

"That was my own name for them," Mac said. "That was after I found out they'd raided Frank's find after his accident. And 'they' is Rob, Derrick, Miller and Val. Val's dead, Miller's in Mexico, and Rob's a MacArthur scholar. That leaves Derrick. I went to the docks to warn him about a bad deal. He was doing amateur work like it was thirty years ago, and there are many professionals in that business now. I managed to get him off the boat before it went up. He'd been beaten and robbed, left to die in the conflagration."

"It's not possible he'd asked Rob to provide him some huacos for the black market, with an implicit threat of going public on past ethics violations?" Jim said, still not entirely convinced that Rob had nothing to do with it, since he had a scar where Rob sliced him. Mari had come the next day to check on him and apologize, and he'd staggered to the door with a blood-soaked bandage that slipped off and went splat on the floor. She'd gotten him to a doctor, given him TLC and that only infuriated Rob more after he got taken on the Chimu Armor. It wasn't like Rob didn't have a demonstrated propensity for violence.

"I think it's more like the nature of the business Derrick was dealing in," Mac said. "It doesn't excuse Rob for the past, but what he did thirty years ago, I don't know about that. He helped to stop degradation of the site at Sipan, and to make it a national archaeological site. It was wrong if he pushed another fledgling out of the nest. I was one of Frank's dissertation advisors. I know that the Silver Llama and a capa cocha discovery would have made his career. He'd have had tenure somewhere for sure, if not at Cal, there'd be a good number of other universities. I should have been more observant, it was a dereliction of duty. I owe him something and you too. You're the one who actually picked it up."

"Yeh, but you don't owe me anything," Jim said. "You gave me knowledge and that's worth more than silver. Anyway under Peruvian law, it should be the property of the state."

"I do think this Silver Llama ultimately belongs in a museum," Mac said. "It was my hope that Frank, and or you, however you decide your respective interests in it, that you'd want to donate it. I didn't have an opportunity to examine it. Of course if it is 1570 A.D. and TASI is for Tupac Amaru, Sapa Inca, then it would be much more valuable than the five thousand I bought it for. The auction house thought the markings were defacements. But Ocros was not so far from Vilcabamba, the real lost city of the Incas, which wasn't discovered until 1964."

"This Llama has been in commerce, you did buy it at a legal auction," Jim said. "So I could donate it, but then it's Frank's money, and he has a say. You don't know of any other prior claims, do you?"

"Claims, uh no," Mac said. "I believe Derrick thinks the piece is valuable for the same reasons you did. He remembers you talking about it at Vinchos. Rob wouldn't touch it now, in fact I thought he might have put it up for auction, to unload it, and Rick wouldn't have liked that. I don't think Rob killed Val, but I still harbor suspicions about Derrick. He's still a big strong hulk. You know he played tackle for Dartmouth."

"And he always seemed so polite, almost courtly," Jim said.

"It's more likely Trujillo huaceros," Mac said. "In any case, it will be a relief to get it off my hands. I'll give it to you tonight."

Mac's plan was that they'd have dinner at the chifa, and around quarter til eight p.m., at which hour Olga started listening to her TV programs, Jim would drop by for a short visit to make sure the insurance claim for the break-in had been processed and paid. She of course would be delighted to see Jim, and he'd prompt her into some of her classic stories, the boxing match in Paris during a Grand Tour in the Thirties when Carpentier knocked out the Englishman in the first round before they could even get to their seats, or getting strip-searched by Republican Customs in Spain and having to swallow all their gemstones to avoid confiscation, later retrieved from a chamber pot. When her program came on at eight, her attention would be fixed on it and speech would not be permitted, so it would be easy for Jim to slip out and open the back gate. Mac would then get the Silver Llama and give it to Jim. They agreed to meet at the chifa at six-thirty to give them plenty of time.

"By the way, where'd you get the tip about that bad scene going down on the General Ordoñez?" Jim said.

"I'll tell you all about it at the chifa," Mac said. "Ask for Hop Sing if the owner isn't in. That's Song Li. So Sing Song, if you need to remember."

Well, at least he was going to get a Silver Llama even if he didn't get The Truth, if in fact it was the same one they'd found hiking around Ocros, at about 17,000 feet when the weather changed and a tremor triggered a slide that nearly killed them. 'Saved by the Grace of God' was what mariners would have said after surviving terrible storms. Another explanation the locals would have had was that the mountain Apu was angry but belched thee forth, because you gave of the llama a good offering.

—ɯ—

Before Jim left for the chifa, he wired his front gate together as best he could, like it was a tin sheet calamina gate in the barrios, and gave Liz his gun for protection in case the excavators returned. Before heading over to the chifa in Pueblo Libre, he stopped by his office to make sure that all the orders he'd put in had executed because the market had been on a real roller-coaster ride up with Clinton not invading anywhere, as had Reagan not done before, maybe except for Granada and Bill the Balkans to know we still had it and didn't want Europe to slide further into barbarism on its soft underbelly. He was happy there was no urgent mail from ministries soliciting bribes, nothing from the IRS, the DEA or any other USA alphabet agency. On the way over to the pension, he picked up a box of chocolates and a bottle of champagne for Olga, and went on to the chifa. Traffic had gotten terrible and when he arrived late, a new man at the bar told him his old friend had gone on to the pension and would meet him there as planned. It had gotten dark and the garua, a heavy Pacific fog, was rolling in by the time he arrived at the front gate, got there by seven-thirty expecting Mac to appear like the shade of some classic hero encountered in the underworld, but no show. He then walked back and forth under the hemlocks on the side street, before testing the garden gate, which he found unlocked but with no one inside, so he went back to the front gate and rang.

Olga was delighted to see him, appreciated the flowers, candy and wine, and they sat in the parlor and talked for a half hour, many of the stories ones he had heard, but a few new ones. She told about huddling in a sierra thunderstorm under the tin shacks with the miners' children at the mine where her Scotch father was chief engineer, from whom she learned her perfect English, in addition to the Spanish of her Peruvian mother, and the Quechua from the miners' kids who were their playmates because there were no other children besides her own brothers and sisters, so she was perfectly trilingual. The storm was like bombs were going off over their heads, and the rain was so heavy it looked like it was boiling on the tin roofs.

A thump sounded upstairs.

"Is Vicente still here?" Jim said.

"It's Dr. Fogle, my only guest now, probably dropped a book in the library," Olga said. "He's a clumsy big fellow. He's trying to prove the Incas had writing, something with quipus, their string abacus. Grand chance of that. The poor blighter's been bouncing around on one year assignments."

"I met this guy once," Jim said. "I'll just nip upstairs to say hello."

"He'll talk your ear off. Don't forget my program starts in a few minutes," Olga said.

"I know the house rules, no talking during Nino, it's like sneezing during the Messiah," Jim said.

Jim took the stairs slow and quiet, having no intention to talk to this pseudo-scientific buffoon, Dr. Fogle, who might have scared Mac away from the garden below. Nobody down there now, everything dark and deserted, the only light coming from anywhere was coming from the library, a crazy-quilt of books American scholars had left behind to make their weight limits on flights home, so Perry Mason mysteries and Louis L'Amour Westerns were interspersed with the biography of Georges Sand, the Warren Report, To Kill A Mockingbird, the Kinsey Report,--it was interesting at the Kinsey Institute at IU they had a condom in a bell jar kept up by forced air—, "Peyton Place", and then a red lacquered Buddha that sat in a three-legged black stand. Rather than distract an aspiring gypsy scholar, Jim slipped by to the back stairs and went down to make sure Mac wasn't waiting in the kitchen or storeroom for lights out. There was nobody downstairs, only fog in the garden and pots and pans stacked up in the kitchen, along with him tripping over a kerosene can and pile of old lathe and papers in the utility room Vicente had ready to take to the incinerator, so Jim went back upstairs, and peeked in the library, on his way back downstairs to watch the intro to Nino and say goodnight to Olga.

Fogle was in the library sitting at a desk with his hair mussed up and his spectacles askew, looking so much like a big tweedy Scotch ape bent over a book, a large fellow who might have thrown the caber at the Highland Games in the auld land, but had gone to seed in the New World, especially had let himself go as regards his mid-section, wherefrom he had unbuttoned his vest, and was dipping into snack bags of Chez puffs, chicharrones and chips. His red hair was queerly grey in the filtered light of the green glass semi-cylindrical lamp shade, and just as Jim was passing, the prof had exhaled mightily and his big head hit down on the book he was reading. He had to feel sympathy for the gypsy scholar pursuing a pet theory of Inca writing based on the quipu. He doubted Fogle'd make his case, yet many amateurs had made great discoveries in Peru. Hugh Thomson was not an academic, yet discovered in Hiram Bingham's field notes in Sterling Library the coordinates for the observatory across from Machu Picchu and up a side valley, another Intihuantiyu altar, very rare, the Spanish priests destroyed them as heathen.

Fogle blinked open his eyes, they glowed as he turned toward Jim, stood up supported by his arm, and smiled at him like he was a fellow patron of the library of the Pension Inglesa. We live in a time of discovery, many hidden secrets will be revealed. What a great time to be alive. Many great books were lost at Alexandria in the great fire there.

"Urh," Fogle muttered, rising up from his chair and looking straight at Jim, as if he were ready to lecture on the Incas and writing.

"Well, hello," Jim said, stepping into the doorway just to say hi and then, sorry, have to run.

"The bath's down the hall," Fogle said. "Hot water is limited, maybe a minute before it goes lukewarm, breakfast seven-thirty to nine."

"Thanks, but I'm not staying," Jim said, stepping away from the door.

"I didn't mean to imply this is a flophouse," Fogle said. "No bed bugs, pretty good food, the broth a bit thin, but it's all clean, no Atahualpa's revenge if you know what I mean."

"I just dropped by to pay my regards to Sra. Olga, she's an old friend," Jim said, stepping away from the door. "Sorry to disturb."

"I'm the one who should be begging pardon for being uncivil," Fogle said, getting up and closing the volume on the desk. "I get wrapped up in my work and can't think of anything but. Why don't you come in and sit down a while? You've heard of the quipu? There's an excellent private collection at a hacienda near Tambo Colorado. Say, don't I know you from somewhere? Oh my God, I met you and Liz Teris after you took her from Frank after his unfortunate motorcycle accident? Or was it later when you came up the coast when you were bonking Mari Emerson? Time goes by. Ayacucho in '69, long time, Jimmy."

"You were on the '69 Proyecto Ayacucho?" Jim said, stepping toward the door. "I don't remember you."

"You might not," Fogle said, grinning at him like a circus sideshow chimp, tugging at his orange beard like it was cotton candy, mumbling soto voce 'got to get this crap off me, it's giving me eczema.'

"Come in and sit down," Fogle said, with a ham-handed courtier gesture toward the chair. "We'll talk about old times."

"I would, but Liz and I are still together, and she wanted to catch 'Clockwork Orange' again," Jim said. "And if Rob sent you to hassle me, tell him it's push come to shove."

"Hear that, he thinks the great scholar Emerson has sent us?" Fogle said.

"Shut up, Rick," a voice behind them said, swinging the door shut. "Sit down, Jimmy. It's truth or consequences time."

Jim turned around and saw a tall man with a gun pointed at him. He was big in the chest and middle, taller than Fogle, but Jim couldn't see his face clearly because he had a Panama hat with the brim down to cast a shadow on his face. Besides that, Jim was looking mainly at the gun.

"You can catch your show if you just answer a few quick questions," the man said definitely.

"So, Dr. Fogle, you're Derrick Stephensen?" Jim said. "After Mac saved you from the fire at the General Ordoñez, did you come here to trap him with a disguise? What did you do with him? You or your bufalo with the gun?"

"The old fox caught our scent at the chifa, and slipped away, much to my dismay, because all I want out of this is the Silver Llama," Derrick Stephensen aka Fogle said. "Did he by any chance tell you where he hid it? I assume it's here because why else would Mac come back to where he got mugged before. All you need to do is tell us where it is. It's no sweat off your brow, is it?"

"He said he hid it in the garden," Jim said. "That's all I know. Now do you mind calling off your bufalo?" advancing toward the door in front of which was standing the big man with the drawn gun. "Pardon me," he said, attempting to go by, but he was thrown backward by a strong arm, with a hard smack on the side of his head with a ham hand holding the revolver.

"You said there'd be no more violence," Derrick Stephensen aka Fogle said.

"Shut up, Rick," said the man with the gun, holding it up and advancing into the light. "Sit down, Hiram. I have a couple other questions you need to answer."

"Oh my God, it's Miller," Jim said, recognizing his particular churlish sneer from back when he came after him when he was down and tired from fishing, coming back to the bar of the Hotel Colmena in Ayacucho. "So the Gang of Four is back. Or I guess now it's now the Gang of Three with Val's passing."

"Maybe you should have worn the disguise, Miller," Derrick Stephensen said. "Look, Val should have never sold the Llama to that huacero in the first place. And for two thousand, then Mac got it for five. I'll give you twenty-five thousand cash on the barrelhead. Dollars, en efectivo."

"I'd give it to you at cost, but I don't have it," Jim said, getting up from the table. "I've got an idea, Rick, like demilitarizing the situation. You, me and Miller go away and let Mac come back and find the Llama in the garden. I'll get him on the phone and tell him the coast is clear. If you want to be there when I make the phone call, that's okay by me. He's promised it to me. I'll give it to you when he gives it to me. Isn't this like a Mexican stand-off? They said you'd gotten up in the world in Sinaloa, Miller. I'm surprised you're hassling me over some old huaco."

"Yeh, I've worked in Mexico and other places," Miller said. "I get around. Wherever the money's good. It can take you from north of Chicago down to Santiago. They say that faith can move mountains, but my experience is money's the first mover. It can buy big ol' Caterpillars. Defoliate your garden so it's like Happy Valley Gone Sad after the giant steals the magic singing harp."

"I think Jimmy's got a point," Derrick said. "Our best plan is for him to call Mac and tell him he's thrown us off his trail, set up another meeting and Mac gives him the Silver Llama. We know where to find him. He doesn't want it. Maybe we need to be practical."

"Sorry, that doesn't work for me, Rick, a few thousand bucks for an Inca piece versus a thirty-five million case," Miller said. "You know what I'm talking about, Jim."

"It's kind of like the same thing with the Llama, I'd give you what you want if I had it," Jim said. "Nothing buried in my garden. You can go back and dig it up again. I guess you've been in the business long enough to know about frame-ups."

"Isn't that enough for tonight?" Derrick said. "I don't know where you get the idea the Llama is worth thirty-five million."

"Shut up, you idiot windbag schoolmarm," Miller said, brandishing the pistol in Rick's direction. "You know what I'm talking about, Jim."

"I'd certainly like it if someone would explain it to me," Derrick said.

"I'll tell you, Rick, if you tell me what you were doing down on the docks with Peter Seymour," Jim said.

"Go ahead, tell him, he's not the DEA," Miller said. "Tell him the short leash you're on."

"As a matter of fact, I've had a few setbacks recently," Derrick said. "I'd been having a romantic liaison which my wife discovered. She was quite upset and sequestered all her assets from me. In the meantime I had become addicted to laudanum and cocaine, which exhausted my professor's salary rather rapidly. If you must know, I had been in touch with Mr. Seymour to purchase cocaine. Quite unfortunately, I was robbed and beaten in my quest. I am thankful Dr. MacHenry was able to get me off the burning ship. Honestly, Jim, I had nothing to do with the assault on him, and it would be an immense personal victory for me to get the Silver Llama. Isn't it something how it's turned up after being missing all these years."

"After you hooked it from Frank and me in Ayacucho," Jim said.

"That was me," Miller said. "It was such easy pickin's, 'cause you and Frank were zonked from soroche and hypothermia."

"You told me Val stole it, hid it all these years, and some huacero killed him for it," Derrick said.

"Let's forget the petty bullshit, and move on to the next order of business," Miller said. "Jim needs to tell me all about Mr. Larsen."

"Who in blue blazes is Mr. Larsen?" Derrick said.

"He was a Seymour Company corporate counsel with a thirty-five million dollar, main man insurance policy on his life," Jim said. "He had his hand in the till and disappeared in Chile about ten years ago. The insurance company thinks he's somewhere in a hammock sipping piña coladas, enjoying La Vida Buena. Others, the beneficiaries, want to prove he's dead. Which side are you on, Milller?"

"On the side of truth," Miller said.

"Funny when bufalos start talking about truth," Jim said.

"People think truth is just one thing," Miller said. "Like Norm Larsen is either alive or dead. That's just a fact. Truth is something bigger. See, my man, whichever way it is, the truth could still be two things, either revealed or concealed. Which makes it real saleable to the highest bidder."

"Now what does Jim have to do with this Larsen?" Derrick said.

"That's what we're going to find out," Miller said, gesturing with his gun. "Now we're going upstairs to my room where I have a tape recorder set up for his statement. You will assist me, Derrick, in the interrogation."

"I'm not comfortable with this," Derrick said.

"I don't care what you're comfortable with," Miller said, bringing the gun around toward him. "Let's all go upstairs."

The TV downstairs was turned up loud with Olga's bad hearing, and the gunfire from the Argentine Bonanza clone horse opera filled the stairwell as they marched up. Only one room existed on the third floor, with the rest a flat cement roof with a low parapet, where he used to come up and read Octavio Paz and sun in a deck chair when he stayed there in the early days. Miller already had a good Sony tape recorder plugged into the outlet, and he told Derrick to tie Jim into the chair.

"Again, I'm not comfortable with this," Derrick said. "Do we have to restrain him?"

"And again, I don't give a rat's ass about what you're comfortable with," Miller said, pointing the gun at him again. "Now tie him down, or you will have no Silver Llama. It'll disappear for another twenty-five years. Maybe I'll go sell it in Singapore."

"Oh, you wouldn't, please God, it's unique," Derrick said. "Certainly, you have some residual ethics from your training."

"What a freak, just do your part, we'll get this over, then Jimmy can call Mac and tell him the coast's clear," Miller said. "We just need to make sure Jim doesn't jump and run. I'm not in shape to catch him, and neither are you."

Derrick did tie him, and Miller checked the tightness of the rope around his first arm, but was preoccupied with getting the mic set up on a side table beside the chair, and Derrick tied his second arm somewhat looser. Miller insisted he also tie his legs to the front chair legs, a heavy maple frame with seat, back and arm cushions, and similarly it was one leg tight and the second leg loose. He then told Derrick to stand outside the door and keep watch, and he did step outside, but left the door ajar so he could see in. Jim felt some assurance from him being there and his undetected resistance to Miller in not tying him up too tight, though he knew from a bit of repositioning that he was not going to be able to slip the nooses quickly and make a run for it. Miller was hitting the 'Record' button to initialize the tape, date, time, location, James Hiram's on Norman A. Larsen, hereinafter known as the subject, testing, asking Jim whether the testimony he was giving was given freely and without duress.

"No," Jim answered shortly.

"Hell, have to erase right off, or should I wait til later to edit," Miller said, smacking him with the back of his hand. "Let's get a clean tape. Now, is your testimony freely given and without duress?"

"No duress," Jim said, though he pronounced it with the accent on the first syllable, like it was in the word 'duro' (hard) so that passed with Miller. And damn, Jim was willing to say whatever Miller wanted said to get out of that inquisition, which of course could always be contested as having been elicited under duress, though also of course if the declarant were deceased (i.e., Jim were dead at time of trial), it would be hard to prove duress. Though he didn't want to say what really had happened, he started in with his tale, yes, Larsen had appeared at his place that Sunday afternoon, and a confrontation ensued between him, namely Larsen, and Pete Seymour and his fiancée Holly, shots were fired between those individuals, though Jim did not see this action, Holly and Pete left shortly thereafter with Griggs, a Seymour security operative, who had been previously knocked unconscious by Pete while trying to take Pete into custody and return him to rehab in Philadelphia, then revived with a cup of java, drove off with them after the set-to with Larsen, who was wounded in the fracas, whether the bullet had grazed him or in dodging the shots, he'd knocked his head against the cellar stairwell wall and temporarily lost consciousness. In any case, he was gone when Jim got back to check on his condition, to see whether to call an ambulance if necessary. So Larsen was gone from the stairwell after he got back from hustling Pete, Holly and Griggs out of there. He said he told the former two they might want to take a long holiday in Ecuador, which was a good place to hide, had a developing computer chip industry and sense of independence, less likely to extradite to either Peru or the U.S. on charges. Pete slipped Griggs after they went to the hotel, and he heard later that Griggs had deceased, and didn't know anything about Larsen anyway, that was not his mission in Peru.

"So damn, I guess the dead really can rise, because I heard somebody say somebody say she shot him down to the ground," Miller said. "How does that work? How does a dead man drive himself to the hospital and get treated for a minor abrasion?"

"Maybe she's not the shot she thought she was," Jim said. "Maybe he had some help. They said he had a local partner, a straw man named Juan Selzer. Larsen was down and moaning when I ran up from my cellar. Yeh, he was down and didn't have a gun up when I went by him. I didn't stop for an examination. My first thought was to see about them, because frankly Larsen had been marching me downstairs to no good end."

"Juan Selzer was an alias Pete Seymour used to help Larsen rob his old man's company," Miller said.

"You know more than me then," Jim said. "There were two SUV's outside my place that night. Griggs arrived in one and got knocked out trying to take Pete home for rehab. After the shooting, I showed Holly and Pete out and they drove away with Griggs. I went back to check on Larsen, and he was gone, and when I went outside again, his SUV was gone. Didn't they say somebody returned his SUV to Avis at Jorge Chavez?"

"Somebody did?" Miller said. "You're smooth, Jim. You've given me a couple of buns, but Where's the Beef?"

"Funny slogan, but it didn't work so great for Mondale," Jim said. "School kids won't need to memorize him on the presidents' list."

"What I'm saying is we need more truth in the mix," Miller said. "You remember a cat named Holub on the flight from Lima to

Santiago that night? A U.S. AID worker from Fresno, actually a CIA operative, so he's not real anxious to make public statements, but he was watching other Americans coming to Chile."

"Holub? I don't think so," Jim said. "I met Chileans coming north to escape the fascist bullshit there, summary trials in soccer stadiums for leftists, prison camps on Isla Robinson Crusoe, but the other way around, going down there when the bulls had the rule, no way. You know it was right after Nixon went to Beijing and he and Kissinger shut down Allende. I don't doubt this guy was CIA. The company was in on that one, thanks to Tricky Dick, even if school kids don't learn it in American History. So some CIA sub-contractor is a witness in your case, really credible evidence since I've had bullcrap backwash from them before. I can tell you more, if you want to check your sources. Check out checkers, check out the Gulf of Tonkin Resolution, man, you were counter-culture back then, you want to believe what they're telling you now?"

"That was then, and this is money," Miller said. "This Holub recalls talking to a Larsen on the flight to Santiago, and I'm wondering why a smart dude like him would use his real name, if he was on the lam with company funds."

"Don't have a clue, man," Jim said, thinking Holub was so damn drunk at boarding and Jim had already dyed his hair jet black and shaved a two-day growth to leave a pencil moustache, also nicely dyed, and had kept his face down from the adjustable pencil beam, and he looked a damn sight like Larsen anyway, they could have been brothers or at least cousins.

"So you never rode his ticket to Santiago?" Miller said.

"What? I flew out of Lima the next day to Arequipa, not to Santiago," Jim said. "I'd already spent like over a week out of the office finding Pete Seymour in Tingo Maria. Next, his dear old dad, who'd come down to bring him home to rehab, dad has the big one in the sierra, and it's left to me to bring the body to Lima in my Plymouth Satellite, great car, customized hemi. Anyway it's left to me to get Dad Seymour's body on a flight home. Larsen shows up at my place wanting the body and shortly after a shoot-out ensues. I was just glad nobody got killed. I didn't need bad press. I had a client waiting in Arequipa with money to put into MicroSoft. So I went to Arequipa."

"Oh yeh, Fawcett did have a record of your return ticket from Arequipa to Lima, but just the return, nothing on getting there, funny, isn't it?" Miller said, noticing that Stephensen had appeared at the door. "Derrick, would you mind checking downstairs? Make sure the coast is clear for a quick exit."

When Stephensen had gone, Miller went to the bed table and was fiddling with something.

"I don't know Fawcett's filing system," Jim said. "Maybe they got one file for round-trips and one for one ways? I did buy them separately, because I considered renting a car and visiting around Arequipa. Maybe you paid for one file, and whoever took the mordida, is waiting for the next installment. Damn, you've been south of the Rio Bravo thirty years and you still don't know how things work down here? They can smell money like a bloodhound smells a convict. Or did Pirisini put you on a budget?"

"I'm an independent contractor," Miller said, turning toward him with a hypodermic needle he was squirting up to make sure the air bubbles were out. "I'm just interested in the truth. Which is why I need to use some truth serum. It's not harmful, in fact a fair to middling high, DynaFlo it was known as in the day, after the first Buick automatic transmission, in fact, if confession is good for the soul, it'll help you unburden your conscience. It makes you powerful windy. I know you like things clean, Jimbo."

At this point Jim did squirm and rise up so he brought the chair off the ground, but Miller easily pushed him back down with his off hand and then used it to hold his arm to the chair arm. Jim managed to rotate his forearm enough that the needle went more into muscle than the veins in the crook of his arm. As Miller turned to operate the tape recorder again, he noticed Derrick, who'd returned and been standing at the door watching.

"No one is down there, and what is this?" Derrick said.

"Just finishing up here," Miller said, smiling and looking around for his gun. "Jim has been most helpful and we just need to verify a few more points."

"You might be next on his list, Rick," Jim said. "After that fire at the docks, I found a photo just like the one they found on Val, except it was you who was circled. Mac didn't do that. I didn't either. Now who might have done that?"

"Don't listen to his crap?" Miller said, flipping away the needle and looking around for the gun which he'd chucked onto the bed and had slid under the coverlet. "Jim is a master of bullshit. Now get back out there and keep a watch."

"This isn't as it should be," Derrick said.

"Not much in life is," Miller said. "Be a good pal and we'll get you the Silver Llama tonite f'sure. I've got a high power boat light and we'll scour the garden. Just a couple more questions for Jim and we're done here. He's unburdening himself now. The truth can be such a burden, right, Jim?"

"Truth is, Derrick, I'd be on a fast horse out of here," Jim said. "After he killed Val, and tried to kill you to create a diversion from this big Larsen insurance case, you think you're going to get away alive? Remember the General Ordoñez?"

"Jim's a lawyer, he can raise a fog to befuddle Sherlock Holmes," Miller said, going back to engage the tape recorder.

"But I'm not lying now, Rick," Jim said, feeling the Dynaflo take him and trying to take the talk back his way. "Hell, I went to the hospital after that fire to make sure you were all right. I didn't call Sylvia because I knew about your pecadillo. She still thinks you're in Ontario doing fieldwork. Miller may have already called an associate in Quebec at Rochambeau Prison to go stage an event, maybe planned to send him a tooth from the Ordoñez fire. You're my only friend here now, Rick. You'll be an easy kill for him, like a dodo for a sailor. See, Miller is money and money is Miller. Open your eyes and Miller's your killer. Run your ass fast, call the cops and ask, is Jim's pal Fregosco in at the desk.

"Crazy ass, I'm a poet and I don't know it," Miller said. "He's trying to dodge a couple questions on the death of my old friend, Norman Larsen. I'm just trying to get some closure, just want to know where my pal's buried."

"Norm Larsen wasn't Hecuba to him, nor he to Hecuba," Jim said. "Think he might have knocked off Val, and tried to get you in the fire on the General Ordoñez just to create a diversion from this big Larsen insurance case. Remember Val, the poor duck got throttled. How do you think it's going to be for you?"

"Jim's a backwoods shyster with scare tactics," Miller said, coming away from the tape-recorder and leaning over the bed to look where he'd flipped away his handgun.

"Call Fregosco, will you?" Jim said. "I've made money for his retirement fund, like JFK said, a rising tide raises all boats, I'm just trying to keep the faith."

"He's talking crap now," Miller said,

"Not all of it," Jim said. "I see why you want that Silver Llama, Rick. Your old lady speaks only to the Cabots and Lodges, and not so much to you. I know what it is to be persona non grata in good society. It reminds me of the joke about the hillbilly who tells the Cincinnati society lady, 'All my people came over on the Mayflower too,' 'Oh rilly, sez she', 'Yep, right over that thar' bridge in a Mayflower move van.' You know Ohio used to be an ocean with giant sharks swimming around, so maybe back to the past soon. With global warming, they'll be raising corn in Greenland. Does it seem warm in here, Rick? Maybe I'm still feeling the heat from the General Ordoñez fire. Preview of coming attractions. I don't think those kerosene cans at the bottom of the steps are for popcorn. And those oily rags—you got a chop shop on the side, Miller? Think you'll dodge the inferno this time, Rick?"

"Jim's talking through his hat again, isn't it clear?" Miller said, going back to the tape recorder and again looking around for the gun he'd flipped onto the bed and and which had slid under the comforter. "He looks so moral but it's a false face. He's been covering up this Larsen murder and lying about it. A couple questions more about that and we're done here. Damn, did you hear a car door closing outside? It might be Mac back to snatch the Silver Llama from the garden. What about that? You whiff on that one, and your ass is grass with the Duchess, right?"

"I didn't hear anything," Derrick said, backing off as if he were attempting to apprehend a distant unverified presence, holding his hand to his ear as if tracing the ephemera of pestilential flatulence, before he broke for the stairs. It was like Jim had just kept talking whatever came into his head, for as long as he could avoid talking about Larsen's fate and his own complicity in the affair, but in a sense we are all complicit by reason of having been born into this world, how he was loath to disclose that, but was not far from telling all whenever Miller got back to his inquisition.

This was as Derrick took a good clue and made a break for it, before Miller fumbling around unable to find his gun on the bed, just took off to catch Rick before he made it to the stairs, the two of them wheeling around like a couple a grizzly bears wrestling, Derrick as big as Miller, two six foot four gringos going at it on the top floor of the pension. Gringo grande was what the locals called them in Vinchos, the serranos were built big in the chest, would make great astronauts, stocky and stronger in the high ground, he'd seen a campesina market lady hoist and sling a hundred pound sack of potatoes onto the back of a flatbed truck. It was like watching wrestling on TV, rooting for Derrick, flexing tight in the chair until he felt the slack on the bonds on his right arm, got it loose, had to look up to see how things stood outside before getting caught half loose and worse off, but surprisingly Derrick was holding his own against the stronger man. He looked like a bulked up tweedy character in the ring at World Wrestling showtime, Dr. Hekyl or Professor Flunkya, it must have been the Dynaflo he'd been given, it seemed unreal as Jim was watching all this while working on the knot on his left arm, til it came loose too and with two hands free he was able to undo his legs while the two big boys were dancing outside. It was a flat roof with a low parapet all around, and Miller had horsed Derrick away from the stairs, working him back and forth like rolling a keg of beer, inexorably toward the front corner where it was a thirty five foot drop to a brick patio. Time to punch off the interior TV and run to life. The chance to flee appeared and Jim made a run for the stairs, but the ropes on the floor tripped him, plus the 'Dynaflo serum' had affected his balance, so he ended up on his belly like a beached porpoise midway between the door and the stairs, trying to do a belly roll push-up when he was stalled out of gas like Beetle with Sarge, just able to turn his head sideways to tune in the fight of the night. He was back in time from his wandering mind to see the blur of the big contestants slow, and right afterwards a scream and the consequent moaning from below confirmed that Derrick had been thrown and was not in good shape.

Seeing this set-to gave Jimmy a shot of adrenaline and he was able to get to his knees and walk, not run toward the stairs, but Miller had already turned and seeing him escaping, was like a wrestler recovering consciousness after throwing his first opponent, stumbled back to Jim, took him by the collar like a fractious schoolboy and started dragging him back toward the room.

"We've still got to finish our interview," Miller said. "Where'd you stash old Norman? Up the street in Sra. Sanchez's garden, you want more backhoes on your block?"

"Deep six, baby," Jim said spinning off and getting further away this time, but Miller sashayed sideways to block his exit down.

"And where is that grave?' Miller said, not picking up on the nautical nature of the metaphor.

"Bloop, bloop," Jim said, doing the Swim, running this way and that as Miller was closing in on him, as he considered jumping into the big fig tree near the front corner, but that was risky, especially in his shape, and Derrick had already been thrown down there. He thought Miller wouldn't kill him until he got him on tape, since even Jacques Cousteau in a diving bell wasn't likely to find Norm's casket in the deepest water this side of the Tonga or Marianas Trenches, just keeping running because every minute the junk was wearing off, but unfortunately Miller caught him and held him over the side. Jim looked down and could see Derrick hung up in the fig tree, his neck in a big crook and his head bent back, no longer moaning.

"Hell, fear works as good as dope," Miller said, holding him out in space with his fat thick arm. "I can make a billar and knock Rick out of the tree with you. Now where exactly is Larsen's grave?"

"About three hundred miles offshore, where that InterCon boat blew up and sank the Sunday before Harry Seymour's funeral," Jim said, glancing downward with a grimace. "Let me go, I'll tell you all about it."

"The insurance guy said that was a rumor about the old man's body being on board that crate," Miller said, keeping his hold on Jim.

"It was a rumor about Harry, but not about Norm," Jim said. "Harry's body was already on a private flight back to Philly. Norm came looking for it because he killed him with a digitalin overdose, which I found out with the help of a med student. Norm didn't want to risk murder charges voiding the big CEO policy. So he came to my place to get Harry and to kill me. Lucky for me, somebody else shot him first."

"Then you pulled the old switcheroo and sent Norm out to sea," Miller said. "Didn't you tell somebody it might have been Juan Selzer who was driving his SUV?"

"I lied," Jim said, glancing downward with a grimace as he heard Rick moan below. "I thought Selzer was an alias. I put Norm in the coffin, drove the SUV to the docks where they were waiting for it. It's like he did his own funeral planning. Then I rode his ticket to Santiago, laid a trail down, withdrawals, sightings, a real estate deal that went sour, Selzer a suspect, good luck finding a man who never was. Stayed at the Hostal Reloj de Flores, where have all the flowers gone, remember that song? Nope, Norm checked out on my cellar steps, one shot to the chest. You can guess the shooter, but since I didn't actually see it, you may have a better idea than me."

"Oh yeh, the bobsy twins, your wayward brother-in-law and his molly doll, they might be my high bidders now, depending on how this shakes out," Miller said. "What say we go back in and get all this on tape? I get the tape, I got the deal to make. Don't worry about yourself. It's never going to court."

After Jim just witnessed him throw his co-conspirator off the roof, Miller's reassurance seemed less than credible as he led him back to continue the interrogation. He was still loath to retell the story of Larsen's watery grave and the subsequent cover-up, but the Dynaflo was hard to buck. His own behavior had not been exemplar, though he hadn't felt much guilt about it. He had just fallen in love with Helen, and did this in part to save her from more emotional pain after her dad's death, and to protect her mother too. If he were ever charged in Peru, just the fact that he considered his mother-in-law as anything other than a pain in the rear, would prove his motives were good-hearted. Larsen was an embezzler who'd killed before and planned to bump off not just Jim, but also Pedro, the med student from the barrio, who used to shine shoes in the plaza, oh but, he didn't want the toxicology report to be known, or the insurance would have backhoes digging in the Haverford Mills cemetery tomorrow, his thoughts were rambling as Miller led him back to the room, and he stumbled thinking that he'd just witnessed Miller kill Rick Stevensen, it wasn't likely he wanted a witness, so he might be next down with a billar as the end game, the story would be they struggled and went over together, just slap another copy of the group photo with Rick circled and Jim made a good suspect in the string of murders, some revenge killings over an bone of contention, an old Silver Llama, that'd make a good motive and Miller could release so much of the history as would support the story.

"Up now, don't mess with me," Miller said, pulling him up like a rag doll.

"It's that junk you gave me," Jim said, thinking the exercise had made it wear off more and flopping back face down to get more time for it to metabolize and fade.

"Dr. Penny's special formula, Pennington, he was my butthole buddy back in the day," Miller said. "We had a perfect operation. Dude died in a shooting in a Lima hotel. He was always ready to party. Never messed with anybody who didn't mess with him. Didn't you have a run-in with him in Cuzco?"

"He was Liz's pusher and she was in bad shape," Jim said. "Yeh, I told him to lay off of her."

'Psst' Jim heard and thought it was Miller at first but as his eyes focused he saw Liz in the stairwell, quite dim as in the shadow of daydream, he had just said her name and under the circumstances, it could have been his hopeful mind playing tricks on him.

"So you're back together with Lizzy, how is that?" Miller said. "Must be nice to have a happy home, and with a garden, I know how you liked plants and potatoes, that farm boy bullshit."

"I got some work to do to get my garden back in shape when I get home," Jim said, blinking his eyes and seeing it was in reality Liz standing in the shadow of the stairwell, holding the gun he had given her when he left home, and she was motioning with her other hand for him to move out of the way, which he tried to do, lurching forward like a sprinter off a block, but Miller had a good hold on his shirt and the net effect was to send Jim's spinning to the floor again.

"Bad move, just when I thought you were being cooperative," Miller said, jerking him to his feet and bringing him upright, and putting his neck in the crook of his arm.

"Let go of him," Liz said stepping out of the shadows with the gun raised.

Jim felt the vise grip on his neck release, but Miller still kept a strong hold on his arm.

"Now step away from him," Liz said.

"My God, it is dizzy Mz. Lizzy, we were just talking about you and your happy home," Miller said. "This here, we were just wrestling. You know boys will be boys."

"It looks a bit more serious than that," Liz said.

"It's not what it looks like," Miller said, taking a step towards her while holding Jim ahead of him. "Jim was helping me with some background research, just a few more questions and we're done here. You don't want this case hanging over you, do you, Jim?"

"Back off," Liz said. "You're a bad ass. One more step and I pull the trigger."

"We're all old friends here," Miller said. "I know you're a pacifist at heart, Liz. I saw you putting flowers in the gun barrels when they called out the National Guard in Berkeley. This must be very hard for you. Why don't you just put down the gun so we can talk? Isn't that always the best way? See, Jimmy wants to get this taken care of, because it's just going to hang over his head like a damn sword. Ask him and he'll tell you. He knows there's big money behind this, and even if he puts a finger in the dyke tonight, the levee's gonna bust tomorrow. Too much pressure on the other side. Tell her to cool it, Jimmy."

"It would have been that way if you hadn't killed Derrick," Jim said. "What say I mail you a tape with all the details, though I may want to leave out Juan Selzer, since I don't want to incriminate my brother-in-law."

"I say we do it now and get it over for good," Miller said, giving Jim a little push in the back and inching him forward. "I can get Derrick away from here, no problem. Lizzy can hold the gun on me while you talk into the mic. I'm not afraid, I remember her in the Sixties, the days of Flower Power."

"She's had gun training since then, working in some rough neighborhoods, not a bad shot," Jim said.

"Damn, maybe what you said before about her shooting Penny wasn't bullshit after all?" Miller said. "Kind of poetic justice since it was his special Dynaflo formula that caught his killer."

"What the hell did you tell him?" Liz said. "Penny was my friend. I was defending him."

"He's trying to confuse you," Jim said, feeling Miller tense up behind him. "Don't let him get into the room. He's got a gun in there."

"So maybe it was Jimmy who did Penny, and he was trying to put it on you, that's why he needs more Dynaflo, wouldn't you like to know, Lizzy, do you really trust everything he's told you, so don't think you're just above it all and don't care to know," Miller said, like a wizard gazing up at the zodiac and contemplating the truth, while he had released his grip on Jim to push him away hard and make his bull rush.

"Watch out, he's comin'," Jim called, as he was pushed aside, though he was able to catch a sleeve and bring the bigger man down over him. Then they were both up and dancing like it had been with Derrick before, except that those two had been like two gargantuan linemen struggling, and this was like Jim was a cornerback in the bear hug of a lineman, trying to keep him from making it to the room, trying to extricate himself from the caveman so Liz could get a clear shot at him, but he knew he was fighting a losing battle, had to make some move not Marquis of Queensbury, so got in an elbow to the head, a knee below the belt, got some separation, and called to Liz. "Shoot now. I can't hold him off any more."

"Stop," she shouted, but she seemed to have frozen and didn't have the gun up.

Miller saw and wasn't stopping, charged straight ahead at Liz. Then she did shoot and he cried out in pain, even as his momentum carried him into her and knocked her back against the wall.

"Oh shit, the bitch shot me," Miller roared, holding his foot, where he was wounded, either by the bullet or the cement its ricochet kicked up. He raised up slowly, but instead of going after her, dazed and down on her side though still holding the gun, he came and got Jim in a hold, and it was back to the wrestling match, and they were heading toward the edge where Derrick had gone over before, again a losing match for Jim, who was being wheeled like the next keg of beer, not as vigorously as before and the shine of the blood soaking his captor's sock and pant leg was visible now, and he was moaning as he held Jim at the side of the roof, and said. "Drop the gun right now or Jim goes over."

"He won't do it," Jim called, as Miller made a move to hold him out over the side as he'd done before, only this time Jim planted his foot on the inside of the parapet and turned the momentum of his attacker against him, managing to slip his grasp at the last moment as he tottered on the edge, shuffling his feet but unable to regain balance.

There was a scream, a crash of branches and a moan from below.

"Oh God, Jimmy, I didn't kill him, did I?" Liz said. "I was shooting low to wound."

"No, he's down there moaning," Jim said. "You sure saved my bacon though. I was losing ground fast. How'd you manage to show up here?"

"Mac called to tell you why your meeting was a bust," Liz said. "When he said he gave Miller the slip at the chifa, I knew I'd better check up since Miller was supposed to be in Mexico. I knew him quite well from the old days. He was a bad ass, anything he could get away with. Hop Sing said you were on your way to the pension.

Can we just go down there now and see that he's alive and call an ambulance?"

"First, how are you doing, baby?" Jim said, cradling her up because she was slumped down against the wall.

"I don't feel so great," Liz said. "I think I hit my head against the wall. He was coming right for me when I shot."

"Don't worry about him, he's strong as an ox," Jim said, caressing her hair and fluffing her North Face down vest. "You know I used to sunbathe and read up here. The favorite song on the radio then was 'Caramelo' and 'Goodbye To Love'. Long time back, like twenty-five years, we're getting too old for this kind of life. We need someplace quiet, like a houseboat in Tahiti."

"I'd get bored fast," Liz said. "Can't we go down and check on him now? If we ever do have a child, I don't want to have to tell the kid that Mom's a serial killer."

"Sure, rest here and let me get a couple things out of the room first," Jim said.

She had a bump on the back of her head, a possible concussion but not life-threatening, so Jim brought her the comforter from the room and then went back in to clean it up. First there was the tape, next the syringe and the ampoules of Dr. Pennington's DynaFlo designer nostrum, especially engineered to sniff out snitches and undercover agents, and having plopped all those into Miller's leather briefcase, he found the gun partially obscured by a fold of the cotton bed cover, and picked that up with a Kleenex, not wanting to smudge Miller's prints. He also found more copies of the Ayacucho project team, the top one with Derrick circled and more disturbing, a receipt from the copy store with Jim's name and address on it, and the note, 'Will Call'. That was the frame. He went back out to Liz, helped her up, and they went downstairs by the back stairs.

When they got to the ground floor, over the gunfire and hoof beats from the TV Western inside, they could still hear moaning from the fig tree at the corner. But it was Stephensen, not Miller, doing the moaning. Miller had evidently hit a smaller limb before landing on the pavement, and was not moving. Jim got out the gun, nudged Miller with his foot, and jumped back in case he was playing possum, but it was like pushing a side of beef. So he knelt and took a pulse first at the wrist, nothing there or at the jugular where he could see the last branch had flipped him so he'd apparently broken his neck.

"They'll say I killed him," Liz said.

"Looks more like the two of them were struggling and went over together," Jim said, setting Miller's gun down beside him. "Even if they notice the wound, maybe he shot himself in the struggle. It's clearly not the cause of death. Listen, I'm going to call an ambulance and the cops. Could you get me a cold Coke out of the fridge before you take off? I recall the antidote to DynaFlo is a soft drink. If you see a bottle of Mr. Boston, bring it along. I could use a Cuba Libre after this."

"I'll bring your trago, macho," Liz said.

While she went to the kitchen, Jim heard a rustling of branches from close behind that made him jump forward. Then he realized it was from above, not as far above as Stephensen had been before, since Miller had evidently displaced him to slide lower, not with a billar or cabezaso or other contact but just shaking the tree, and his second stage of falling had brought on sharp pain that woke him. Rick was now just over head high, with repositioning his leg bent back in an unnatural position and all scratched up like he'd been horse dragged, hung by mega-shrikes in a Druid tree. The pain had brought him to consciousness, his eyes were wide and looking straight at Jim as he tried to form words out of the moan.

"Oh God, my leg hurts," Derrick said.

"I'm getting you an ambulance," Jim said.

"Don't leave me, please," he said. "Miller will kill me. He wants the Llama for himself."

"Miller's dead," Jim said. "After he threw you off the roof, he lost his balance and fell over too, broke his own neck."

"Oh, my God, how terrible," Stephensen said. "And the Silver Llama? It'd break my heart to be this close and lose it."

"I'll bring it to you in the hospital, I promise, no crosses count," Jim said. "I need to go call the ambulance and the cops."

"Oh, do you really have to call the police?" Rick Stephensen said. "There's a morality clause in my tenure contract. It's bad enough with my pecadillos, but a murder could end my career."

"No murder here," Jim said. "He was going to kill you and me after he did you. It's called self-defense. You saved me, Derrick. Thank you, man."

"He was off his rocker, thirty-five million for the Llama, how did he get that, I couldn't raise that even if Pookie were still behind me, and she isn't, she's quite peeved I couldn't keep my zipper up around the young stuff," Rick said, speaking in short phrases whose caesurae were filled with a refrain of groans, until the words became less distinguishable and merged into a general murmur. "I told him I wouldn't countenance his actions against you, but he was insane. Thinking you were selling it for thirty-five million to some Chicago insurance man, who'd have no idea of its value. How could he?"

"He was a crazy mother all right, and a narcoterrorista—if anything, you'll be getting a medal from the government," Jim said, feeding him another pain pill and a swig of Coke to take it down.

"You don't suppose you could poke around the garden for the Llama, just in case Mac is put off from coming back," Stephensen said, groaning and proposing. "Mac might not return after a second attempt on his life. He'll say third time's the charm, I'll not risk it now. I'll be back next summer, but suppose Mac has the big one before then and the Llama's lost again. Ouuu, Ouuu, I can't bear to think of being this close and losing it again. It's like I can see it on the edge of a chasm and it could go over with any gust of wind. Silver beauty, my little hobbyhorse to ride back to the top. So sad about Val, but such things can't get in the way of science, these huaceros have no sense of any worth beyond the monetary, and Miller is no better than any of them, so we all make our deal with the Devil. It was at an anthro conference in Los Angeles, I heard you were Mari Emerson's prix chevalier, had maybe taken the Llama for yourself, llama, my llama, llama."

And then Rick passed out cold.

Jim went inside to the kitchen, where Liz had located a cardboard six-pack of the old, small Cokes in the fridge, the kind each little bottle with a shot of caffeine as strong as a big cup of Joe. He took one and took it down with quick gulps.

"Don't you want some ice?" Liz said. "I found rum for Cuba Libres."

"Nah, I just want to come down so I'm basically rational when the cops arrive," Jim said. "That DynaFlo is insidious. The quickest way down is sugar pop. When I talk to Captain Fregosco, I don't want to spill beans that are better left unspilt. Miller is dead, Rick is passed out and Olga's still inside watching her horse opera. She didn't see you come in, did she?"

"No, I came in the back gate, and snuck up the back stairs," Liz said.

"Here's my car keys, it's the blue Plymouth in the next block past the chifa," Jim said. "Before you go, you got any more Dilaudid in your hiney pack? Derrick's in bad pain."

"Here, take the bottle," Liz said.

She carried the opiate for kidney stones, which would form with a combo of heavy drinking, dehydration on long sierra treks, cream of spinach soup which she loved and was full of calcium oxylates, so she carried a bottle of twenty-five strong dosage with her, no problem in Europe or Peru, had gotten hassled as a possible mule on the way to her father's funeral in Iowa, maybe a good thing since she had somebody official to be pissed off at besides her dead dad, who couldn't correct or direct her any longer. It was stark weather on the prairie when they laid him in the deep loam, frozen half down, twenty years and she was still thawing to Jim's steady warmth, all right she liked to be on top, but then he could bring her bum down.

"Hola, estoy llamando al capitan, me llamo Jaime Hiram, con un poco de emergencia," Jim said, when Capt. Fregosco's wife answered and said he wasn't in, but when she learned it was Jimmy, she went and got him from in front of the TV. "Two gringos, both down, I'm calling an ambulance."

The story he told El Capitan was that there'd been another incident at the Pension Inglesa, not fifteen minutes away from him, again involving American Scholars, this time two odd-ball gringo professors who'd gotten into a fight at the Pension Inglesa, over some Inca idol, you'd think there was a curse, and Fregosco, whether it was he remembered the Chinese food Jim had brought to the last break-in there, or because he liked Jim, a turco like himself, or the schoolboy quiz games, Sennacherib, a snack of ribs, whatever, he said he'd be right over.

Next, he called the emergency squad and the ambulance got there before Fregosco, who arrived as they were getting Derrick down from the tree with a ladder Jim found in the tool shed. Jim told the captain that he had been over to visit Olga, had gone upstairs and heard the two professors arguing over a Silver Llama, whose it was and what it was worth, and was poking his head up from the stairwell when he saw the two of them get into it up on the roof, were wrestling with each other and Derrick Stephensen, the man they were taking off to the hospital, got thrown off by the man who was dead, who'd lost his balance after that and also went over. He'd called the dead man 'Miller' as they argued and later fought, and yes, there had been one gunshot downward and Miller had cursed, but Olga had the TV set turned up and he just saw a barrel flash, and they went over, one-two like that. Anything else, oh yes, Stephensen was a noted professor, married to an heiress, and it sounded like Miller was trying to get money from him, because at one point he asked how much it would take to get Miller to go back to Sinaloa, and he answered how about thirty-five million. What did the professor say? He just laughed.

"This appears to be his pistol," Fregosco said, picking it up with a handkerchief and giving it to his assistant who bagged it, then looking over the body, lifted the right pant leg with an unsharpened No, 2 pencil. "Evidently they struggled over the gun, this Miller shot himself in struggle, Stephensen bent over trying to wrest the gun away, was easily thrown over, but managed to grab the arm or shirt of his attacker, who was not as lucky in his fall as was his victim. Do you know what they do in Sinaloa?"

"Make tortillas, make TVs, microwaves, a lot of stuff with NAFTA, does GM have a plant there, must piss off the UAW," Jim said.

"Las drogas tambien, it's the center of a big cartel," Fregosco said.

"Wait a second, you remember that group photo from the '69 Ayacucho project, there was a guy named Miller who dropped out of the graduate program and was up in Mexico, rumor went he was doing all right in that very business you refer to," Jim said. "It's a common name so that could be wrong."

"I'll need to talk with Doña Olga, have you informed her of this?" Fregosco said.

"I didn't, because she was happily watching her favorite program, 'Nino'," Jim said. "She had so much stress with the first break-in, and her ticker's been erratic, I didn't want her to have a hissy fit before things were under control."

"It's 'Nino' I was watching it when you called," Fregosco said, sending his assistant upstairs to check things out, and take some photos while he went in at a commercial break to say he had responded to a call about a fall of Professor Stephensen, whom Jim explained she knew as Dr. Fogle, who had maybe been using an alias to avoid this Miller, who had broken in through the back gate, no problem now, the ambulance was taking them away even as the commercial ended and the program came back on, occupying their attention as Jim went to the storeroom to remove the kerosene can, the papers, the oily rags and the scrap lumber. In the last category was a rickety old box for 'sapo', a game in which iron quoits the size of sugar cookies are tossed toward the open mouth of the sapo, a brass frog's head affixed to the box, hopefully to pass through the opening to land thump within. Well, he thought it was old quoits stored inside, that were sliding around when he lifted it up. It was only one thump though and heavy like a shot-putter's shot. When he opened the box, he saw it was not a sapo quoit, but visible through the translucent bubble wrap, was the Silver Llama, its legs somewhat splayed out, looking more like a rocking horse than a llama. Relief more than exultation was his reaction when he found it, because he wouldn't have to wait for Mac to call, and that made things much simpler. He had no time for celebration, and put the statue in Miller's leather briefcase with the other crap he'd collected, which he'd stashed in the bushes by the garden gate, and went inside to see how Olga was doing.

Nino had finished on TV and Olga came out onto the terrace, identifying Derrick as Dr. Fogle, the quipu expert, before the ambulance took him off to the American Hospital. A second ambulance arrived to take Miller, whom Olga recognized as Professor Metz, who had previously visited Dr. Fogle there, though she had not seen him that night. They took Miller/Metz to the Lima morgue. Jim had cleaned up upstairs pretty well before Fregosco arrived. At least the big gringos had inflicted damage mainly on each other, and not like before with the mess of the broken chumpa and the mummy on the crapper. If there was a homeowner's claim on this one, Jim would handle it too. Olga, the old dear, had suffered enough trouble, shouldn't the last years be passed in tranquility and not in strife. He made a mental note to get Frank to buy her a new big screen TV with stereophonic sound after the disturbances she'd endured with her pension serving as a mise en scene for recent lethal incidents.

When Jim got home, the first thing he did was put in a call to Mrs. Stephensen at her place in the Hamptons, and left a message that Derrick was in the hospital.

After he got off the phone, he called the chifa and left a message for Mac that he'd found the present in the box and not to worry, and that Derrick was in the hospital. He didn't know anywhere else to get in touch with Mac.

Liz was unusually calm after her shoot-out at the Pension Inglesa, was fixing him a BLT in the kitchen, and he poured himself a stiff drink to sit on something hard. She said she didn't want one, unusual since she usually had a nightcap.

"Scared you straight, huh?" Jim said. "You really have reformed. Health food, quinoa salad, running, and no Kickapoo Joy Juice."

"Not really," Liz said. "It's just that, um, well, I just feel better without it now, it's got all those free radicals."

"Not me, baby, after a long day grappling bozos like Miller the Oaf, I want my rum ration," Jim said. "I'm no evangelista. No hooch for them. Like the Mormons, though they won't let you have an extra woman, even if you marry her. They're almost up to ten per cent now. They helped put Fuji in. Changes keep on coming. Tommy's been working on a story on the Colina Group and Tigre 96. It's like violence is all around and it lands in your garden. It's like blood splatters from an old crime. After ten years and not being guilty, you'd think the blood would be dry. If the houseboat in Tahiti isn't an option, and the shit keeps coming down here, where would you go?"

"Back to Holland, I guess," Liz said. "But don't you see a glimmer for Peru, to rise out of the violence and the corruption? I'm happy here with you. Christ, you made it through the civil war, it's got to get better. The economy's getting better."

"Yeh, over five per cent last year, Wall Street would die for numbers like that back home, and new big energy contracts like the Camisea gas fields, Halliburton's in the Amazon now, not the Near East, which is always touchy, and Newmont's mining gold in the sierra, I don't know how that'll work out when the campesinos see their sacred mountain pushed down in the valley," Jim said.

"Listen, you remember I said I needed to make one more quick trip up to Ayacucho to cover some gaps," Liz said. "It might not be a bad time now to make that trip, considering this evening's events. If the police start asking around, the SIN has a file on me. Up for a quick road trip."

"I'd love to go back to Ayacucho, but I can't get away now," Jim said. "I've been out of the office for so long. There's Stephensen, who's in the hospital. He needs emergency surgery. I've got to make sure his wife gets word. There's Miller, who's in the morgue. Captain Fregosco is no dummy. The question will have occurred to him, why was Hiram there at the time of this confrontation. Was it solely to be visiting Olga to check on the insurance claim? Maybe he asks around the neighborhood, goes to the chifa, and finds out you came looking for me. So it might not be such a bad idea for you to take a short trip. My world is in chaos. I can only take so much disorder. My garden looks like it was saturation bombed. My fig is smashed like a brontosaurus sat on it. I'm thinking of leaving the hummocks and installing a koi pond, or maybe piranhas or crocs for security. You might as well go because I plan to spend my weekend up to my bippy in mud, stinking of chainsaw oil and gas. I won't have much left after a couple days of that."

"So, unwinding in our own ways, you in your garden, me on a high country hike with my camera," Liz said.

The phone was ringing, and it was the hospital calling because he'd told them he had contact information for Derrick's wife and he needed emergency surgery. Fortunately, he had all the info in a current file, S/L/1.70, thanks to Rad, his Chicago rat dog dick, and had just called the phone number in Massachusetts. Smiling as he read the margin notes, 'mo' shekels than Rocky on wife's side, pet name, 'Pookie', Vassar grad. Field hockey, watch out, boy.' Ten minutes later, the phone was ringing again and it was Pookie.

"Mr. Hiram, this is Sylvia Stephensen," she said. "I'm very confused. I've just gotten a call from the American Hospital in Lima saying my husband is there and needs surgery. There must be some mistake. My husband is an archaeologist, but he's doing fieldwork in northern Ontario now."

"He was, but he actually arrived here on a mission of mercy to save some classic Inca art," Jim said, playing up Rick's noble quest to save it from a huacero, basically a grave robber, and giving a thumbnail of Miller, also including narcoterrorista, they used the huacos for ready cash, his joust and throw-down from the roof of the pension, Derrick surviving the lucha libre with a broken leg, the villain dead from a broken neck. "I happened to be there visiting the owner, a dear old friend of mine, when the ruckus broke out upstairs.

Yes, Derrick's going to be all right. I remembered him from Ayacucho in 1969. I've met many American scholars down here. I know you want to get him home a.s.a.p., but I talked with the best surgeon in Lima, and he said it would be best to operate before moving him, given that it's a multiple fracture. His nickname is Dr. Lazaro, he'd be happy to talk with you, he speaks English well, in fact, he did a post-grad fellowship at Johns Hopkins. Rick is under heavy sedation for pain, and they'd feel better if they had spousal consent."

"I'll call the hospital and the doctor right after I'm off the phone with you," she said. "I'll book the first flight out to Lima tomorrow."

"I think that's a good idea," Jim said. "I doubt if there'll be any inquiry about the death. I told the investigating officer that Miller was the aggressor and it was self-defense on Derrick's part."

"Can you tell me more of how it happened?" she said. "It's still somewhat unreal."

Jim said he was talking with Olga in her living room about an insurance claim and heard noise upstairs, went up and saw the light on in the third floor room and heard the two men arguing, just snatches of conversation, including the Silver Llama, which Derrick wanted for its archaeological value, and Miller seemed to be holding him up for money, talking about millions, and then they struggled on the roof, a flat roof because it never rains in Lima, a couple inches a year, so there they were in a dim profile above like a couple of wrestling bears, getting closer to the edge, then a gunshot, Miller cried out, evidently shot himself, and in the process of throwing Derrick off, he went over too. Fortunately Derrick had better luck and landed in a fig tree. It was definitely self-defense, he had no problem testifying to that if it came to that, and he knew the officer.

"Derrick was defending himself," she said. "They can't call that a crime, can they?"

"It's a clear case of self-defense, but I can't guarantee what they do here," Jim said. "I'm mainly in financial planning now, but I'm an attorney, and though not an expert on Peruvian law, I do know how things work down here. I don't think you want to get involved with the legal system. Costs can run as steep as in the Silk Stocking and the Gold Coast. I told the responding officer it was self-defense, but he may still have questions. I'd bring travelers' cheques, fifties and hundreds are good. Don't dress up or wear much jewelry. Be careful of your purse in the airport and on the streets. Thieves cut the straps, or drag you behind the Vespa until you let go. In fact, wearing a money belt or a girdle is best."

He could tell from the tone and tenor of her voice that she had sensed the imputation of bribery, and that the suggestor was perhaps in some scheme to skin her, whether in concert with Derrick or some other con artists, so Jim mentioned he had already advanced three hundred to the hospital to make sure her hubby got a private room and good attention, he always carried enough cash in his wallet that the rateros would know he was somebody and wouldn't kill him, dropped a couple of names that Helen had known from back to the days of the Seven Sisters, and told her he once went skiing in Poughkips when it snowed, nasty weather all weekend. It was nice in Lima now, but bring a sweater, or buy a nice vicuña one here, perfect for an evening chill. She knew Rob Emerson, and Jim said he knew him too, very sharp, actually knew Mari Emerson better, very nice, a better reference for him than Rob, explaining that knowing the scholars was not always loving them, since their lovability quotient varied greatly, a general truth she could relate to personally.

"Did he say anything else, anything about me?" Sylvia said.

"He was rambling on before the ambulance and police arrived," Jim said, speculating that Miller, who was rumored to be mixed up the Sinaloa Cartel, might have drugged him, and since he had been assiduously restoring the shine of professional honor to her wayward hubby in saving precious endangered Inca art, why not add a romantic reason to season the bread of mercy. "Um, do you know anybody called 'Pookie'?"

"His pet name for me is Pookie?" Sylvia said.

"He was rambling on about Pookie before the ambulance and police arrived—I think he thought he was dying," Jim said, speculating that Miller drugged him with a talkative substance known as DynaFlo, to make him malleable and cooperative, but he had resisted, was a big strong fellow, and threw the villain over with him, the vice with his gun and lathe, and that Rick had told him when he thought he was in extremis hanging from a tree, to tell Pookie I love her and she was right, the little bitch who had her claws in me, I was getting away from her when I came to Peru to save the Silver Llama. "The main message was he loved you, Pookie, and was sorry if he ever hurt you."

"He can play it up," Sylvia said.

"I don't think he was acting, in fact he kept rambling on about Pookie until the ambulance took him away," Jim said, saying that DynaFlo had an effect like truth serum. "She was just a bit of fluff, I cut it off, I knew enough."

"My poor big Pooh bear," Sylvia said, and he could hear her sniffling in the background, as she recovered from the idea that her seriously injured husband still loved her, what the hell, Jim could understand that, the seabirds on the cliffs of Miraflores still called for their mates, his trouble had been that his birds had all flown away, Helen had been in Philadelphia for two years now, the native Pocha had expatriated to Europe during the Terror, the Iowan Liz was on her way out of town with another possible homicide investigation pending, she really didn't need that with her file, so two weeks in the sierra wasn't such a bad idea.

—ɯ—

Having just committed justifiable homicide on Miller and done a reputation rehab of his co-conspirator, Derrick Stephensen, for the well-feeling and being of his spouse, who did arrive that next morning though she checked in first at the Sheraton before she went to the hospital, Jim had another surprise when he met Pookie there in the waiting room.

His first impression was, well Princess Grace was a beauty, but Pookie is very pretty, God, Derrick, you're a complete idiot, a rich, lovely woman who is jealous of your love, why, because she's a model with mileage, yeh, you're an archaeologist but you're just like all the business execs who need a young trophy wife. It's a predictable pattern, twenty years out the professors divorced the wife who put them through grad school and took up with their grad student twenty years younger, it was alpha males needing fresh young stuff if you're having trouble getting it up and off, got to trade her in for a new model, just like those vampire stories that had become so popular in current American Literature and TV, maybe not such a bad central metaphor, in Peru there were legends of those witches who drank the blood of others. And President Velasco had spoken of the landlords no longer living off the poverty of the campesino. He thought there must be some fatal flaw about Sylvia, was she psychotic, a Wicca, a sister of Lesbos, a total bore, a puritan prude, but no none of that, in fact, quite knowledgeable about art, knew the Boston Museum of Fine Arts collection well, knew art maybe not as well as Helen, but it was fun to talk to her about it. He took her to the Granada for lunch, it was small and intimate, but with those high colonial windows that had sills below knee level and went up ten feet, and had excellent photos of the Cordillera Blanca and the Cordillera Negra, and a deli case with fresh fish on ice. He had the blackened sea bass and she had the pollo a la milenesa which he recommended with an Ocucaje cabernet sauvignon, nice body, smooth finish, and with a kick from the equatorial sun. It was a good choice, and she opened up about the frustrations she'd experienced with Derrick over the past two years, well, two years without sex and Jim felt more like he was Cary Grant in a glitzy thriller on the Mediterranean Coast, oh wave to Ari and Jackie on their yacht, is that a bikini, though he managed to gull her into accompanying him on his weekly visit to the soup kitchen, they got into cooking the day's stone soup where everybody brought something and all of them shared in the sustenance. Then on to Sister Rose, in her Notre Dame sweatshirt, she was a saint except for that, he had a running bet with her on the Michigan game, Woody wouldn't play N.D. because he didn't want to risk losing recruits from the parochial schools in Ohio, or just losing, the Irish were pretty good in the day. She ran a charity for street kids and tried to feed them and give them basic education, so feed the body and the soul, she'd take in the difficult cases, like the crippled boy with a speech defect whose mouth the other street kids stuffed with mud and left him on the pavement. He'd called ahead to her to tell her he had a big fish visiting, and the kids were great, bright-eyed they recited a poem for their visitor, and had drawn crayon pictures of trees with suns and them playing. They sang to her, a little ditty about a bird called Puquicitu, and they all stood up and said Bienvenido, Sra. Stephensen, and muchas gracias for your help. When she had tried to pay Jim back for his deposit for Derrick at the hospital, he had told her to divert it as a donation in my name, explaining the tax advantage would be better for her in her bracket, and was stunned when Rose came over and told him she'd upped the ante to ten thousand, and thanked him for what he'd done.

Since that was right after their first intimacy, it felt somewhat like being named gigolo of the barrio, not that he felt a hell of a lot of guilt about it. It was kind of like he was single and she was obviously contemplating divorce and getting revenge for her hubby's waywardness. When the prim angel said shame on him, he was reminded of Voltaire's Last Words, to the priest who implored him to renounce Satan: "Now Is Not The Time To Make Powerful Enemies." A corollary of that for Jim was 'Now Is The Time To Make A Rich

Friend', a special friend in Pookie, since she had a net worth in excess
of the capitalization of the insurance company with the policy on
Larsen. She had a bit of exhibitionist tendency, oh, did aristocrats
ever ignore their Pookie babies, probably better than abusing them;
it merged into his nightmare set back in Olde Durfee trying to find a
bathroom after a night ramble, it was all different, new shacks and the
dorm had been occupied by a Commune and they had hot plates, TVs,
microwaves, Internet, had to go through side passages, ménages, tent
cities, pull-down stairs, it was like the Paris Commune, and when he
got to the top, there was a commode, mission fulfilled, but Pookie
slipped in ahead of him, when it was his turn and he really had to
go, yeh, like do they still let maids attend you in Poughkeepsie, and
bring livery. Can I find a bathroom where I can be alone? A producer
came through from the adjoining suite leading a goat and smoking a
cheroot, scratching his beard and looking for talent while you were
questioning the meaning of existence when your every waking hour
was theirs taken up for the texts they had chosen, St. Anselm, St.
Jean-Paul's Huis Clos, Gammer Gurton's Needle. You were charged
with conscience, but not with wisdom, and to question the wise men
was risky. Pookie had asked how he landed up in Lima, which was
where they sent him instead of St. Elizabeth's, because he was crazy
and didn't play dominos by the rules, the people in charge who had
beat Hitler and Tojo, they didn't see things the same as him with the
Soviets pushing in Cuba and the Third World, thought containing
communism was job one, while he thought defeating poverty was
more important than the Dulles Doctrine. Of course the state had
the machinery to control its enemies. A group had broken into the
FBI office in Philly in '68 and found the files on antiwar dissidents,
and the FBI promised Congress it would cease and desist busting
on the dissenters, but word was slow to get out to provinces of the
heartland, damn, they would stifle in the fight for freedom, and their
paramilitary civilian corps was also strong, so they deduced he was
somehow in with the Quakers who broke in, because he'd once dated
a Bryn Mawr girl who was involved in the antiwar movement, and
somehow knew about their informant, Mr. Buer, a Philly wealthy

individual active in the movement, who'd murdered his female partner in a paranoid rage, and then expatriated to Europe to avoid prosecution, not that they were so anxious to bring him back. Yeh, the FBI wasn't above getting into your undershorts, or telling about your family, screwing with your personal life and professional reputation, they'd spread the rumor in Paris that Jean Seberg was pregnant by a Black Panther. There was a law in Uruguay against writing anything derogatory about high officials of another country, maybe from the days when banned journalists fled Peron to Montevideo, where they could keep up the good fight. It was kind of funny that that law meant Jim could be tried there for saying J. Edgar Hoover was a blackmailer, and plotting to paint a moustache on his portrait, his defense, disappearing ink.

So Lima was a cosmopolitan city, despite the poverty of the urbanizaciones, it was nearly eight million now, about the same population as New York City had when he went East in '61. He'd found a niche in Lima after a couple of false starts, first in international law, then in journalism doing mostly travel pieces like the one on the Brazilian homing parrot, at three hundred bucks a throw that wasn't going to make it, so by serendipity and thanks to Mari Emerson's dad, who was a Chicago stockbroker, Jim received good training to get into stocks, and he'd made some friends getting them into MicroSoft early, including his old buddy, Frank Mathiessen, who'd grown up in Minnesota and saw the people who'd invested early in 3M, who had their big cabin cruisers on the lakes, it had pulled back recently and there were new darlings, but the thing Frank was up against if he sold MSFT now, he'd have a huge tax because he had like a thirty-fold profit on it, and the U.S. capital gains rates were high and steeply progressive then, so Jim was advising some college trusts and charitable deductions for him.

Yeh, Jim knew enough about law to think it might have been a hard row to hoe back home, the move south had been well advised, after Kent State it was pretty clear the powers that be were serious when they said, 'America, love it or leave it.' It was brave but sad, his Mom's riposte, 'America, love it and change it', this after the IRS audited Dad's estate tax return, 'Yeh Milhous wasn't the first to use the IRS, m' fallow Mercans, you know how we treat liars, cheats, and hippie draft-dodgers. Hope she never believed any of their crap about him. Sad ending now for a wonderful woman, in a nursing home like Helen's mother was, the mind disintegrates with Alzheimer's, she who was your faro when the world was dark and chaotic, is now crumbling into the Lethean stream. I am left to stand. But me, right now I wish I didn't remember things so well, didn't see them quite so clearly, because I have not been without sin since then and feel I have much I'd like to forget.' The affair with Sylvia was something he really enjoyed. He had briefly entertained the illusion of going back to Boston with her, sure, he could become a Patriots fan, even get premier season tickets with her funding, you needed a fat sponsor, enough to pay off that Cambridge parking ticket he got at the Tute years ago, then stop in at the inn with the Black Madonna portrait and quaff an ale. Some dreams, eh, it soon became clear she wasn't staying in Lima. What he hadn't understood was her love for Derrick, whom he had viewed as a sententious buffoon, definitely a fool for having estranged her. He'd been under heavy sedation for most of the week after orthopedic surgery, having had a stainless steel pin inserted in his femur, but when he was out of it, she would visit and they would talk for hours until he fell off again. Rick was quite anxious to speak with Jim, and of course, talk would inevitably turn to the Silver Llama, a subject whose whereabouts he did not wish to discuss at this time, so he'd been dodging coming in to the room. Sylvia was fine with that after their nonce coming together, having asked Jim not to mention anything that had gone on between them. Of course he would vouchsafe her that, he wasn't a rat. After several inquiries from her recuperating husband, he finally scribbled a note: 'Rick. Llama is safe. Mac went to garden. J.' There was neither a causal, nor a temporal relation between the two sentences, though one might be assumed. He needed to talk with Frank about the ultimate disposition of the piece, because he agreed with Mac that it was best that it should be in a Peruvian museum. So there were Frank's interest and Derrick's expectations to be dealt with. Derrick was still in a full body cast, he'd broken a couple ribs in addition to the leg, but in a week and a half the doctors thought he could be moved, and Sylvia was planning to take him home as soon as possible. She made it clear to Jim that she wanted to cool it between them, and he gave her his thumbs up to that, included a soft shoe rendition of 'Just One Of Those Things', (It Was Great Fun, but it was just …), a kiss on the cheek, his business card, put her on his client list to receive his fortnightly newsletter, which he hadn't gotten out for two months now. He'd blame it on El Niño.

—∿—

Helen called that evening to tell him her mother had fallen and broken her hip the previous week, had contracted pneumonia, and was seriously ill, they didn't know if she'd make it, and she seemed to have lost her will to try. He told her he'd come back to be with her because he could hear the anxiety in her voice when she asked him to. He needed a couple of days to catch up at the office. It was a convenient time to go, and the last evening before leaving, he got a call from Mac. It was good he called, because Jim didn't want him visiting Derrick and telling him he didn't have the Llama. Mac didn't even know Rick was in the hospital, nor that Miller was dead, so it was news to him the story about their wrestling on the roof, and Jim finding the Llama in the sapo box when he dragged it from the pile of scrap wood.

"The Llama wasn't worth anybody dying for," Mac said. "If I'd just given it to them…"

"It would have come out the same or worse," Jim said. "Miller admitted to Rick that he killed Val. He was one aggressive dude and was not going to be appeased. He'd have probably melted the Llama in the fire he was planning for us. Now it'll go to a museum in Peru if

I have my way. I have to finesse Frank on this. Let me know where to get in touch with you, so I can invite you to the donation ceremony."

"I'm at the Hotel Bolivar now," Mac said. "I wanted someplace with security after all this."

"It's not going to be tomorrow," Jim said, because he had decided to take the Llama with him back to Philadelphia to get it checked at Penn and have a copy made for himself if he was giving the damn thing to Peru. He also made a note to call his writer, L. May out in New Mexico, who was working to turn his notes into 'Tihuantinsuyo Quartet' and have him revise his version of the '86 shoot-out at the Bolivar when Liz had wounded Haberman, an ex-SS officer and art dealer, after killing his driver, Otto, which he had in his notes described as having gone down in the old 'mistress wing' of the hotel, then under renovation, and the wounded Haberman falling down those lovely marble steps toward the lobby with its exquisite crystal chandeliers, evoking a scream from one of the British women playing bridge in the lobby, of course, a total fabrication—he visualized those scenes in the Bolivar for effect, the events had actually taken place down the Colmena at the Hotel Crillon, another top downtown hotel whose big claim to fame was that John Wayne had stayed there when he was filming in Peru, but Jim wasn't a big fan after Duke said all the protestors were fags and posers, had the wool pulled over their eyes by the commies and liberals, yeh, the military was already shunting blame for the defeat onto the liberals pulling funding, not blaming a flawed strategy, they thought it'd be another Korea, but no, a lot of differences, Indochina had been one of the worst-administered French colonies, then the Japanese took over, against whom the communists were the patriotic underground, and now the Americans arrived in the shoes of the French. He'd read Bernard Fall and Schoenbrun, and that was enough to turn him against the war before Walter Cronkite announced there was a credibility gap. No, the Bolivar was a still top-rated hotel, and though it presented a classy mise en scene for the gunplay, he didn't want the book May was writing to get him in trouble or defending a lawsuit, one aim he had was to benefit Peru in some small way, and anyway the Crillon was getting pulled down to make way for new construction, so they wouldn't be suing him over business reputation any time soon.

Note one was 'change (arrow Bolivar to Crillon, claim to fame, Duke slept here). Note two concerned the Silver Llama, which was in his carry-on case, and he was preparing to defend to customs officials as a world heritage object which he had first discovered and had recently saved from narcoterroristas, but they didn't even hassle him in Miami about it. Note two was to call Rolfe and get a duplicate or two made of the Llama, because Jim had made some money. So one thing was to have a copy that could be a souvenir, he still wanted the original to go back to Peru where he felt it belonged, and the next was to have another copy for Frank, who'd paid him to get it for him, and could be possessive, or for Derrick, who was obsessed with it, but whose position was still subject to some leverage, no need to make more copies than that, Rolfe, kind of want to keep this in the family.

Oh, and who was Rolfe, an artist, actually an art forger aka the Black Forest Dwarf, who had helped Helen identify a Durer which she thought was suspect, verified it was a forgery, for which the Paris museum that she worked for then, which had been preparing to pay millions for it, had been quite grateful. Rolfe had gotten in trouble in Europe after having expertly reproduced Hellenic koroi, archaic period stand-up straight ahead statues, closed form, even rarer than much finer work such as Discobolus or The Winged Victory, and had scammed a major museum for millions for pieces now lingering in its basement, having used marble from an Attic quarry and aging the statues in a slurry of donkey dung. Rolfe had begun his art career in the time-honored tradition of copying various masterpieces of European art and was so good at copying that he had produced his own personal German economic miracle, not without attracting the attention of the authorities. Jim helped him with his visa application, and had seen him at work in his studio near the Delaware Gap, it was incredible what he could do to recreate art from ages past. He had done some Knights Templars' jeweled daggers and chalices, which were good sellers, so Jim trusted him to make a copy of the Llama, actually two or three, didn't want to mass produce them.

"It doesn't look much like a llama," Rolfe said. "Looks more like a Brancusi hobby horse, quite stylized, except these few marks on the belly."

"I assure you it's authentic Inca," Jim said. "Don't scrape off much patina, but maybe just a tad, if you could pick up those marks, I'd appreciate it. You might keep it in your safe when you're not working on it. A couple of men have died trying to get a hold of it. Another got sent to the hospital. I'd lock the gate and leave the Dobermans out tonight."

"Ach, if you scam a museum, they don't kill you or break your arm," Rolfe said. "Is it so valuable?"

"I'm not sure, it's not unique, it's a standard votive form, I couldn't say twenty thousand or fifty thousand, it's not a Van Gogh, but the people after it are somewhat nuts," Jim said, inflating the value so he'd take care of it, explaining it could be worth more if it were shown to be from the half century immediately after the Conquest, and those marks were inscriptions, Roman letters, Arabic numerals, a cross, had all been suggested, but it was possible it was corrosion of the silver. He tried to give a thumbnail of the syncretism of Andean religion, so you could still find platos of food to feed the spirits of the place alongside the Christian cross, which they knew had been a cross for them to bear in their history, even as they believed in El Señor, Christ the Savior, they knew what burdens were, still carried a small rock along up a steep path to deposit at the summit pass on an apacheta pile as a symbol of the journey and the weight they carried up and were relieved of. They had had ghost dances to pray to be rid of the curse of the white colonizers, just as the Sioux and other North American tribes had, and he could imagine a capa cocha ceremony to apu in Ocros, praying to the old gods and inscribing on their votive Llama the marks of the invaders, possibly as a contra, a spell against their spell.

"So, belt and suspenders, right?" Rolfe said. "Yes, I'll look very carefully at these markings. Do you plan to sell these copies? I may need Peruvian silver if you want make sure they'll pass for authentic."

"The original's going to a museum," Jim said. "I just wanted a copy for myself, and another for a friend, maybe three in all is good, I might have a problem with the guy who's still in the hospital. He was hot to get it before he got thrown off a roof. He's married to a very wealthy woman so I should take him into consideration. And on the topic of wealth and being aware, you know Seymour Industries is going through a transition period with its Chicago investors. Some problems I've experienced in my little Garden of Eden, might trace back to those problems. Helen doesn't want to deal with them, she's got her mother to worry about, and she puts it off to me, and I say, look, we don't need it if it's a hassle, you'll get pennies on the dollar for your stock if they push it into bankruptcy. You need your own bankruptcy expert, and I get her a name, and she doesn't call of course. And her brother is a total black sheep, not just a cocaine addict, but a compulsive gambler, it's like an open spigot on the money barrel. Speaking of balance sheets, did you see that about their accountant who went overboard and drowned while yachting in the bay. Hey, you know why Washington crossed the Delaware? You may need to know this for your citizenship exam."

"To get to the other side?" Rolfe said.

"Actually to slaughter Hessian mercenaries asleep after a nice Christmas dinner and heavy drinking, lock your gate," Jim said, thinking back the Llama was indio and the Native American peoples were referred to as savages in the Declaration, the Crown has failed to protect us from the savages, and the Brits' response, armies are expensive, thus the taxes, though no Yanks in Parliament. Ah, so great to be back in the Cradle of Independence, though Hartford took the cake as far as insurance companies. "I would keep this locked up in your safe. People have been digging around in my garden. One of the men who died going after this statuette, used to work for the Mexican mob. He'd been using it as bait for a bigger case, namely, a $35 million insurance claim for a former Seymour Co. exec who disappeared in Chile. You know Vince, he's been with the company from the Creation, ever since he graduated Penn State, he said the new elements now hold the upper hand."

"New elements? Are we talking about the mob?" Rolfe said.

"I'm sure it's all legit biz now, but just lock it up, man, and maybe make five copies," Jim said, counting on his fingers, thinking what if Emerson, the other survivor of the Gang of Four besides Rick, wants the Llama, and Frank, a classic A-type, may not be on board with this donation gift idea, besides if I get more heat off the Larsen case, I might want to sell the copy to Rick for a hundred and fifty thousand, that'd be something toward relocation expenses, oh, but I couldn't do that to Sylvia, I could do it to Rick, but not to her. Rolfe does such a nice job. I'm going to need a backhoe in for my garden, and those things aren't cheap. Yeh, he could sell two copies to Emerson and Derrick, give one to Frank, give one to Rolfe, who'd make one for himself even if Jim didn't suggest it."Yeh, make it five copies, four for me and keep one yourself. I may have some silverware you can melt. I only use stainless now."

It was past eleven when Jim got back to Haverford Mills, Helen was waiting to go to the retirement home, but the golden lab, Chessie, burst out the screen door and greeted him with an effusion of tail wagging. He had to go back in the house to lead the pooch back in and distract her with kibbles while they both slipped away. Helen looked preoccupied, and somewhat dejected, so he told her she looked lovely, and she squeezed his hand, and allowed a passing smile as she turned to watch the old house with its overgrown Weigela and grapevine, disappear behind them.

"Steel yourself," Helen said with a neutral-vacant intonation that chilled him. "She was doing better, but then she had another fall. Getting out of bed to go home. They don't like to restrain them, but she went over the guard rails on the bed. Another drop down mentally and they may have to put her in the dementia unit."

"I'm sorry," Jim said.

"I thought she might have a couple of reasonably good years in assisted living, but no such luck," Helen said. "I even thought she might come home after a couple of weeks. But she declined very quickly."

They went in to the nurses' station where they encountered a pleasant elderly woman patient sorting the records. She'd been a head nurse in her real life and was always coming down to the desk to try to run the show. That wasn't bad compared to the man who sang "Home On The Range" over and over again, and the woman who screamed all through mealtime.

Here it was in glorious Technicolor, the kick in the rear Life gave you at the finish, and the experience of another dim, depressing shade toward its end. Not that there was anything wrong with the nursing home. It was top of the line, good food, very clean, high ceilings and good HVAC system, minimizing the scent of urine that was pervasive at places not so well run.

"I keep wondering if I'd been here, she wouldn't have hurt herself," Helen said.

"Don't hit yourself over it," Jim said. "There are people here whose children never visit."

"She doesn't always recognize people, even me," Helen said. "Don't feel bad if she doesn't know it's you. It's happened with me."

"I know it's rough," he said, hugging her before they went in the room.

"So that's life," she said. "Another load of crap dumped down."

"It's like the old German peasant saying," Jim said. "Life is like a chicken ladder—short, steep, slippery and full of shit. I offer you that folk wisdom from my Cincinnati kraut ancestors."

People frequently said 'things could be worse' in a general way, but it was the specific examples such as the man singing "Home On The Range" over and over that brought it home. The idealist philosophers like Kant could ramble on for chapters about categorical imperatives without a single example from life, so the reader was forever waiting for the one last chance example at the edge of a cloudless desert of vast metaphysical dryness, but there were plenty of examples around of how things could get worse. Just fall down or soil yourself and descend to the dementia ward; it wasn't as bad as a solitary cell on Devil's Island, but then not much was. There were countless ways things could be worse, and hanging around Peru had given Jim ample examples. The nurse's aide had dressed her mother nicely and she was wearing the simulated pearl necklace she thought was the real thing, an anniversary gift from Harry, she thought it was really time they went home because he would miss her and set up a ruckus. She did look quite frail and needed them each to support her on either side on their way to the dining room for the old folks who still had their marbles, and had lunch at an excellent buffet with shrimp on ice, roast beef, breaded pork chops, kielbasa with kraut. Helen cried a little in line as she got her mother's plate, then was trying to keep her from having a second pudding because it would send her blood sugar through the roof. So Jim pulled the old one where he said, 'oh, go ahead, Joan', and she replied 'Did you have your eye on it? Go ahead and take it." The highlight of lunch period was the 'banana run' when the fruit tray was set out, because the residents liked to take a piece of fruit back to their apartments, so they all rushed, hobbled and wheeled to it like lions to a fresh kill. Due to his courtesy, Jim didn't get a banana for Joan, because the elderly all had it timed perfectly to get theirs, but it was just as well with her diabetes. She obviously had enjoyed the company, and conversed during lunch, despite forgetting things that had just been said a few moments before. It appeared she remembered him but when they were saying good-bye, she asked Jim what his name was.

"Such a nice young man you've brought home," Joan Seymour said. "You must introduce him to Daddy."

"I already did, Momma," Helen said.

"Well, he didn't tell me," Joan said. "I'll give him what for when we get home."

"You know they're painting the house, and the smell would give you a headache," Jim said. "I told them not to cut any of the shrubs because you wanted them just as they were."

"I want none of the bushes cut," Joan said, emphatically thumping her small fist. "You must make that perfectly clear to them, Mr. Horan. Harry would be beside himself. I can hear him now. Who ordered the scalping?"

"I'll make sure nothing is cut," Jim said. "Helen's been taking care of everything."

"She's put on some weight I think," Joan said.

"She can carry it, she's got the Devereaux height from you," Jim said, giving her a hug. "It makes her curvaceous."

The Wurlitzer organ was booming out a lively rendition of 'Alley Cat' for social hour assisted aerobics when they left the Scarlet Oaks.

Helen cried quietly for the first quarter hour on the way home, and then made him promise if she were bed-ridden like that, he'd make sure she'd have the music she loved, 'Moonlight Sonata' and not 'Alley Cat'. It was late afternoon when they got back to Haverford Mills, back to the old Shingle Style mansion with big wrap-around porches overwhelmed up to the roof gutters by vegetation from rules set down by those long since passed from managing the house. The weather had changed with a nor'easter dropping down from New England, turning a scintillating day into one haunted by shadows and the storms for sinners in the hands of an angry God. In short, the place reminded him of the House of Seven Gables, and not in a good, picturesque way, more like hauntology. He'd seen her the night before walking on the wing with the swing he'd unearthed stored in the garage with its long chains put in canvas bags that showed through rings of rust, renovated with polyurethane and Rustoleum, happy memories of swinging as a child, then sad with the ghost of a nice-looking college boy in wingtip cordovans, the steps fading away, that was where she lost it. That was the trouble with old ancestral mansion houses—they could support you or haunt you.

"It was a rough day," Jim said.

"I hope I die quickly and don't have to exist in a half-life for long," Helen said. "Just give me a gun."

"The Catch-22 is that once you get senile dementia you don't even know enough to pull the trigger," Jim said.

One plus about the depression the visit had created was the desire to live and enjoy that it spurred. They managed to make it back to her bedroom, with its oversize, ultra-plush four-poster bed and Empire bed curtain, dimly lit from a cloisonné Tiffany lamp on the bed-table where a copy of Anais Nin's Delta of Venus lay. It was like being in the overpouring mist of Niagara, her soft loins receiving the prow gliding into port, thumping hollow against the pylons of the dock. All the depression about her mother's decline and the terra incognita of their future seemed to have dissipated in the release of coitus. They were lying side by side afterwards, holding hands with eyes closed.

"Remember when we were first together, we used to talk about having a family," Helen said. "You used to talk about having someone to play toss with."

"Yeh," he said, thinking 'oh God, she was talking to her analyst about the miscarriage and now she's on a guilt trip, just close the door on it'.

"It might yet happen, I'm pregnant," she said. "I'm four months gone. The other time it was at six weeks, so the doctor said things look okay."

"That's great," he was able to say after pausing agape in a state of complete surprise. "How do you feel?"

"I feel strong, some morning sickness, at the moment I'm just depressed over mother," she said. "I didn't want to tell you in case I lost it. You know my biological clock is ticking. And I didn't know whether you still wanted a child."

"Of course I do," he said, running his hand over her belly, and thinking 'Oh, this is the big change, she won't come back to Lima, and I'll have to sell my practice, and now don't you feel like a cad having slept with Sylvia recently, well, at least she's a likely client if I repatriate, Frank would stay with me, and several others from Lima, and if I could get her to leave Philly for Miami, they'd come through on their way to Disney World, but she wouldn't go to Miami before Joan passes in any case'.

"What are you thinking?" she said.

"How happy I am, darling," Jim said, thinking 'oh Lordy, I don't have any birth coverage in my insurance, if she has complications, it'd cost a bundle, and I'll have to carry the ball anyway for money, with Seymour under adverse possession, and she won't go back to work for five, six years, maybe never, maybe if Rolfe could make about ten copies of the Llama, I'll need to find a buyer for my practice, Rosa Billups, that State Department employee, her husband was an econ major at Michigan State, and was looking for something more than teaching English, but they might be moving again if she stays in the foreign service, though they were talking about starting a family. "Just how happy I am, baby."

She was sleeping well, having told her natal secret and seizing a natural carpe diem moment after the Lunch of the Ancients at the nursing home. In the subsiding amorous aftermath Jim saw in his mind's eye the pure deep blue of the sierra sky and a red sandstone canyon with miles upon miles of pines beyond. He even knew where it was. He'd seen it at a train stop on the line north from Arequipa. Nearby he'd seen guanaco come rushing up out of a dry arroyo, small wild cameloids fast as antelopes, moving so fast he couldn't count whether they were three or five, disappearing in a second like smoke wisps rising and caught by a strong wind. It was just past the water stop up the long climb around the back of Chachani. It was right after exams and one of the drunk university students passed out and got his boots robbed by three macho gauchos who got on and were playing cards. Jim wasn't going to cry thief or mess with them, he was there to observe, not intermeddle, and they looked like hard dudes. It was like in that Dylan song, or in that Van Gogh painting of a pair of shoes, his own or another peasant's was the question, and it looked like it could be either way. There were immense pine plantations right after that stop, where he'd eaten a hot guiso stew with oja and quinoa, and down to the left from the tracks he could see a series of finger lakes in the pines and remembering he'd vowed back then to ride that line again, maybe hop off with rod, reel and backpack to see if any of those lakes contained good-sized trout, that train carried soldiers with submachine guns during Manchay Tiempo, maybe he'd make one last tour when he went back to wind things up in Lima, it was a real trip, Henry Meiggs had built Peru a great rail system, he could see a photo of him with his macho indio crew, a son of the Old Sod, fled San Francisco after a bond scandal, but paid it all back before he died, laid to rest in the Protestant cemetery in Lima, a good child of the patria, Jimmy dreamed of an honor ceremony where he could cry over how good he'd been, but he was out tossing ball with the kid, and the sky was so blue, sometimes things were deep blue and green after love, with war and strife it turned to red. No, there won't be one damn trout in all those lakes, just stay home and play toss ball with the kid.

—⁂—

Haverford Mills, PA

The phone was ringing, ringing off the hook, and he was surprised to hear Frank's voice at the other end when he picked up. Liz had called him to see if Jim was there when she arrived back in Lima and found the house deserted, with his impromptu concertina wire and tin gate after the break-in and bulldozing.

"Sorry I didn't phone you sooner, but I did manage to get that silver llama on auction in Miraflores, actually Mac bought it and gave it half to you, and half to me, because we found it together," Jim said, trying to prepare him for the idea of a joint donation. "I have it in my possession. I'm looking for my sketch of it and I'm getting a carbon dating. If it comes in at 1570, it may be worth a lot more. Mac thought it would be a good idea if we donated it to a museum in Peru."

"But I gave you five thousand to buy it," Frank said, in that type-A Mr. Business tone, which before had convinced Jim not to go up and work for him even when things weren't going smoothly in Lima.

"Well, Mac got to it before me," Jim said, describing the events that had led up to his discovery of it in the sapo box at Olga's pension, and the surrounding lethal and injury consequences, Derrick wanted the Llama enough to sell his soul, and when he got out of traction, he'd be right back on track to get it.

"My first impulse is I want it, why should this bum, Derrick, think he should have it?" Frank said.

"Just think about it, man, that's all I'm asking, you'd have a nice fat tax deductible charitable contribution if it's what we thought it is," Jim said, not pushing the fact that he had actually been the first to see it in the volcanic outwash near Mt. Ocros, and by Mac's donation, was co-owner or joint owner of the Llama and had some say in its disposition, no need to say all that, because the situation was still developing, Jim had found his notebooks from Peru '69 stored in the garage, and somewhere in there was an Acuario school notebook with a sketch of the Llama they'd found. "I'm not even sure it's the same one we found, but if it is and it dates to the 1570's, and the marks aren't just something a collector put on, it may be necessary to build a museum just for it. Think about that. Aren't you already building a conference center near Nazca? Talk about a draw."

After they got off the phone, Jim couldn't go back to sleep, he was still suffering jet lag, so he went to the kitchen and made himself a salami and cheese sandwich with the brown mustard they used on dough pretzels, and gave a scrap of salami to Chessie.

He himself was preoccupied with the prospect of fatherhood. He thought of his desire for a son, or really a child, he could play toss with a daughter and teach her how not to 'throw like a girl', need to step into it. I can get her a Phillies ball cap and she'll toss like Robin Roberts, who had a record like Whitey Ford in the day, even without the Yankees' batting behind him, but coming home there would be different now. They'd had the block occupation and the police bombardment and fire at their black commune, and it wasn't like Peru didn't have bias, mainly anti-Indian and the contra, but it was more like Woody Allen described the ethnic condition in the neighborhood of his youth, everybody hated everybody else, so it all balanced out finally (joke).

'Where will we live, I don't want to live here, this place needs major renovations before it goes on the market,' he'd already encountered the mountain of past crap stored in the large garage, big as most houses, formerly the old carriage house so big because it was a stable with remnants of harnesses and tack from when her progenitors were cautious about prospects for the internal combustion engine. Horsehair cushions were still the norm in Harry's office, he evidently had a bomb shelter out there because Jim found a case of Jack Daniels in the closet out of which flew bats when he opened the door. He'd put many of his memorabilia files and law files in bankers' boxes stacked chest high with tarps, and pulling down the old Peru files was such a drag, he'd sent those back to Philly when Sendero was coming to Lima after eighty-five, thinking it was time to leave then, but now with a birth at home, there was something more compelling for him than fleeing violence. It was time to leave back then, they'd heard Bob Marley's 'Exodus' at Runaway Bay on their stopover in Jamaica on the way back for a visit, now it was past due, though he'd gotten used to siestas and the pace of Latin life. He was imagining getting some land a ways outside Taos and building his own house; he'd seen in 'Mother Earth News' a straw bale house and thought he could construct a file box house faced with adobe or stucco, but maybe not, after hassling bats, squirrels and raccoons in the garage, he could see it as a perfect nesting spot for all sorts of creatures, besides the kid would have to go to school. He was drifting off when Chessie set up a ruckus and was about to bust out the back screen door.

"Chessie, come," Jim commanded her without effect. "Bad dog. Very bad dog."

Chessie was not content to sit back and take his criticism, but surged through the door and instantly out to the carriage house where she'd been with him when he was into some old Peru boxes with a soapstone ekeque model of a farmstead to ensure prosperity and a charm with a llama fetus in a bottle, very interesting to her and possibly to some nocturnal critter, in any case she charged up to the old office. The barking increased and the sounds of a struggle, a howl and a whine as she came rolling down the stairs, landing right at his feet. Before he could grab her collar, she was on her way back upstairs. He flicked on the lights in the office and saw the mess, a couple of the Peru boxes opened and papers all over, including the Arcetura family tree, Olga was a distant cousin, another photo of Don Pedro El Progresivo on the balustrade of a hotel on the Cote d'Azure, April, 1912, a military quality map of Ayacucho province, he'd have to take that to Liz, whom he hadn't thought about today, but she'd understand when he told her about Helen, she knew he wanted a child, even as he knew Liz didn't. As he surveyed the mess, a back door opened and somebody went running down the stairs, the dog bolting after, and out across the big lawn that sloped toward a row of evergreens, catching up as the intruder was about to take the rough-laid stone wall, then a yip and a howl. She was breathing but not moving when he got there, so he wrapped her in his coat, ran back to the house for his keys and wallet, drove over the lawn and got her in the car, went back in to phone the vet, got the answering service and explained the emergency and they said they'd phone the vet's home and get her to meet them at the clinic. The dog had recovered enough to whimper in the back seat and he comforted her on the way, saying 'good dog, very good dog'. After the vet patched her up, found no broken bones, Jim took her home and carried her in to her bed. Helen had slept through the entire thing, so Jim went out to the garage office. He'd been thinking about the break-in, recalling talking to Frank about the Silver Llama right that afternoon, wondering if Derrick had pursued his obsession, had somehow learned that Mac didn't have it and Jim did, had hired some local talent for surveillance, perhaps a phone tap not judicially authorized. If Derrick was behind this cat burglar, Jim had put a shine on his reputation for Sylvia, he could put him right back in the doghouse. No, it was not right, these break-ins, beating their dog, with his wife pregnant. She had talked lovingly of her Lab, her companion on long nights when Rick was at the library, supposedly. It couldn't be Emerson, he'd seen gold Chimu funerary masks from the north, objects more valuable than the Llama. It would be good to get a donation ceremony on the drawing board, but he wouldn't tell Frank about tonight because it would just make him more possessive. Once the Peruvian antiquities authorities learned the background of the piece, it would be on their radar and not going to any private individual, not leaving the country.

And then, as if thought and act were melded in the moment, a manila envelope that had stuck in a box flap, popped out and on in was written in his hand, "Notebooks—Vinchos & Ocros, June-Sept, '69". Inside was the aquamarine "Acuario", with the water-bearer, a school kid pocket notebook that he had taken on the Ocros hike. It contained descriptions of the Hog they rode out there on, the Witch of the Woods, who sold them the llama charm, and there the sketch he'd made of the Silver Llama with the detail, oh, he felt like calling Rolfe and saying he was coming right over to pick up the piece before there was another break-in, no need for any copies, he wanted to return it to the nation of Peru where it could be assessed by a competent archaeologist, of which they had plenty, though not with the money the Americans had. Now he'd be able to see if this was the same piece they found near Ocros about thirty years before. He could donate his notebook to the exhibit, with an account of how he sketched the Llama on the terrace of the old Arcetura hacienda while recovering there and with Doña Lucita sipping maté through silver straws.

"Oh, my God, Chessie, what happened to you?" he heard Helen exclaim as he was going in to get another jacket, and he explained to her, Chessie had gotten into it with some wildlife creature in the garage, and she had recovered enough she was able to wag her tail a bit and try to stand up. No need to upset the pregnant wife, oh yes, they'd cohabited in Ohio before common law marriage was outlawed, and would have married in the National Cathedral but for Sendero bombing it the month before the date, a bad omen, must have been around the time they moved Pizarro, he'd been resting for four and a half centuries there, now in a nice glass case still in his dress armor cuirass, not a tall man, like the armor in the Tower of London showing men were generally shorter then, an illiterate pig-farmer an indigenista critic called him, but quite a brave soldier, a smart tactician, he won the Seige of Lima against a resurgent Inca army with the help of his princess concubine's tribe, formerly Inca subjects, taking a page out of the book of Cortez, so not the Tarzan did it single-handedly of Conquistador myth, yes, ruthless, avaricious, but smart, as the campesino saying went, 'smarter than an orphaned pig'.

He needed to make a list, talk to H. about wedding, no I'm not going to have a bunch of preppie snots being snide about my child, need to call Frank about donation plan, I'm inclined to give my half, you want to cut it in two, Solomon, need to call ADT about security system upgrade, they can laser the entire perimeter wired to a storm warning alarm and kliegs, got to run over to Rolfe right now, though it was dark and he had those Dobermans, it can wait til tomorrow, better not call if there's a wiretap, need to make a plane reservation to Lima, drop by the hospital and see how Derrick's doing, if Rolfe's already cast two copies, I could give one to him to keep working, or give the other to Sylvia for Derrick, she could keep the secret until the donation ceremony, it'd be nice to wear one of those silk sashes with a do-dad medal, one for Rick too, after all he rediscovered it after it was stolen, no need for all the details, hey they could use a charitable deduction. Need to get the gears turning before any new untoward evenement on the large insurance policy on Norman Larsen—shot in Jim's garden, et in Arcadia, tu, morte, morte d'Norman. Llama, llama, llama, a name, a flame, a camel.

Before he went back to Lima, he got together with Vince Scarlatti, who was always up for a good tennis match, and sharing the latest scuttlebutt re Seymour Inc and family shareholders. Of course Vince knew Larsen as Chief Counsel had a big insurance policy, didn't know all about the beneficiary designation or a pending case in Wisconsin, knew that Holly was separated from Peter, but they were still married, yeh, a good idea to preserve marital privilege, not to put too fine a point on it, but Vince already knew he had ample reason to distrust his brother-in-law and Holly, who had access and a big enough interest at stake to plant bugs and phone taps at the Haverford Mills family mansion, it had been right after he talked to Frank about the Silver Llama and the Ocros notebook that the cat burglar showed up in Harry's old office in the garage. So Vince said, sure, he'd drop by and check on Helen while Jim was away, bring Chessie some chew treats, she was recovering well, she was just good-natured, yes, dogs had temperaments just like people. She was a puppy when Harry had his fatal heart attack, and now she was over ten, old in dog years, so another for Helen to have to take care of. Vince was on the cusp of retirement from the company, so he didn't want it to go into Chapter Eleven, an option currently being kicked around, as by consequence might affect his executive pension, images of a nice retirement home in Florida with the pool and tennis court and boat in the slip, yeh, Vince would come around to check up.

On the plane back, Jim read the journal of Don Pedro Arcetura, the poor cousin who began in the late Eighteen Hundreds with a very small share of the original vice-regal grant in Ayacucho. His wealthier relatives had already moved to Lima, and they viewed Don Pedro as a handsome provincial, quixotic to speak of the beauty of the sierra, which in their opinion was cactus-infested desert populated by feral pigs and cheating indios who sapped profits due the Arceturas as absentee landlords. Don Pedro seemed to have a genuine love of the sierra, and instead of abandoning his small slice of a bad pie, he had been going around buying up for next to nothing his cousins' shares of that scrubby, high desert, periodically subject to drought and famine. But in his travels Pedro had been taking soil and mineral samples, all precisely labeled as to location, which he had analyzed in Sheffield, England by a young Scottish mining engineer, Edward Ingersol, similarly impoverished, whom he convinced to come out to Peru. That was Olga's father, yes, she was a Scot before she married a successful Limeño dentist and collector, all the great names of American Andean anthropology had stayed at their pension, the great Stanley Robe, Mac MacHenry and a bunch of others the grad students mumbled praise to as if they were the sainted. The old place had been much larger, a mansion in fact, with a formal European garden with a fountain in the center and overlooking it, a stone balustrade around an elevated terrace fronted by French doors like the set of L'Annee Derniere a Marienbad. After her husband's death, she sold it because she couldn't afford the upkeep, and then you needed to watch to keep from getting stuck with long distance charges to the States and unpaid liquor tabs, but she kept the Pension Inglesa going on a smaller scale, still able to hold forth as the grande dame and virtuoso raconteur on her slightly reduced stage, well it was somewhat shabby with the cats using the chairs and curtains as scratching posts, one might say 'frayed gentility', of course she thought Velasco a martinet, and of course he was a general who took power by a coup, but he had a serious reform plan for Peru, agrarian reform that helped liberate and enfranchise millions of campesinos, though of course there were losers, and she'd say these government bonds aren't worth the paper they're written on, five per cent, do you know what inflation was last year. A photo from 1912 showed Don Pedro as a dapper, well-dressed man with a neatly trimmed moustache and a silver-headed cane, standing outside a Riviera casino, a smile but subtle like Mona Lisa, the eyes having a sadness of having seen his own early hard times and the severity of the sierra. He'd give Dona Olga those books back along with the stock certificates and mineral rights deeds, of questionable value given the usual civil law treatment of subsurface rights, give them back because he was going home. He did want to make sure she got compensated for damages or loss of business, thought she might like a new big screen color TV to see 'Nino' on. Unfortunately she'd been checked into a hospital by her doctor for tests when he dropped by on his way from the airport, so he made a note to visit later.

Liz was at home and came out to greet him at the gate, and he kissed her after he made it through the barbed wire. He somehow felt she'd understand when he told her about Helen, because she knew he'd wanted a kid, she'd said she never did, because she thought she'd be a terrible mother, she loved to go on long hikes, take off at a moment's notice, liked her freedom, liked to run around, liked to mess around, enjoyed getting high, liked to have fun, all the things you needed to warn your kids about, so why even try when failure as a parent was inevitable.

She'd calmed down some as she got older, but was animated telling him about her last trip to Ayacucho, where she'd photographed another ceremony of campesinos whose village had been decimated by raids of the Sendero rebels and the government counter-insurgency forces, who in remembrance of their dead family, friends and neighbors had gathered in a procession that wound up an inclined plane of road hugging the side of a treeless mountain barren, some shots in black and white, some catching the vibrant Andean colors of the chullyus, the mantas and the full skirts, against grey background, like a scene from Pilgrim's Progress, it was quite moving for him, the campesinos knew the value of a ceremony.

"You didn't have any problems with the authorities afterwards?" Jim said. "Either there or from that night at the pension?"

"No problems in either direction, but sit down, honey, we do need to talk," Liz said. "I did have to go to the hospital when I got back. I thought I might have a vaginal infection, but the doctor told me I was pregnant. I suspected before when I'd missed my period twice, but there it is. I'm knocked up. I won't make you marry me, but you have a right to know. I've decided to have the child. Even if you aren't ready to be a dad to it, I know you were at one time, but things change, and you know I've always been keen on freedom. I don't plan to abandon travel. So I'm having the child."

"Of course, I can't tell you how happy I am," Jim said, because he really couldn't tell her that and the happy meter was fluctuating like crazy, thinking a bun in each of two ovens, this complicates things exponentially, I thought if I married Helen, I could get birth insurance, but two wives, this requires advanced juggling technique, maybe one common-law marriage with a separation agreement and the other a ceremony in the cathedral, it's vacant now they moved Pizarro, oh, what kind of mess have I gotten myself into Ollie, but I was so alone when Helen went back home, and Liz was there for me. "Darling, I can't tell you how happy I am."

"I'm so relieved you're not mad at me, because I didn't know whether I could go through with this alone," Liz said. "I don't know how good a mother I can be. I may need help. I never liked the idea of being tied down."

"That's okay, you can go off on your trips, I know how to heat bottles, burp babies and change diapers, what else is there, play peekaboo, play ball, take her or him fishing, maybe she'll be able to run like you, remember running from your senior skip day when you thought you'd lose your scholarship to Berkeley for drinking beer with your weird friends?" Jim said, hugging her. "My little runaway, I'll be there for you."

Whew, maybe best not to have back together again sex right now, Jim thought, escaping to his study to put away the Silver Llama as Liz fixed lunch for them, she could cook quite well when she wasn't cropping and printing negatives. He put the Llama in his safe along with his Ocros '69 Acuario ringed notebook, and took the four excellent copies Rolfe had made, each within a few grains of the original, and with a slight sulfur additive to mimic the Inca original, how he got the patina was an alchemist's secret, took those copies down to the basement behind his big oak door. It smelled like garlic, onion and soy on pork chops when he was coming upstairs, and he sniffed and gave her a pat on the butt, glad not to be having sex when he had been thinking about bigamy in our time, how could he have lived through the Sexual Revolution and gotten screwed by it now.

As if things would never calm down, Frank called him that afternoon and Jim was sure he was going to reject the idea of a donation of the Llama, he'd mentioned he already had a new glass case for it, but surprisingly he agreed that a donation would be the best disposition, so victory, but there was a wrinkle, nothing could be simple. Frank had business interests in Peru, had diversified from shipping into construction and was building a resort/conference center south of Nazca, but within a half-hour jitney ride, the tentative name being Cabanas Nuevo Mundo, to appeal to the New Age crowd that had already acknowledged the presence of celestial energy in the Nazca Lines, some wondered how and why figures not discernible from ground level had been constructed on the coastal plane, Liz thought it had been a initiation site, she thought youths rode the winds like Icarus from the bluffs above, they had cotton and knew sails and weaving intimately, perhaps the neophytes walked the lines before and then rode the wind above them on para-sails or balloons for the revelation of their pattern. Strange, in out of body experiences, yogins described seeing things from above as if flying, and if they, why not the shamans of the Nazca culture. Man seemed to need to escape consciousness at times, since we were always seeing the limits of what we could see and know. Anyway, the Cabanas already had a long house finished where the side road from the PanAmerican Highway entered the property in back, that was going to be a convention room/ reception center/alien teleport station, with a big fireplace at one end, high ceilings. The five completed housing units were nearer the bluffs over the beach, the pool was under construction, and Frank's idea was a private museum with a 99-year lease to the government, add the silver manta clasp he had kept from Ocros, and it would be a tourist draw to the south coast; these New Age people from the U.S. had money to travel and it was like a spiritual quest.

All Frank asked was that Jimmy take care of setting this up, not a given that the authorities were going to buy this deal, since the law, though widely ignored, was not finders keepers for antiquities, nor any right that a private facility could house them, but he immediately put in a call to Tommy Davila, whose column could use some human interest relief, after drilling without anesthetic into the BBQ Massacre of Grupo Colina, the desecration of the corpse of Mariela Barreto, shades of Tupac Amaru II being drawn and quartered in Cuzco, there's progress, surgical tools rather than draft horses. This could be like a feel-good story, two young gringos discover a Silver Llama thirty years ago, its shady and convoluted history, now one of those two, a millonario businessman in La Paz proposed to donate it to Peru on condition it be housed in a private museum on the south coast. The other gringo, namely, Jim Hiram, now a Lima financial planner and lawyer, and the one who first sighted the Silver Llama, said he had no doubt that the piece belonged to Peru, though he added he had seen the facility at the Nuevo Mundo Cabanas his old friend proposed as a museum to house the piece temporarily, and considered it a first rate facility, with barometrically monitored glass cases, and a strong security system, and would also discuss conveying the museum site to the nation or a lease with reversion to the state, the benefit to the nation being that it was a tourist draw and, like the museum that housed the Senor of Sipan north near Trujillo, it would be a stimulus to south coastal tourism, Peru was more than just Machu Picchu, saying he considered Peru his second mother, having lived there almost as many years as in the U.S., though of course he accepted any judgment of the republic.

In Peru you were able to be not only the godfather of a child, but also of an event. Frank also knew that putting money up front, made it more likely that such plans were considered likely to come to pass. He already had the place for it, and after the capa cocha discoveries of Reinhardt, a single silver llama in the classic Inca votive form wasn't considered especially unique, without the other evidence of the burial, and it wasn't a prime artifact because it recalled child sacrifice, the thinking then had been perfectly logical, the lord of the mountain, apu, was appeased, and the soul of the child resided in a high spiritual region, so now not such a popular fact, now with Toledo, the first president of full Indian blood to take office, it was another quite moving event to have his inauguration at Machu Picchu in Quechua, the tongue of the Incas, after four and a half centuries of oppression. Things were changing, but one thing endured, it was still good to have the do-re-mi.

—⟋⟍—

Three months later
South coast Peru
Nuevo Mundo Cabanas

Proceeding down the Pan-American Highway south of Nazca, Jim took a left on a gravel road to the Pacific bluffs where Frank's Cabanas resort was located, driving slowly because both Liz and Helen were complaining of feeling bloated and queasy and all he could hope for was that neither broke water before he got them to the resort suite. Up top around the first knob of granite were cantilevered condos perched like the rectilinear volumes of Neutra or with the landscaping not so clean-shaven, more like multiple Falling Water's without the Crafts Movement influence. In the center strip, beside the pool was another long house, whether Ojibwa or zen inspired, suggesting communal living, with just one employee at the desk, a cousin of Frank's Lucita, who told them there was ice down the corridor and a continental breakfast in the lobby. When he had the ladies settled in, he went outside to look around. The architect had produced a magnificent plan with terraced gardens and palms and willows overhanging the water along an acequia that came down from springs or drilled wells on the heights above. The designer had incorporated the images of parrots and monkeys, of jaguars and anacondas from the jungle, the highland Incas and the coastal tribes too, all the way back to Carel, were fascinated with the jungle, they still danced the Jaguar Dance in the sierra fiestas, every morning its ember eyes rose out of Amazonia and the outline of its teeth was the first silhouette. To the West the ocean and images of Orcas, of marine iguanas and seals, the concept for the resort being that environmental awareness, would appeal to New Age types, what marketing majors might call an overlap. Frank had already placed a few of his collectibles in display cases, and created a juice bar where you could get pleasantly juiced. A Caterpillar had cut out a sheltered crescent past the pool, black volcanic earth for clay courts, not much different from greensand, with green mesh screens on the fences with Lombardy poplar windbreaks, and tack-down white cotton lines already installed. Maybe Frank thought he'd lure Carlos back from Stanford in the summers to be tennis pro here, if he was intent on getting away from the paternal shadow, since it was clear his older two liked it in California and only visited once a year.

The road up to the upper big house was eroded in pencil gullies on the side berms, and Jim was thinking 'Damn, I wish I were big shit like Frank and had a bulldozer or even just a Bobcat,' though consolation was available at the bar at the end of his hike. He was sitting there nursing a Black Russian, when a guy behind him ordered a double Jack on the rocks, and the voice sounded familiar, like Milt Takita, one of the gang in Ayacucho in '69, not allied with the Gang of Four, he arrived that summer after Frank had been injured in his motorcycle crash, and they'd taken his Hog over many back roads of Ayacucho department.

"Hey, buddy, don't I know you from somewhere?" Jim said. "Maybe a Grateful Dead Concert in San Jose?"

"I don't think they ever played San Jose," Milt said, getting up and returning his compadre hug.

"I never liked friggin' jug bands anyway, bad associations with folk music, former girl friend a folkie and I was a rocker, it would have never worked, and those Dead concerts were like open fishing trips for narcs for kids dropping LSD, you know people did hard time for that in federal prison, and where's the band's responsibility?" Jim said. "And Altamont, man, Jerry says everything's cool, we got the Angels doing security. So whatchu been up to?"

"My latest thing is retooling a DC-3, this baby could land on a snowfield at eighteen thousand feet, just like in 'Lost Horizons' and Shangri-La," Milt said, who in his teenage years had retooled big-block Chevy's for drag racing. "I'm happy working for Frank. It's not every employer who understands the working alcoholic. You know this is an open bar. I'm thinking three day blow here. I will contact the ancestors when I am unconscious."

"Before you get to that state, I want to thank you for that last tape," Jim said. "The one with Hendrix 'Angel' had kind of a personal meaning for me. It was after love appeared miraculously and saved me from lonely despair."

"Jimmi was great, a poet like Collins or Shelley, seemingly fated to die young, after this creative burst," Milt said.

"So what do you think of your paisano, Fujimori?" Jim said.

"He's not my paisano, I've never been a fascist, and I hope they get him and find him guilty as hell," Milt said.

It was auspicious since soon afterwards the President, travelling to a trade symposium in Brunei, had felt enough heat from new revelations about his looting of the treasury, he didn't go home and ultimately was given political asylum in Japan, which refused repeated requests from Peru to extradite him to stand trial. A few years later, on a trip to Chile which he evidently considered a safe place given its own swerve hard right away from communism, was surprised to be extradited to Peru to face charges of theft in office, bribery of congressmen, and murder of Tupac Amaru rebels after their surrender in the Japanese Embassy hostage crisis, to mention just a few. He'd written a book detailing his micromanagement of the tunneling under, the surprise attack in which only one hostage died, and all the Tupac rebels died, except that another hostage testified that he had seen rebels alive after surrender, who were later found dead, shot execution style, the witness a former minister of his administration, it must have been galling to El Presidente, and incomprehensible to him that anyone could have any sympathy with terrorists, but the people were tired of violence, wanted peace and prosperity, also not to be run by privateers, it coming out he looted the national treasury of some $300 million plus, they were still freezing accounts in Miami and looking in Switzerland and Singapore. This rivaled the sum stolen by his former, SIN intelligence chief, Montesinos, who had been tracked down to Caracas, despite the repeated denials of Hugo Chavez that he was there, and not long after occupied a prison cell not far from that of Abimael Guzman, the former leader of Sendero Luminoso, a fearful penal symmetry, though neither was a Lamb, more like a brace of tigers, as if to say threats to the nation, whether from left or right, will be defended against.

Milt always liked to have somebody to get drunk with, and began to talk about his older sister, the one who taught him to swim by throwing him in Lake Tahoe after they got out of the camp in Arizona, the first accounting Ph.D. in California to make a perfect score on the CPA exam, and a poster child for the conservative Nipponese soul, Born To Save ethic that in the old country was stalling out Japan's massive economic engine, anyway it was good he was reliably and remuneratively employed now, and not just a rummy and a no-count hippie. Success is relative and when people used to ask Jim why he got into financial planning, he said it was because he didn't have the personality to become an accountant. It was good to see Milt again, and hear Frank had arrived in Lima, was now doing business and would be there later for the ceremony at four that afternoon. The catering trucks were rolling in with buckets of iced shrimp and oysters, lobsters and crabs, crates of wine and boxes of Jack and Jim Beam, champagne and silver buckets.

"Frank sure knows how to throw a show," Jim said.

"Reminds me of a New Guinea hog roast," Milt said, this from anthropology, (one of his seven undergraduate majors—he said he'd been on a quest for universal knowledge), referring to the Polynesian custom whereby a headman would sponsor a big feast like for an event such as a bungee jumping initiation, and thereby gain prestige. It was also the way for a fiesta in the pueblos jovenes, where a nine box of beer quarts per man was the estimate for a good party, and for chasers, cañaso, cane liquor, what a kick, like 300 hundred proof even though proof numbers only go up to 200, they'd never have passed Prohibition in Peru. They drank more beer per capita than Germans, so probably many alcoholics, and maybe a greater tolerance of a drinking man who held a job. It was good to hear he was now engaged to the 'Pepper Princess', a Japanese-Brazilian young lady he'd been seeing off and on for some time, her nickname from her family's pepper plantation. The family hadn't been exactly crazy about him, maybe after the time he came into Minneapolis in a long queue, began the weekend early with champagne the stewardesses had found, and got busted for alcohol by FAA inspectors, well, dishonor to the family and all the mores, but she loved him evidently, and that was what could save him from self-destructive impulses, eros ascendant over thanatos, he was smart and funny and had had a lot of experiences, they talked about the fiesta del condor when he was drinking like an Andean peasant, and had released the condor, got thrown in the hoosegow and Jim had to play the jailhouse lawyer for him, when he didn't much like being around places of confinement himself. Sometimes it seemed like he had a death wish, because life could throw all kinds of curves. There was some concept of honor Jim didn't fully understand, which gladly hadn't resulted in Milt becoming suicidal, unless one considered he might be killing himself with alcohol.

He got a bit more of a perspective on the honor thing after reading a story on the failure of a Tokyo securities firm, which described the rolling effects of the failure, the bankruptcies and suicides, saying every week there was some failed businessman who'd thrown himself in front of a train. It was tough to conceive. Jimmy had handled many bankruptcies when he practiced, he knew U.S. businessmen who had danced through several company or corporate shells, with no apparent guilt over disappointed creditors or investors. The Japanese took things entirely too seriously, but then the U.S. for all its openness was escapist. A sad, nasty, incomplete haiku occurred to Jim—

'Pale moon on Tokyo Bay, blood on the rails, inconvenient wait on the morning commute.'

He was glad Milt had found the right woman. He said he didn't drink while he was around her, and Jim believed him, but he definitely made up for it now that he was on his own.

"Frank sure knows how to festejar," Jim said, watching produce go in the kitchen, artichokes, avocados, cherimoya, super-sweet with a paw-paw custard taste, cases of limes, crates of oranges and potatoes, mushrooms, the chefs came out to look it over and tell them where things went. "Listen, I'll see you later, and we'll reminisce about the old days. I promised to swim in the Pacific. I don't go to the shore around Lima to swim, too much effluent."

—m—

The beach was nice below Frank's Nuevo Mundo resort, and the water was clean. Both Helen and Liz were now big as beach balls, sunning on the lawn chairs near a roadhouse replica of Bimbo's where in '69 the Ayacucho team recreated on the coast with cold beer, iced shrimp and volleyball, while waiting for the uprising in Ayacucho to calm down, five killed by troops after throwing rocks, many wounded, carried off into the boondocks by relatives who didn't want them going to the hospital there. It was a warm day, it seldom got hot in Lima though it did get foggy. Two young Mormon lads on mission, easily recognizable in their clean white shirts, ties, and dark slacks, took the cut-off from the highway and pedaled down on their bikes. They made their spiel, and Jimmy invited them to sit down.

"Like a brewski?" Jim said, flipping open the cooler. "My wives can't drink with me because they're both embarrasada."

"It's his fault, he likes to keep us barefoot and pregnant," Liz said, kicking off her sandals, and getting up. "Here, there's gaseosas, Coke, Fanta orange, Bimbo flavors."

"I promised each of them I'd marry them," Jim said. "I know it's binding because I used to be a lawyer. Did you know when Justice Holmes wrote the opinion that outlawed Mormon polygamy, wherein he said 'monogamy is the bulwark of Western civilization', by then he was on his fourth wife, or was it the fifth. A pretty young thing, I think he picked her up at a Seattle drive-in, you know the kind where the waitresses on roller skates bring your burger and fries around to the car. So a few bad struts in the bulwark of civilization. There's no justice this side of Eden. I'm thinkin' I'd like a small ceremony, no Rev. Moon mass wedding, something intimate. Anyway why not explore an American model. You got any literature on sister brides in there?"

"Jimmy, you're being inappropriate," Helen said. "Don't mind him, boys, he's snookered again. He's keeping a low yardarm, if you know what I mean. Give him literature on the evils of drink. I think my sister and I will go for a swim,--Elizabeth."

"She is correct that I did imbibe with an old friend at lunch, and she knows I ordinarily never drink until after supper and mainly on weekends, except today there's a big celebration at the resort up those bluffs," Jim said. "Ah, she's so pure, she's from Philadelphia, she was pure as the driven snow, but then she drifted. You know W.C. Fields once tried to deduct his booze as a business expense on his taxes. When he got audited, he said, 'You ever try to be funny without it?' Of course, the IRS denied it."

"Well, as to your question, sir, we don't practice polygamy now," the first Mormon lad said. "In the early days, it was because there were so many more women than men among the original converts."

"Maybe because my Ohio forebears were busy oppressing your people, you ever hear of Kirtland, they burned you out of there, said move on West, to that mob in Nauvoo that lynched Joseph Smith," Jim said. "Ah tolerance, the First Amendment guarantees it."

"Maybe I will have a coke," the first Mormon lad said.

"If you have a lemon-lime, I'd like that please," the second Mormon lad said. "Are you on vacation from Ohio?"

"About a twenty year vacation," Jim said. "I need to go back soon and get my bearings straight. Or maybe the Bering Strait? Alaska da questions, and you giva da answers. Y'know with this global warming they're gonna be planting corn in the Yukon soon. I may get a job selling combines to Eskimos. Right now I'm in financial planning, so when you prosper, I know how Mormons have gold stashed away in those mountain vaults along with the genealogies. Always looking for new clients. I'll need to keep working til I drop in the hafts. Have you seen the cost of plastic diapers lately, and these gals ain't gonna do no washing or cooking, they're high class ladies."

"Don't believe his baloney," Liz said, snubbing her nose and running the bottom edge of her suit as she prepared for her dip. "He's been telling stories since he was knee high to a grasshopper. Come on, Helen, doesn't his rank hypocrisy bother you?"

"I've gotten used to it," Helen said, standing up so they were like sister Nereids on a mission, and they walked off in stride together, just to go down to the sea for a quick dip.

"They're something, these sisters," Jim said. "I hope my joking didn't offend you. I didn't mean anything by it. Hey, if you're hungry and you can get your bikes up that road, a friend of mine, an American businessman named Frank Mathiessen, owns the resort up there and there's enough food for an army, there's a big reception for a museum, tell 'em Jimmy Hiram sent you."

The young men thanked him and took off on their bikes, as he turned and watched the ladies wading out to their knees and splashing to cool off. It was good to be out in the sun, Lima was often overcast, and a slow hot breeze was coming up off the sand.

—◦◦◦—

The reception was very nice, Derrick was also honored for having rediscovered the Silver Llama and saving it from huaceros, with a red silk sash and a medal with a llama on it, a more realistic rendering like the one on the sol de oro coin and not stylized like the Inca piece. Of course Rick had first squawked when he heard the llama was going to be donated, but it was better to have it in a museum where he had access to it, than in Frank's private collection. Besides, Jim had included one of the excellent copies and copies of his field notes and sketches from Ocros, that verified it was what they had found there, though he hadn't had time to study the markings. Sylvia was there also, and they danced a couple of numbers to light salsa swing jazz and mickey music like a request, 'Just One Of Those Things', talked about getting together when he was back in Philadelphia, she needed to ask him about stocks, and then she and Helen sat at a table and talked, they'd both grown up in similar milieus, were well educated, knew art and enjoyed talking about it, so a potential client.

The band turned to a zarzuela and then a marinero, the national dance, and Rosa Billups rose to the occasion and took the floor with Jim because they knew this number. It was a very sensuous dance, involving flirting with a handkerchief in a lascivious manner, including capturing the woman by putting the kerchief over her head and down to her butt and bringing her in close. She'd brought along her twelve-year old niece, who was standing there wide-eyed beside Uncle Ricky, who was talking to Davey Crenshaw, the Brit photographer that Frank brought in for the ceremony, also a potential client since he had bucks, pounds, lucre from his days as a London fashion photog. Jim told him that Davey was a hard sell, from his days as a tush stuffer and waiter, his experience was that Brits were the worst tippers, oh much worse than black people, they were the main reason continental restaurants had service included on the tab, and of course Davey said the Scotch were much worse, moths flew out of their wallets when they were opened.

Speaking of inglesas or Scots, Olga was not able to be there, but there had been good news for her. A large American mining company, Newmont, was constructing a large precious metals mining operation there, was buying up land and rights in the area of the traditional Arcetura lands. Yes the Agrarian Reform had taken lands from the family domain, but mainly in the few fertile valleys, so the high mountain cactus desert now had worth, and she was glad she hadn't thrown away the old deeds or the share certificates since Newmont was buying land and mineral rights, anyway he was glad to inform her about good fortune coming her way after having witnessed two break-in's at the pension, not to mention Miller's death. She was not in the best of health and getting up in years and didn't need that kind of trouble, so now she might not need to take in guests.

Captain Fregosco was there with about fifteen of his extended family, the kids all dressed in Sunday best, and immensely enjoyed the buffet. Fregosco had been in the U.S. once on a Peruvian fellowship that paid in Peruvian soles, which was when he first discovered the mysteries of exchange rates and devaluation, which allowed him to afford one meal per day at McDonald's, this for a man the size of a mature Italian tenor playing Falstaff. It made Jim feel bad inside thinking of the big guy going hungry in the land of plenty, like when his Dad told him about frying eggs on the iron in his room at the end of the month in college during the Depression.

"Ah, Jimmy, this is grand, but I did have just one more question for you," Fregosco said, while Jim suddenly shifted to considering alibis, hoping this query wasn't about finding a bullet that didn't match Miller's gun, he had heard one shot and not two, right? ah but the TV was on with the Western, bang-bang, and look, there's Derrick Stephensen right across the room, lurking over the Silver Llama with his tongue hanging out like a hungry wolf, about to run back to Sylvia and ask her to buy it for him, why not ask him if he remembers another shot, but no problema, Fregosco was playing academic quiz bowl, an old game they enjoyed. "What is the capital of Outer Mongolia?"

"That would be Ulan Bator," Jim said. "What do I win?"

In fact there were no further questions for him from any quarter about Miller, or about Norman Larsen, no more questions though there was big news later in a call from Rad. The insurance company had offered a twenty-eight million dollar settlement, and Holly had accepted it on behalf of her ward and benefactor, Gertie Pinaro, who was now in terminal nursing care. Maybe having his garden excavated and them finding no evidence of crime, was worth it. Holly had heard about the big dig in his yard and later tried to tell him that she had nothing to do with that, she thought they were landscapers he'd hired, and had taken off when they brought in the backhoe and bulldozer. It must have been the insurance company she later surmised, when they next saw each other, which was at the fourth birthday his daughter, Julie. He just laid a finger aside his nose like a Dickens' character, 'Mum's the word, luv', and gave her a goose, his cuñadita tan cariñosa, who'd tried to seduce info from him on the Larsen case. She seemed cool with silence on the subject, had her own yacht now and Peter hung around on deck like a useless puppet, like Peter Lawford after Frank and the Rat Pack shunned him. Julie offered Jim an escape from the webs of lies previously woven when practicing to deceive, when she rushed up in her party dress, already soiled with ice cream and disheveled from soccer with her younger brother.

"Daddy, it was a good kick, he ran in front," she said, throwing herself on his lap and presenting an image of winning to Jimmy, Junior, just three and with tears welling in his eyes.

"She kicked me and it was a foul," Jimmy Jr. said.

"Did not, and he kicked me first," Julie said, showing a crescent of blood on her shin.

"Hey, are you my Macho Duck?" Jim said, referring to a Donald Duck take-off on Village People's 'Macho Man', a cartoon the kids liked to dance to. He'd have to tell his writer to cut the disnero reference, in case his book got discovered, but what chance of that—it took the American literati seventy years to discover Moby Dick. "You know Macho Ducks don't cry."

"I am not crying," Jimmy Jr. said, sniffing into his sweatshirt.

"Now, can you practice together without hurting each other for five minutes while I tell Aunt Holly good-bye, and get your mom to referee, Liz, where are you? The kids want to play soccer again," Jim said bumping them up off his knees and watching brother and sister run away, having duly lodged their mutual complaints against siblings, and having been sent back into the game. "Sorry, Holly, I better referee this match before there's bad blood. I don't know if they get it from me, I always liked to win, or whether it's because I'm Daddy for both and they each have a different mommy, Taos is very tolerant, there's no Murphy Brown backlash here, but they do know it's somewhat different, our ménage a trois, actually has worked out well since Liz is always itchin' to go, and when she's away, Helen's here, and she never gives Julie a bigger dish of ice cream than Jimmy. Anyway, I'm not overly judgmental and letting sleeping dogs lie is not bad advice, when we all have our sins. I don't doubt you had your fair share of abuse from Norman when he put you out on the street for him? You deserve every penny of what you got. My only regret was not sleeping with you, because you're such a fox. I just couldn't risk falling under your spell. Frankly it looked to me like you were exposing yourself to unnecessary risk when you already had a strong case, which is how it turned out, right? You know it wasn't because I didn't find you attractive. It was just that it couldn't be, under the circumstances then, and now I'm a married man, so game over."

"Sometimes I think you understand me better than Peter does," Holly said, folding into his embrace and snuggling before the kids started yelling for him to come and play. He gave her a good-bye kiss, though personally not that broken up to see her leave since he was concerned about the kids, just his mother hen instinct in the aftermath of relief when he heard of the settlement of Norm's big insurance policy, actually the second shoe to drop in the sequence, the first being over the Silver Llama, now happily in the museum south of Nazca, oh and then its copy stood on his desk, the kids called it the horsey from Peru and knew not to play with it. Peru was someplace magical to the kids, like Shangra-La or Machu Picchu, where Mom Liz went to take pictures of the Quechua people, who were the grandchildren of the Incas. She brought photos to parent's day at the kids' daycare, Jimmy, Jr., was especially proud. They were there half-days mornings, it was good to be with other kids, and they liked to spend afternoons with Jim because he took them fishing and sledding and got fast food and milkshakes, told them tales from the mythic land of Peru, remembering how much he'd loved Kipling's "How So" stories as a child, tried to do the same with Andean materials, like they knew now if you happened be out at night in the Andes and in the moonlight saw a string of llamas laden with packs, it might be the ghost train of the Inca gold, and you had to follow that train because it led you to the gold. And if you saw a crazy Spaniard with a washbasin for a helmet, tilting windmills on his faithful steed, Rocinante, that would be Don Quixote. The only real bears in Peru were not Paddington, but spectacled bears and why were they spectacled? So they could read the morning paper just like Daddy. They would get a chance to see Peru when they were a little older and Mommy Lizzy would be their guide, because she worked there and knew all about it.

Things were working out in Taos. He'd lured Helen there after they visited all the galleries and went to the Georgia O'Keefe Museum, and after her mother passed away, she was ready to leave Philly herself. A deli there had the big fat baked soft pretzels and Philly mustard, creamed herring, smoked salmon, fresh oysters from the Gulf, and the video store had favorite New Wave films on VCR cassettes, "8 1/2" with the scene of Marcello Mastroanni as lioness-tamer with his whip, "L'Aventura" and "Shoot The Piano-Player" with a poster cover of Aznavour at the 88's.

For Liz it also worked out well, she was just a hop and skip from Houston or Dallas and they had international flights to Peru or occasionally to Amsterdam to visit friends, and she felt assured with Helen there that she wasn't neglecting her son, and Jim made sure he didn't feel that way, spent time doing things with both the kids. He'd made enough he was only working half time out of his home office, besides Seymour Industries had not gone into bankruptcy, was paying its seven per cent preferred dividend, and Helen didn't have her brother continually mooching off her now with Holly's recent inheritance. Liz was also contributing to family expenses, so they were doing well and all happy, the kids were bright, what's the Ivy League cost a year, forty thousand so in fifteen years, maybe three hundred thousand a year, $1.2 million times two kids would be $2.4 million, it looked like he'd be working into his seventies, maybe a pony now would be a good investment if one of them became a cowboy or cowgirl, I feel distressed as Micawber, a penny away from the poor house, where they serve thin soup.

"Whatchu thinkin'?" Liz said, coming up and putting her arm around him.

"Just how happy I am, happy with the kids, happy we've been able to make the transition here," Jim said. "Don't stay away so long this time. It affects Jimmy Jr. more than he lets on. He gets possessive and argues with Julie."

"It won't be as long this time, I promise," Liz said, and they went out to the back lawn, singing a ditty from the barrio about a legendary victory of Peru in Mundialito play, 'Gol, gol, gol del Peru, Cachito Ramirez es el autor', very catchy and also interesting the concept that a soccer player could be author of a goal. Speaking of author, he just had to call his amanuensis, L.H. May, and get him his notes and corrections so he could finish the last novel of the Tihuantinsuyo Quartet. It already seemed like a strange dream, conjured by a Prospero, or like Don Quixote regaining sanity just before he died, though Jim knew he was suffering from that temporary insanity known as culture shock, but each day he saw the kids and that helped him want to get better, he remembered so much, like the kids' ditty of Cachito which Liz and he sang, and made sure each child got the same number of goals and the game ended in a tie, and thought if he got a chance to dedicate the Tihuantinsuyo Quartet, he'd dedicate it to 'Progress and prosperity for the nation, and good fortune to the children, they are the future.'

Printed in the United States
By Bookmasters